Spoiler Alert

If you have not read AK-239 (Book I) and Project 252 (Book II) you will miss much of the backstory on which this book plays. You should still be able to enjoy this volume on its own but you will not have the backstories to better understand the humor, motivations and history of each character.

I highly recommend that you read the first two volumes first. They are available in both e-book and print forms at Amazon.com.

Cheers,

Roger Ellis, Esq.

1. AK-239 The Enemy is Already Here (JD I) John Denning (Book 1)
2. Project 252 (JD II) John Denning (Book 2)

Thank You

Once again, saying thank you to some very special people by name seems also to be trivial, without whose assistance this book would not have been possible.

There are several active and former individuals who either work or worked for a "department" in the federal government with Sensitive Compartmented Information (SCI).

These people work with information that is beyond "Top Secret" and known only to a handful of people, so obviously they could not be named individually.

I thank them for their invaluable insights.

These brave warriors have gone about in silence doing their jobs without much recognition and considering the dangers and risks to their friends and family, they, selflessly, continue their work. They, like Navy personnel, commanders, SEALs, officers, and enlisted personnel do their jobs, courageously, every day and do not want to be thanked publicly.

But thank you anyway!

Without each of these warriors' assistance I would be relying too much on my own craziness.

With regard to everyone below, except for my family, they are not in any particular order and I certainly don't mean to slight anyone.

All of you are at the top of my list and I can't thank you enough:

Editors are the final writers of your book so I do thank my wife first and foremost:

So thank you Mary, for "helping" to keep me grounded in some reality (for over 35 years!)!

My children: Robert, Rebecca & Bethany

John Dunham 1957-2016
Ann Dunham

David XXXXX
(You know who you are and so does your family!)
Former U.S. Navy SEAL

The United States Navy
Navy Special Warfare Command (NSW)
Special Warfare Combatant Crewmen (SWCC)
Navy SEALs - Active and Retired Personnel

Ruth Ann Dyke Zirkle
Jeanne Petrie Lampi

All the wonderful people of Cunard's Queen Victoria Cruise Ship -
Southampton, U.K. to Monaco and Rome, Italy (Sept. 1, 2018)

I especially want to thank, but it's certainly not limited to:
Andrew (Lloyd Webber - NOT)
Richard
Helen
Kev
Alen I
Vivian
Alen II
Sue
Wayne
Mongo
Christian
Lisa

And all "The Beautiful People" who helped me from Ketchikan, Seattle, Paris, and
Moscow to Monaco.

AK-239 (2016)
The Enemy is Already Here
JOHN DENNING VOL. I

PROJECT 252 (2017)
JOHN DENNING
VOLUME II

For more information go to:
www.RogerEllis.biz

Veteran Suicides

I'm shocked and saddened at the high suicide rate for veterans. It's currently (2018) nearly twice the rate of suicides in the U.S. compared to the civilian population.

If you need help please call the VA's confidential Veterans Crisis Line at 1-800-273-8255.

It's open 24/7 for veterans and those concerned about a veteran.

If, for whatever, reason, that number is not satisfactory please look for a crisis suicide center in your state or online. There are some great people out there who want to help you, your friend or family member.

Don't hesitate!

If you think there's a problem, don't wait!

DO IT TODAY!!!

Table of Contents

1

I'm sitting in an ordinary looking hospital room in New York City.

I'm seeing the best doctor in the world for brain surgery and paint is peeling by my 12th story window?

I find it hard to believe, based on the evidence so far, that this is "the best doctor."

I stare out the window thinking about the literal whirlwind of disasters that overtook the planet only months ago and now — nothing.

I turn my attention to the TV and turn up the volume. A New York City reporter is on a boat in front of what's left of the Statue of Liberty. A scaffolding surrounds the bottom half of the former statue. No woman holding the torch of freedom, just thousands of ugly looking scaffolding rods.

"As you can see, repair work is well underway. It's estimated this will take at least a year, maybe more, before the statue is rebuilt. That's with over 5,000 workers, working around the clock. In a gesture of goodwill, France has supplied New York City with a team of engineers and construction workers to help restore the statue as close to its' original beauty as possible."

Bet this "kid" reporter doesn't even know that the original statue was a dull brown.

The original statue was made from copper.

Here's a fun fact:

If they use the same copper and leave it alone it will take over 30 years to once again turn it to the greenish color we all would recognize.

It's gonna take the equivalent of 30 million pennies to build that statue again.

How did I know that number without looking it up?

Well, it's always good to start a story at the beginning.

Many cities around the world recently experienced devastation of Biblical proportions. Some still say it was the work of Russia. Of course, Russia denied this and all major Russian news agencies claimed that the United States was behind the attacks.

I turn my attention again to the reporter. She says, "It's unbelievable the senseless, worldwide destruction of our major cities and famous national treasures. There have been repeated denials by at least 10 separate United States government agencies. The White House press office has repeatedly claimed that 'neither they nor anyone working for them had anything to do with this senseless taking of life and property.' This is Ruth Cortez reporting from the Statue of Liberty."

I change channels on the TV then see a very strange site.

Melissa McCarthy and Kristen Wiig, dressed in complete *Ghostbuster* garb are being interviewed. As I turn up the volume on the television the Bus Boys Song "Cleanin' Up The Town" is playing in the background. Melissa McCarthy says, "Ya well, we came out here today to show our support for New York City and to help clean up 'da town. We also want to say that whenever these ghosts come back, we're ready for ya!"

Kristin Wiig steps in front of Melissa saying, "Ya, I ain't afraid 'a no ghosts." She then gives a cheesy smile to the camera.

Melissa's not happy with her.

She stares at Kristin while there is dead air.

After forever, Kristin goes back to being the sidekick and takes a step back.

This pleases Melissa and the star looks at the camera, still saying nothing.

The nervous reporter tries to take the microphone away, as Melissa McCarthy grabs the mic and keeps it in front of her face. The reporter finally gives up. Melissa smiles, turns to the reporter and calmly says, "Tawny, would you like to say anything else?"

The reporter, very upset that Melissa stole her mic, remembers the age old rule: Stars are never wrong! — Even if there is only dead air.

Tawny composes herself, while Melissa continues to hold the mic. Melissa finally looks at her, prompting her silently to speak. After a disgusting look the reporter says, "This is Tawny Elliott reporting from Midtown Manhattan."

"There, that wasn't so bad now, was it, Tawny?" says Melissa.

Tawney doesn't know what to say. She's upset but this is Melissa McCarthy, so Tawny bites her tongue and puts on a fake smile.

Melissa then looks at the camera and smiling says, "Are we clear?"

The cameraman playfully eggs on Melissa by nodding the camera up and down.

Melissa says, "So now I can say any fuckin' thing I want?"

My television screen immediately goes to the station sign off, multi-colored, test pattern.

I look at the TV in disbelief. I don't think Americans can tell fake news from real news any longer. More importantly, I don't think most care, so long as they're entertained. Most people are not watching this. They're too busy trying to earn a living or taking care of their families.

Others would rather tune out and live in their alternate realities of facebook, twitter or a million other entertaining distractions.

I think back to the level of mindless worldwide chaos that was wrought only months ago by, Elena, one very insane woman.

The world has literally gone to hell. Many large cities are still trying to recover months after they were partially destroyed by, for lack of a better word, ghosts. Fortunately, Elena, no longer has access to supercomputers and the infrastructure necessary to duplicate her destructive powers. However, it's a race against time to find her before she's able to recreate her destructive capabilities. With quantum calculations and expertise from the best and brightest, she was able to inflict tremendous damage and infect numerous computer systems worldwide before she disappeared.

Neither CIA, FBI, NSA, or about 15 other three letter government agencies can figure out how she did it, or where she is now.

I'm very proud that my SEAL team helped stop the murder of millions in a near nuclear holocaust.

All I know is that human nature is amazingly resilient. I can think of thousands of historical examples where humanity seemed forever doomed. Somehow, decimated peoples banned together and overcame the monstrous behavior of a few who were given too much power.

From Cain murdering Abel to Hitler murdering millions, some wondered, how can we go on?

Yet we do.

And we will continue to do so.

So, I'm sitting in this hospital room staring out the window trying to stop the trillions of crazy thoughts from going through my head.

I'm not successful.

Much has happened in the weeks since Jen and I flew back to the United States from Paris.

We are in this hospital because my brain was implanted with something no larger than a quarter.

Let's just say it gives me more brain power and memory than any living human — and maybe the brain power of probably a few thousand humans combined!

I haven't told anyone else but Jen about this.

Now Jen thinks I've turned into a jerk.

Maybe I have. But when you have the brainpower of a few thousand people —
that can really go to your head!

Literally!

Jen walks in the room so I have to pretend this "thing" doesn't worry me.

It does!

But I can't discuss it with Jen as I want to leave this chip in, for now, and she wants me to see her brain surgeon friend to "discuss" removal.

Whoever can mass produce these things will change the world forever — for
better or for worse, depending on who controls them.

And whoever controls them may be able to control us.

That's what worries me the most.

I agreed to speak with Jen's surgeon friend and have been assured he can be trusted to keep quiet.

Jen walks into the room and says, "Okay, he's on his way."

I sarcastically answer, "That's what all doctors say. Then they abuse your time like they're gods. That's with a little g, a very little g."

"You really hate doctors, don't you?"

"Hate might be too nice a word."

Jen looks at me, disgusted, as her father was an MD and her mother is a nurse.

The doctor walks into the room. He's a husky man, who also looks to be in great physical shape.

I wonder if this was an old boyfriend of Jen's?

Who cares?

If Jen trusts him, then so do I.

The doctor is looking over some papers. I look worried. The doctor notices.

"Don't worry. These are your brain scan results. I wiped the files and these are the only hard copies. I thought you'd like to know what your brain looks like."

"I do. I do," I say with enthusiasm.

The doctor holds up a color scan of what I think is my brain. The doctor says, "This activity is the activity of a normal, healthy, male of approximately your age."

There are several areas that are lit up in yellow, red and purple. I say, "Okay."

The doctor holds up another color scan, "This is your brain."

My mouth goes open as my entire brain is lit up red or purple.

"In case you're wondering, I've been doing brain scans for over 30 years and I've never, ever seen a brain all lit up like yours."

Worried, I ask, "What does this mean, doc?"

The doctor looks at Jen, then at me, pauses, then says, "It means you're using at least 90% of your brain power and that chip seems to be encouraging it. Beyond that, I don't know."

We all look at each other several times before my sarcasm kicks in, "What do you mean you don't know?"

The doctor intently stares at me before repeating, "This thing is like nothing I've ever seen before."

"Well, that's great!" I say throwing my hands up in the air and looking at the TV. "So who might know?"

"If you don't want anyone to know about this, my hands are tied. Everything seems normal except for all your brain activity. I've never seen anything like it."

Jen interrupts, "He never stops eating night and day and he never gains a single pound."

The doctor jokes, "Sounds good to me."

Neither Jen nor I laugh.

"Sorry," says the doc.

Now Jen and I smile.

The doctor gets very serious saying, "I can't take it out without scheduling you for surgery."

I look long and hard at the doctor, "I can't do that just yet, doc."

The doctor says, "Why? Maybe someone put a ticking time bomb in your head. Why would you take that chance?"

I quickly answer, "It's maybe our only hope of finding the person who did this."

The doc asks, "I know you've described how the device was implanted and how it makes you feel like you have extraordinary knowledge but..."

I interrupt, "The temperature of the room is exactly sixty-nine degrees. There are exactly 2 air conditioning vents in this room. There are..."

The doctor has been looking on his smartphone and now interrupts me, "That's all well and good but what if I were to ask you something like, in what year did President Lincoln give his address to the Young Men's Lyceum."

I respond, "Just the year? Lincoln gave the speech on January 27, 1838. That was too easy. Abraham Lincoln at the time was a 29-year-old member of the Illinois State Legislature, and was worried about the, quote, mobocratic spirit, unquote, of his time. Lincoln said in the speech and now I'm quoting:

> "... At what point shall we expect the approach of danger? By what means shall we fortify against it? Shall we expect some transatlantic military giant, to step the Ocean, and crush us at a blow? Never! All the armies of Europe, Asia and Africa combined, with all the treasure of the earth (our own excepted) in their military chest;

with a Buonaparte for a commander,
could not by force, take a drink from
the Ohio, or make a track on the
Blue Ridge, in a trial of a thousand
years.

 At what point then is the approach
of danger to be expected? I answer, if
it ever reach us, it must spring up
amongst us. It cannot come from
abroad. If destruction be our lot, we
must ourselves be its author and
finisher. As a nation of freemen, we
must live through all time, or die by
suicide..."[1]

The doctor and Jen stare at me.

Finally, Jen can't take it any longer and picks up where my sarcasm left off, "You see why I want it out? He used to be a smart guy. Now, he's a smart ass!"

Doc looks at me and sees I'm smiling. Only then does he smile and say to Jen, "He's not, by chance, a big Abraham Lincoln buff, is he?"

Jen says, "Uh no, he wouldn't pick up a history book if he had a gun to his head."

"She's tried though!" I see that no one is laughing so I move on. Since that day with Jen at the Eiffel Tower no one has forced me to say or do anything but I'm like some kind of superman. It's like I have Google attached to my brain, only it's better. It's instantaneous.

 A very worried doctor says, "This has to be reported. We need more tests. We need…"

Jen sees my worry and quickly interrupts, "You promised to give us some time."

I point to file footage on the TV of a great tornado taking out the Statue of Liberty. "You see that? The person who planted this, also did that. No one can find her faster than me, especially with this," I point to that thing in my head.

Jen says, "But you've had this thing in your brain for months, runnin' all over the place and nothing."

Exasperated I say, "No, but I'm close. I'm really, really close. I need a little more time. Please." Thoughts rush into my head as I think back to Paris. "I was in Paris looking out the window at the Eiffel Tower. I couldn't stop myself from saying 'it really is a beautiful sunset.' The thought was there and I said it, however, that thought wasn't my thought. Someone planted it in my brain."

Jen speaks up, "I was there. I said that. Maybe you were just copying me."

I smile and to make her feel better, I agree, "Maybe."

Jen then says, "I have this really bad feeling that Elena is somewhere trying to build this stuff all over again."

I look at Jen knowing she's right. I head for the door, "Thanks doc. We'll be in touch."

2

It looks like any other unassuming, glass, office building in America. However, this is the headquarters of the most Top Secret military facility in the world. The address (675 N Randolph St, Arlington, Virginia, USA 22203) is public knowledge on Google. But even if you're across the street you could be arrested for simply taking a picture of this highly sensitive building. Over the last few years, several people have been arrested by the Arlington police. Their cameras were confiscated and never returned!

One person was so angry that he filed a federal lawsuit to get his "$70,000.00" Canon DSLR camera back. "Somehow" the government "lost" the camera but paid the man his $70,000.00 anyway.

No questions asked.

That's how paranoid the government is about this facility.

DARPA, The Defense Advanced Research Projects Agency is an agency of the U.S. Department of Defense and is responsible for the development of Top Secret, advanced, emerging technologies.

Every military in the world would love a tiny peek into this facility. In fact, most would love to brush shoulders with anyone in this building, or acquire some paperwork, or even find a stray email.

This building had already been infiltrated and breached by some very sophisticated operators, so a number of new security measures have been added.

You couldn't work here unless you had a specialized clearance above "Top Secret" called Sensitive Compartmented Information (SCI). Even people with "Top Secret" clearances are not allowed any knowledge or access to these secret programs. Even though he's Commander in Chief, that even included the President of the United States!

The president never asked about this agency, as he didn't even didn't know about it!

One of these SCI programs is called NLD (Don't you love the government — everything is a three digit acronym!). What that stands for is unimportant. Everyone dubbed it: "Night of the Living Dead." This is based on the 1968 movie where corpses from a graveyard begin attacking humans. Sounds like a bad Frankenstein movie, right?

Well it goes to show you what the DOD people working on SCI at nights thought of NLD!

Follow me so far?

Well, I think I lost myself!

One day two co-workers were messing around in the break room acting like Frankenstein zombies saying, "I'm going to kill you."

In walks the Director, of the NLD program, Doctor Sam Mustafa. The good doctor didn't like his programs being made a laughing stock, even if it was only among other scientists with Top Secret clearance.

He told them, "Cut it out or you'll be looking for other work."

No one cut it out, they were a bit more careful when and where they made fun of NLD.

Every employee with SCI clearance on NLD could no longer speak with family and friends. They were now part of the night of the living dead, isolated in the building. That's right! They could not even leave the building! Most of these people were loners who had no family and that's exactly the type of employee the government was looking for on this project.

They were the ones dubbed "The Living Dead" as the night shift seemed to have the craziest things going on. That might be because none of the handful of Congressmen who know "something" about the project would be here at 3am!

It's much easier to blackmail and gain access to someone if they have friends and family that they love.

These people had no one!

And that was by design.

Genius!

Evil!

Design! – (GED)

Many were so loyal that one died of "unknown causes" in this building and "several" others had to be hospitalized for "unknown and/or classified" reasons.

NLD is an extremely "sensitive" program. One that initially had been conducted "offshore" to avoid any possible legal liability. There were rumors about questionable testing on humans. The animal tests had all been completed and had proven extremely valuable. But when they started testing on

humans this should have set off bells and whistles in anyone
with a moral compass intact. However, people recruited into
the NLD program appear to have a very skewed moral
compass.

What am I talking about?

Well putting this information in a book could put my life
in jeopardy. Rumor has it this group is experimenting on people
in violation of all sorts of moral and legal norms, as I'll soon
explain.

My beloved country appears to be rapidly spiraling out of
control, thanks in part, to a tiny group of worldwide operators
that have infected the very core of many governments around
the world. My suspicion is, "The Snakes" might have already
infected the NLD group as well. Now before you put this book
down and say, "You're crazy," hear me out.

Two years ago I proved a cover-up in Alaska of
monumental order.

Last year I uncovered evidence of the secret society of:
"The Snakes."

Now I've pretty much given up trying to write in the form
of a diary. I'll try to give you immediate, firsthand accounts of
how serious the threats are and the people behind those threats.

Meanwhile back at the DARPA lab a secretary, long past
ready for retirement, walks into Dr. Mustafa's office and
disgustedly says, "They're here."

The good doctor immediately closes a file and disgustedly
answers back, "Great!" He stands and heads out of his office.
As he walks down this sterile looking white hall, a ceiling
camera is outside of each door; about 20 total. This looks a bit
ridiculous, but when you have a black budget with tens of
billions of dollars in it, the terms overkill, padding, and billions
are rounding errors.

As the doctor rounds the corner he stops swiftly. Inside a glass conference room are the CIA's Henry James and an old friend from SEAL Team Six, Skull. His real name, and I'm not kidding, is John Smith — John A. Smith!

There's an entire story that goes with this but let me say that "Skull's" parachute wouldn't open and he landed on his noodle!

Now, I consider Henry an old friend too but I have to admit, the guy's a real nerd. There are very few people that I'd trust with my life. These guys are at the top of that list.

Mustafa swings open the glass conference room door and says, "Ready?"

Henry and Skull follow Mustafa out of the room and down the long hall.

They walk up to a set of large double doors and Mustafa sticks his eyes in front of a retina scanner. Two huge doors open, revealing another world.

This darkened studio looks more like something off a Hollywood set. The room is set up as a theater. There is a stage in the middle of the room surrounded on three sides by seats. It's complete with dark, movie blue, lighting on the stage. It's rather beautiful. Again, when your budget is essentially unlimited, you can do almost anything.

On stage sits a young man in his 20s. Next to him is a small table. He appears to be very calm, almost in some sort of trance.

Behind him, behind the stage, are huge banks of computer servers. Next to the servers sit several scientists, working on the supercomputers. Huge, black, trunks of cables run from the computers into the nearby servers.

Mustafa walks to some seats midway down the empty theater and says to Henry and Skull, "Please, please. Sit, sit!"

Henry and Skull take their seats. Mustafa then says to the young man on stage, "What is your name?"[2]

"Peter, my name is Peter."

"And Peter do you know why you're here today?"

"Yes, you're doing some stress tests on me."

"And knowing that, how does that make you feel?"

Without hesitation Peter answers, "I dunno."

"Well Peter, are you nervous?"

"No."

"Are you worried?"

"No."

"Are you ready to begin?"

Peter calmly and almost with a bit of excitement says, "Sure."

Mustafa motions to some men in the dark. Two men in full flame gear walk onto the stage. They are carrying what looks to be a flame thrower.

Mustafa says, "Peter do you see those men?"

Peter smiles as if to say, you think I'm an idiot? But Peter instead says, "Yes."

"And what do you think those men might do?"

Peter, "Are you going to have them set me on fire?"

Mustafa smiles back, "Well, do you want to be set on fire?"

"No, not particularly."

"But if I told them to do that, what would you do?"

"What do you want me to do, sir?"

"I want you to hold your arm out in front of you."

Peter answers, "Yes, sir."

Without hesitation and very calmly Peter stretches out his arm.

Mustafa then nods to his men and they proceed to throw flames toward Peter's arm for a second. The men look to Mustafa who again nods and the flames are stopped.

Immediately, two paramedics rush the stage and one shoots what appears to be flame retardant onto Peter's arm.

Peter stands there as the second paramedic then douses his arm with a liquid.

Mustafa says, "Peter, did that hurt?"

Peter answers, "Yes, very much."

"But you aren't screaming?"

Peter acts a bit surprised as he says, "No, no I'm not."

"Those guys are gonna get you fixed right up, okay, Peter?"

Peter nods in the affirmative.

Mustafa motions for another man to go on stage. This man holds a Glock 22 pistol in his hand. Mustafa says, "Now, Peter, if I told you to shoot yourself in the head would you do it?"

Again without hesitation Peter says, "Sure."

"And you understand you would be killing yourself, correct?"

"Correct!"

"And why would you kill yourself?"

"Because you told me to."

"And you would do anything I told you, wouldn't you Peter?"

"Yes, yes I would."

"And why is that Peter?"

For the first time Peter hesitates before saying, "I don't know."

Henry and Skull stand up. Henry says, "I hope you don't expect us to sit here and watch this."

Mustafa sarcastically says, "Oh come now Mr. James this won't be as bad as some things you've done for the CIA."

Henry says, "I never allowed anyone to commit suicide, let alone encouraged it."

Mustafa then taunts Henry, "How do you know that gun's even loaded?"

Henry answers, "We don't."

Mustafa then says, "Peter fire one round into the ceiling."

Peter without hesitation then fires the Glock into the air. Peter is obviously not trained for this and he flinches after shooting the gun.

Henry disgustedly says, "That's it. We're out of here. I will recommend to the director and the president that this little operation of yours be shut down."

Mustafa says, "Wo. Wo. Wait. We're not animals. We're Americans." Mustafa then looks at Peter saying, "Put the gun on the table, Peter."

Peter gladly does so. Mustafa motions to a scientist who then quickly retrieves the gun and leaves the stage.

Mustafa catches up with Henry and Skull who have now briskly walked to the back door.

"Don't you see what this means? We now can create SEALs, spies, soldiers who feel no fear and have no hesitation to do an assignment, no matter how dangerous."

Skull says, sarcastically, pointing to Peter, "Uh ya, I don't want to be that person."

Mustafa says to Skull, "Why not?" Mustafa then looks at Peter and says, "Peter, how do you feel?"

Peter quickly answers, "I feel great. Just great."

Mustafa looks back to Skull, "Why not? We can make you feel great?"

Henry speaks up, "I don't know what kind of zombies you've created in here but I can see all sorts of legal and ethical problems with this program."

Mustafa says, "We're carefully conducting everything, safely, in this facility. We take the utmost care and precautions for all personnel, especially the ones who've had magneto-thermal stimulation."

Henry is now curious, "What exactly have you done to these poor people?"

Mustafa is surprised at Henry's attitude, "We've given these people more memory and less fear. Who wouldn't want that?"

Skull once again raises his hand, "Uh, I wouldn't!"

Henry quickly chimes in, "Ya, neither would I."

Mustafa stares at Henry saying, "Don't knock it 'till you've tried it."

Henry stares back saying, "Have you tried it, doc?"

Mustafa happily says, "Why, yes, yes I have."

Skull interrupts, "And you let them shoot flames on your arm?"

Mustafa suddenly stares at Skull before ignoring his question and saying, "We've implanted specially built DNA strands which attach to specific neurons in the brain. This creates a brain that can override your thoughts or endure any pain and…"

Mustafa stops as there is some commotion going on in the darkness. Skull and Henry look to see but can't as it's too dark.

Peter wonders back onto the stage with the Glock, puts it to his head and shoots himself. His body drops to the stage floor, with a thud, as people scream.

Henry and Skull look at Mustafa.

Skull dripping with sarcasm says, "Well… looks like he's feelin' great now."

3

We're airborne out of Hill Air Force Base only minutes outside Salt Lake City, Utah.

Nestled about a mile high in the Colorado Rocky Mountains is a vast prison complex. It's known as ADX Florence, Florence ADMAX, or the 'Alcatraz of the Rockies.' This supermax facility houses the worst of the worst. From the Boston Bomber to Ted Kacyznski, Terry Nichols (one of the Oklahoma City bombers) and a number of other well-known terrorists, this fortress near Florence, Colorado keeps these monsters, in human form, from hurting anyone else.

So this is where we're headed but I doubt we'll make it.

Our Blackhawk helicopter is swaying back and forth like a tiny bug in a tornado. The noise of hail hitting the windshield is deafening. Luckily, we're all wearing headgear or we'd never hear anyone say anything on this flight from hell.

As I'm sitting here, feeling nauseous, a large chunk of ice smashes into the pilot's "unbreakable" windshield. Things don't startle me much but this made me jerk back into my seat. My eyes darted toward the noise. I could feel air rushing into the cabin from where the ice cracked the windshield. The pilot jerks the cyclic to the right, making the chopper move right and we head into a steep dive.

All sorts of warning sounds, sounds, bells, voices, whistles begin to, annoyingly, chirp.

It seems that almost immediately the voice says, "Pull up, terrain, pull up."

The pilot then says the words no one on board an aircraft ever wants to hear, "Mayday, mayday, mayday... This is Zero... Mayday, mayday, mayday!

The pilot is in such a panic he couldn't even cough up his call sign.

The co-pilot is sweating and looks too terrified to speak. The co-pilot is struggling more than the pilot with his cyclic.

We're definitely dying!

I can't die in Colorado!

Not this way!

Not tonight!

"Terrain! Terrain! Terrain!" is going off again in my ears. The sound is deafening.

This is probably the last thing I'll remember.

What am I talking about?

I'll be dead!

About a million other thoughts ran past my so called "90% brain."

Lots of good that did me! I can't do anything.

I hear both pilots let out blood curdling screams.

A huge thump hits our windshield.

Is that snow?

Next thing I remember is — nothing!

My "90% brain remembers nothing!

21

We're still airborne!

I think.

Neither pilot is saying a word.

Both appear frozen in their seats as they continue to fly into nothing but blackness.

No more ice.

No more snow.

Only the sound of wind whistling through about a huge cracked windshield.

The pilot and co-pilot look at each other and then to me as I think —

Unbelievable!

I try to speak but nothing comes out!

It looks like they're trying to do the same thing, instead, we give up and we sit in silence.

The only thing I remember is the deafening sound of wind whistling through my empty head and between my ears — figuratively speaking.

Now, I'd like to say the weather here is really "rocky" but that's merely a bad pun, so I won't "say" it.

I found out later that we hit the "peak" of Cottonwood Peak, 13,588 feet high! Fortunately, there was only snow there and by the grace of God we didn't hit the side of the nearly three mile high mountain.

Nothing but clear skies were on the other side of this peak — for a while.

I finally took a really deep breathe.

It seems like I hadn't taken a breath for about 20 minutes.

Before you say, that's impossible, look it up!

The world record underwater was achieved in 2012 by German freediver, Tom Sietas. "They" claim he held his breath underwater for 22 minutes and 22 seconds.

I don't believe it!

In SEAL BUD/s training we were only required to be without oxygen for a maximum of about two minutes.

But I've heard the competition today for SEALs is much tougher. Four guys have actually died in BUD/s training so I doubt I could pass today.
I barely passed BUD/s in my 20's when I was in top shape. The guys today really are superhuman but 22 minutes?

I don't think so!

Most well trained Navy SEALs will pass out after about 3 minutes!

I would rather have driven my old 1945 Willys jeep from Oregon up here. They claim the top speed in a Willys is 65 miles per hour. But if you claim to have driven an original Willys at 65 I'd say you're 'high' in Colorado smokin' somethin'.

More importantly, If I drove my Willys up here at least I, probably, would have ended up alive. They use the term "white knuckles" to describe people too scared to speak. I'm looking at my hands that are sweating.

My knuckles are the whitest I've ever seen on any person still breathing!

I've made fun of Skull, from my SEAL team before for having white knuckles but mine look far worse.

Air sickness is not something you should tell anyone if you're a Navy SEAL and — especially if you're a Navy SEAL commander! As I think I might vomit onto the floor of this wet, nauseating whale, a voice comes over my headset: "Two minutes, commander."

Two minutes? If I'm alive in two minutes I'll kiss this dirty, wet, floor!

I try to say that outloud. My mouth opens but, again, nothing comes out! That's good because I am afraid the burrito I ate earlier might be the first thing to move past my cold, blue lips.

Those two minutes lasted for about a day and half — at least so it seemed. We drop into the prison yard as rain and hail suddenly start pounding. As we land, I see several men with rifles trained on our helicopter.

Go ahead shoot!

Put me outta my misery.

Shut up JD!

Man up you big wimp.

You've been in worse. Far, far worse.

I see a tall man in a suit running toward our bird with two other men.

There must be twenty guards now, with rifles pointed at us.

In the good ol' days (which never were really that good) my word would have been enough to keep the dogs chained. But I understand. These two Russians were not in a supermax prison without reason. They snuck into America, drugged and killed people in Alaska, while sneaking nuke materials into the U.S. (JDI).

As they near our helicopter the only thing I could think of was:

Don't throw up on them — for God sakes, just don't throw up!

Nikolai Alexi, was the second in charge of the *Severstal* (*TK-20*), the largest nuclear submarine ever built. *TK-20* was taken by the Americans in Alaska. Kapitan-Leytenant Casmerov was third in charge of the *Severstal*. These guys killed one of their own and tried to kill me before escaping into America. So you'd think I would not be very happy on retrieving these guys. You'd be wrong!

24

I'd also know you don't know what already happened to me.

As the Russians drew near, I could see they appear to have been treated well. They were dressed in jeans and polo shirts and look like any other American guys. In fact, I think Alexi has put on some weight. So the first thing out of my mouth (thank God it wasn't my burrito) was, "My God, you've gotten fat!"

Alexi doesn't smile and Casmerov doesn't either.

I realize my joke didn't go over too well.

Alexi, after staring at me, says, eventually, with a smile, "I laugh on inside."

We stare at each other as I try and figure out this crazy Russian using double dangling prepositions. I've studied Russia for years and, If I learned one thing it's that, what's going 'on inside' is much more important than what any Russian will show on their face.

After a very long stare down, Casmerov laughs and says, "We kid. He bluffs. We got you."

I smile as if I got the joke.

Both Alexi and Casmerov laugh.

I sarcastically think, *Yes, that was good Russian joke?*

I then think, *Never in a million years will I understand you crazy people.*

With my added brainpower, I also thought of about a thousand other things I could say but I didn't.

There were much more pressing issues at hand. I look over to the tall man in a suit dripping wet under the huge rotating blades of this rusty old bucket that barely made it here. He hands me some paperwork and says, "I need you to sign this."

I take the soggy paperwork, look it over and say directly, "You do know, warden, that these guys both have been given presidential pardons, right?"

The tall, dripping wet suit says, "Yes, but I'm protecting myself."

As I read over the paperwork it's silly and meaningless legal dribble trying to protect himself from anything and everything.

"And you're aware as a federal employee you are already indemnified against all of these contingencies, right?"

"I'm dotting all my 'T's."

"You mean crossing?"

I sometimes answer people before they finish making their mistakes. This is why Jen now calls me a "smart ass."

The warden seems confused so I help him as I sign the paperwork and hand it back to him while I'm saying, "I think, you mean you're dotting all your 'I's and crossing all your 'T's."

The warden only cares that I've signed the paperwork. I'm reviewing his file in the huge database I can now retain in my head. His file says he's been in the federal penal system for 10 years and is almost qualified for retirement. I'm sure he cares more about getting his "Two FERS" than saving America. A Two FERS is a bureaucrat that has worked at least two government jobs long enough to collect from two retirement plans. This guy will make more money in retirement then when he was working! But who cares? It's not my money! Right?

What a country!

As our chopper lifts off so does my burrito! I almost forgot about my air sickness. I pretend to ignore it as the Russians again stare at me with their game faces. At least I think these are their games faces. They could be their happy, sad or angry faces. All Russian faces look like this.

Casmerov is trying to say something but with all the rotor noise it's impossible to hear anything. I point to the headset hanging right beside them. They each put on a headset.

Casmerov has been staring at the cockpit and says, "What happen to window?"

Both pilot and co-pilot look at me as if to say: Don't!

I shrug my shoulders and play dumb.

Alexi says, "You do realize that you and your president are now colluding with Russians, right?"

I didn't even hear what he said. All I'm worried about is my burrito.

4

Cloudy day at Kremlin but as Stalin used to say, "Always sunny on inside."

My God!

I'm starting to talk like a Russian too!

The newly elected President of Russia is Vladimir Putin. President Putin had grown up in the old KGB as an intelligence officer. He was one of the smartest guys our CIA said they'd ever watched.

When he became a politician it wasn't any wonder that Putin rose through the ranks quickly. His street smarts, wit and cunning tactics helped him acquire the highest job in Russia: President!

The Snakes had gone into hiding as their plot to overthrow the Russian government had failed. A Russian investigation found Admiral Victor Perchinkov was to blame for ordering the assassinations of the top Russian leadership. It was determined the Moscow explosion was ordered by Admiral

Perchinkov. This assassination took out, not only the former president of Russia, but almost all of the top leadership.

When that coup d'etat failed, Perchinkov fled the country. The Russian Federation issued an extradition demand from Barbados, a small island in the Caribbean, where Perchinkov was hiding. Admiral Perchinkov, by then, was nowhere to be found. He knew Russian agents had been tracking him but he lost them somewhere in the waters between Barbados and Grenada in a cigarette boat with V8 engines.

Cigarette boats are very fast, flat bottom boats with powerful engines. They got their name "cigarette boat" because many carried illegal contraband, such as drugs and cigarettes. They were built for speed and maneuverability so they could outrun the cops!

The GRU agents had no aerial assets and didn't think the admiral suspected that he was being followed.

The admiral not only suspected, but had people following those Russian agents while they were following him.

Admiral Perchinkov was a key player in "The Snakes" but he had disappeared off the face of the earth for the past few months. No intelligence agency could find his whereabouts. President Putin, on the other hand, seemed a much more reasonable person than any other politician vying for the job. Putin won the presidency easily, with over seventy percent of the Russian vote.

It's important that the United States and Russia keep talking to each other. Especially considering the United States and Russia have thousands of nukes pointed at each other.

Both Russia and the United States were embarrassed by having their systems hijacked and nukes launched toward each other by "outside forces." Both sides have put more "systems, personnel and communications" in place to avoid this, near disaster, from ever happening again. At least that's what I was told. Do I believe that?

Hell no!

Nothing's foolproof!

Especially with "the government."

People would be scared out of their minds if they read the President's Daily Brief.

It's better known as the PDB (Again, the crazy "experts" with their annoying three letter acronyms).

Why do you think presidents go into office with dark hair and come out grey?

Viktor Sokolov is now the assistant to President Putin. Apparently, no one could prove this "Snake" was involved in the plot to kill the old Russian president. Viktor Sokolov was a serious man with immense power.

Sokolov was also, young, handsome and very ambitious. And, currently, President Putin trusts this child prodigy with his life. CIA and Russian GRU units have warned him against trusting Sokolov but, like Donald Trump, when Putin likes someone no one can come between them.

Loyalty is actually a characteristic of a great leader. Loyalty produces trust. However, unless you give me a damn good reason to trust you, I trust no one.

Russians are not gonna pay any attention to some American Navy SEAL like me trying to warn them. But they have to know that Sokolov had been instrumental in helping to assassinate the prior Russian president. Had it not been for Sokolov, President Ivan Mironovich would not have been in the right place at the right time.

So Sokolov sits in this beautiful office made of Italian White Carrara marble and African black woods. This room exudes class.

Behind the president's desk sits President Putin while Sokolov briefs him, "All of the suitcases are now accounted for except one."

"Is that the one we recovered in Oregon?" asks Putin.

"We believe so. Yes, sir."

"And we haven't been able to get an answer from Colonel Katrina?"

"We have not been able to make contact with her or that unstable, American, math professor, George Ruddy. We believe they recovered the nuke before the Americans captured them and sent them to Guantanamo Bay, Cuba."

"Don't we have someone there?"

"We're working on it, sir."

"Did they leave us any clues?"

"Agents have looked over their home in Portland, Oregon, Ruddy's workplace and Portland State University, but they couldn't find anything. There's an asset at another university in Oregon we're trying to still reach. We don't think the CIA's found anything. Katrina assured the Americans that the suitcase nuke has been removed from their country. We do not believe that is true but we have told the U.S. State Department that we have this nuke safely in our hands and back in Russia."

"But that is not true, is it?" replies a concerned president.

"No, sir, it is not," answers Sokolov.

Putin then says suspiciously, "We don't have any more disasters like *Proyekt AK-239* that I don't know about, do we?"

"No sir."

Putin, in an even more questioning tone, says, "Are you sure?"

Without hesitation the young man says, "Yes sir. I'm sure."

Putin continues, "Well, good. We don't want to draw attention to ourselves. Use as many assets as necessary to find that suitcase. I don't want to start a nuclear war with that crazy man in the White House, Donald J. Trump, especially when I'm meeting with him."

"Yes, sir."

"Now what about Alexi and Casmerov?"

"They've been recruited by the Americans to find Elena."

"Good. Good. We want the Americans to know we're helping them as much as possible."

"You mean for now."

Putin then says condescendingly, "That's right, for now, Viktor, for now."

5

The grain is waving in the hot Nebraska sun. It's almost summertime in amber waves of grain country. A pretty country farmhouse is set back from an old dirt road surrounded by trees and a small stream in the backyard. Most kids would have died to have grown up in this environment — at least 50 years ago most kids would have loved to grow up here.

But, today, farm life in America isn't the Norman Rockwell environment it used to be. Automation and high tech have made the family farm very different from 10 years ago let alone 50 years ago. The internet is everywhere. And farm kids these days spend more time on electronics than they do on chores. Automation, for the most part, has been a good thing. Combines are harvesting the wheat as "farmers" drive in air conditioned cabs. Someday soon these things will probably be driving themselves but not the old timers' rigs. Most of them still like to drive the combines themselves!

However, some values here still ring true. Nebraska's motto is: "Honestly, it's not for everyone."

An old car comes barreling down the road kicking up dust in its wake. As it pulls to the farmhouse it stops, backs and turns around ready for a quick exit.

Out steps a woman with a scarf and wearing a big pair of Hollywood sunglasses.

The woman, dressed way out of place for Nebraska, cautiously walks to the front door.

Meanwhile, over a mile away, above the farmhouse, a Reaper drone is watching. And in The Situation Room at the White House Fred Turner and Jerry Fredricks are watching too.

The Reaper drone is capable of being armed.

It isn't.

Armed drones are not allowed to be operated in U.S. airspace.

On a giant screen in front of them they watch the woman knock on the front door of the farmhouse.

"Go to camera 3," barks Fred.

On another screen the front porch is seen from a camera. This is a closeup shot of "Miss Hollywood." It's been hidden between cracks in the old wooden porch.

On Jerry's computer he's running a face recognition scan on the woman.

New computer systems are so good that even with a scarf and huge sunglasses facial recognition systems today can easily find a match.

"Nothing yet," says Jerry.

A woman opens the door hesitantly, "Yes, may I help you?"

"I was wondering if you and yours have life insurance?"

Suspiciously, the owner says, "Thank you we're already are covered."

As the woman inside the house tries to close the door, she's stopped by a forceful hand from Ms. Hollywood.

The women in the house begins to act scared, "If you don't let me close the door I'm callin' the cops."

Ms. Hollywood slowly takes her hand out of the door and says, "Are you sure I can't talk with you for a minute about life insurance?"

The door slams closed.

Jerry's computer has come up with a large red block across his screen and Ms. Hollywood's face that says: NO MATCH.

Fred and Jerry look on with far less interest as they switch to several cameras inside the house. Jerry asks another young kid who's monitoring the screens, "If anyone else comes on the property, get us, okay?"

The kid answers, "Yes, sir."

Fred and Jerry stand and begin to walk out of the room. Jerry asks, "Have you tried the brisket?"

Fred answers, "Is that all you ever think about... food?"

Jerry says, "Donald has them make it with mashed potatoes at all hours of the night. It's fabulous!" Fred shakes his head and walks away.

This is the home of Captain Valentin Vasili. He was the commanding officer that convinced most of his Russian submarine crew to defect to the United States (*JD I*). That is, except for Captain Alexi and Captain Casmerov.

Captain Vasili's wife is now a widow thanks, in part, to his daughter Elena, better known to the world as the mastermind behind a near nuclear war between the United States and Russia (*JD II*). Her own brother and sister were killed in the crossfire trying to escape the CIA. Her father was killed by me in probably the most difficult split second decision I've ever had to make. That decision will haunt me for the rest of my life.

Fred and Jerry began their careers at the NSA. They were moved up to the CIA and eventually to the White House. It would seem, then, this babysitting job of hoping Elena would try to meet her mother would eventually pay off. However, after months and months of extensive surveillance — nothing.

What Fred and Jerry never saw was the note that Miss Hollywood passed to the captain's wife as she stuck her hand in the door.

A FISA (Foreign Intelligence Surveillance Act) court had signed a "Special Secret Surveillance" order on Mrs. Vasili and her home. However, Mrs. Vasili had already swept it for cameras and bugs. Captain Vasili and his wife lived and worked under Communist rule in the old Soviet Union for decades and neither of them trusted anyone! So Mrs. Vasili knew where each and every camera and hidden mic were in her house. She also knew they never put a camera or listening device in her bathroom.

So Mrs. Vasili walks into the bathroom and closes the door behind her.

She opens the note.

All it says is: Post Office Noon.

The situation room in the White House is empty. Even the kid, who was supposed to be watching Mrs. Vasili is gone. Everyone's probably off somewhere eating "The Donald's Brisket."

***

Burchard, Nebraska has one main street. There isn't even a stop light on it. There are a few old, white homes and a whole lot of trees. You have to pull off the main road if you actually want to see the tiny town.

Everyone knew and liked Mrs. Vasili. She baked pies and attended all the square dances and church gatherings. She also had a post office box in town.

As she steps out of her old, white, Ford F-150 pickup with a rusted door, she looks around to see if anyone is following her.

She didn't see anyone.

Little did she know over a mile above her, the Reaper drone was still watching.

Meanwhile back in the Situation Room, Fred and Jerry are casually eating brisket.

"Could you pass the sauce?" asked Jerry. Fred doesn't take his eyes off a book he's reading and passes Jerry some sauce.

Meanwhile Jerry doesn't take his eyes off his brisket as he grabs the sauce.

Nobody seems to be watching a women, who looks identical to Mrs. Vasili, as she walks out of the Burchard post office. She hops in her old truck and heads away from town.

The Reaper drone is controlled like a video game from Randolph Air Force Base in Texas.

A voice comes over the speaker system in the Situation Room from the Reaper pilot, "She's on the move."

Fred and Jerry, bored, look at the screens.

What Jerry doesn't see is the real Mrs. Vasili, with changed clothes, walk out of the post office and get in an old blue car. She drives North away from the Reaper's prying eyes.

Moments later, Mrs. Vasili pulls up to a grain silo and building, cautiously stepping out of her truck. She looks around before walking inside the old, abandoned, building.

She quickly walks inside a flimsy, unlocked door. There is nothing inside this building but rats and dust.

But she's about to reunite with the biggest rat on the face of the earth.

As Mrs. Vasili walks around, she's making a whole lot of a crackling sounds under her shoes. For anyone that's grown up in grain country, you know the sound. The floor has so much old, dry, wheat chaff that someone could hear her coming from the other side of the building.

And that's the point.

Mrs. Vasili, feeling and sounding a bit scared, says, "Elena? It's mom, are you here?"

Out of the shadows with an iPad walks Elena. She's very intent on looking at its screen.

"Their drone went in the other direction. Good job!" says Elena to mom.

Her mom now sees Elena as she steps into the light. The entire right side of Elena's face is hideous. There are shotgun pellet scars on her face from a year ago. I was aiming for the space right between her ears when my stupid gun misfired!

Her mother looks at her daughter in shock looking at her hideous face.

She says hesitantly near tears, "Elena, what do you want?"

Elena can see her mother's staring at her facial scars. Elena tries to cover the scars with her hair and change the subject.

"Whatever they told you, it's not true," says Elena acting very abrupt and defensive. She attempts to touch her daughter's face.

Elena, annoyed, pushes her mother's hand away as if she's a small child.

"It wasn't my fault. A.T. (Anatoli) and Lana (Svetlana) were shot by the CIA and this…" Elena points to the scars on her face, "… this was given to me by a U.S. Navy SEAL by the name of John Denning."

Mrs. Vasili practically collapses from those words.

Elena watches, emotionless, as her mother almost falls.

Mrs. Vasili says, "John? John Denning?"

The Vasili's and I spent many days rocking on their very old, Nebraska porch hammock. We discussed literally anything and everything. They were very different Russians. I thought I understood them better than maybe anyone I'd ever met, except for Jen, of course.

They loved me and I loved them. However, when I went to tell Mrs. Vasili about her husband and his last words, she threw me out of her house. I certainly could understand her anger and pain. I can't imagine the pain I must've caused her. I thought I had the courage to tell Mrs. Vasili that I killed her husband but I couldn't bring myself around to spit that out of my quivering lips.

Poor Mrs. Vasili stares off into space as if she's no longer in the room.

"Our whole family was wiped out by the Americans." says Elena.

Mrs. Vasili doesn't hear this as she stares at some object, seemingly billions of light years away.

Elena confidently speaks, "And I intend to do something about it. I need to know: did dad put away any papers?"

Mrs. Vasili barely even hears what Elena just said but asks, "What do you mean?"

"Did he have papers... any that he might have hid somewhere?"

"I don't think so."

"Did he ever bury anything around the house?"

Mom thinks long and hard, "I don't think so."

Elena is stumped and about ready to give up when mom says, "But he did get a new computer and backed it up every night on a little thing that he hid in the basement."

"That's it! It must be," says a suddenly excited Elena.

"What?" asks mom.

"It's gotta be the missing calculations dad promised me.

"Is it a USB drive?" asks Elena.

"I don't know. It's only about this big and plugs into the side of his computer," says Mrs. Vasili.

"That's it!" exclaims Elena gleefully. Elena continues, "I need you to bring the drive to your post office box and put it in there for me."

"Your father told me not to give that drive to anyone. The FBI took his computer so they probably have this information already," says Mrs. Vasili.

Elena answers, "Knowing dad, probably not! It won't do them any good. The U.S. is way behind my team in quantum physics."

Mrs. Vasili looks long and hard into her daughter's eyes, "Where are you going to go?

"It's best you don't know. I need that USB drive," Elena says sharply."

Mrs. Vasili finally looks at her daughter in the eye and simply answers, "All right."

6

It's a beautiful day in Helsinki, Finland. It's seventy five degrees and a perfect day for two world leaders to meet. The Presidential Palace sits on the grounds where there was an old 19th Century salt warehouse. The interiors have some of the most valuable woods and stones found anywhere on the planet. Some of the world's greatest designers and craftsmen have built a warm, beautiful office and residence for the president of the Republic of Finland.

As you walk into the majestic State Hall with its gorgeous chandeliers you are immediately impressed by its beauty.

Much of the detail the craftsmen put into the rare woods takes your breath away.

However, when Donald Trump entered the room he whispered to Melania, "I still like our lobby in Trump Tower better."

Melania looks at Donald and wonders whether he's kidding or not. No one knows. Maybe not even 'The Donald.' President Putin and President Trump had 'finisht' (a little Finnish humour) a round of private meetings.

Now both presidents were in front of the cameras and commenting. Mr. Trump is asked a question by the Associated Press. It went like this:

"AP: Just now president Putin denied having anything to do with the election interference in 2016. Every U.S. intelligence agency has concluded Russia did. My first question for you, sir, is who do you believe? My second question is would you now with the whole world watching tell president Putin—would you denounce what happened in 2016 and would you warn him to never do it again?"

"TRUMP: So let me just say we have two thoughts. We have groups that are wondering why the FBI never took the server. Why haven't they taken the server? Why was the FBI told to leave the office of the Democratic National Committee? I've been wondering that. I've been asking that for months and months and tweeting it out and calling it out on social media. Where is the server? I want to know, where is the server, and what is the server saying? With that being said, all I can do is ask the question, my people came to me, [director of national intelligence] Dan Coats came to me, and some others, they said, they think it's Russia. **I have President Putin. He just said it's not Russia. I will say**

this. I don't see any reason why it would be,
[EMPHASIS ADDED] but I really do want to
see the server, but I have—I have confidence in
both parties. I really believe that this will
probably go on for a while, but I don't think it
can go on without finding out what happened to
the server. What happened to the servers of the
Pakistani gentleman that worked on the DNC.
Where are those servers? They're missing. Where
are they? What happened to Hillary Clinton's e-
mails? 33,000 e-mails gone, just gone. I think in
Russia they wouldn't be gone so easily. I think
it's a disgrace we can't get Hillary Clinton's
33,000 e-mails. So I have great confidence in my
intelligence people, but I will tell you that
President Putin was extremely strong and
powerful in his denial today. And what he did, is
an incredible offer. He offered to have the
people working on the case come and work with
their investigators, with respect to the 12 people.
I think that's an incredible offer. Okay? Thank
you."[3]

The conference is quickly wrapped as President Trump notices his security team, including Dan Coats, Mike Pompeo and Melania have left the room.

"Mogul" (Donald Trump's Secret Service code name) is whisked into "The Beast," his private multi-million dollar limo, that is "claimed" to be able to withstand a nuclear blast!

Do I believe that?

Hell no!

Why, you ask?

Because it's never been actually tested for a nuclear blast!

Dan Coats, Director of National Intelligence, has a file which he holds in his hand.

The President doesn't seem to be paying any attention as he waves to reporters outside his limo.

Dan looks to the other two in the car, Melania and Mike Pompeo, Secretary of State and former Director of the CIA. They all look like they want to say something but also don't want to go first.

All but Melania.

Melania sees this and says, "Donald?"

Donald looks to Melania, "What honey?"

Melania looks to the guys.

Dan and Mike, both powerful men, look at each other in a brief stare down.

"What? What did I do now?" says Donald totally confused as to why they don't want to speak.

Mike speaks up, "Well, I thought we agreed we weren't gonna make any broad positives or negatives about Russia at this conference, right?"

Donald is confused, "Ya, so?"

Dan jumps in, "So you said to the world you didn't know why Russia would be meddling in our last election, right?"

"Right!" says Donald confidently.

"You said that Russia didn't interfere in our last election."

The Donald is still confused, "Ya."

"Remember that big file we gave you that showed all the ways Russia meddled in our last election?"

"But you said it didn't make any difference, right?" says a confused Donald.

"Right, but we agreed you wouldn't make that conclusion publicly and in front of Putin."

"Oh ya," says a slightly confused Donald.

"Why did you say that?" asks Dan.

"I don't know. I didn't even mean to say that. I don't know what came over me," says "D man."

Mike, Dan and Melania look at each other with grave concern.

Trump all of a sudden grabs his head and winces in pain.

Melania, concerned, says, "Oh Donald, are you all right?"

Trump, in clear pain, "I, I have this shooting pain in my head."

7

If you're ever in Washington, D.C. late at night and want to party, Heist Night Club is the place it goes down. The club is on Jefferson Place off Connecticut Avenue in North West, D.C. You'd never know this place is here if you drove or walked by here during the day. Things usually don't start really happnin' 'till after about 11 p.m.

Henry and Skull are out with my SEAL team trying to have some fun. Henry put together a full report on Mustafa's Night of the Living Dead program where that kid shot himself in the head. Henry's CIA supervisor, an even more nerdy and uptight bureaucrat than Henry, didn't seem to care. Worse, no one at DOD or Justice seemed to care either.

"So what the hell? If they don't care, why should I, I'm havin' a night out," said Henry. "Screw the system. They're gonna do what they want to do or don't want to do anyway."

Zeke, Tommy and Spider, my SEAL team, are all partying hardy.

Skull is the center of attention telling a story, "I was standing in that spot, last night, when a woman... I say woman... she was off the charts 10 plus..."

Zeke interrupts, "Are you telling us her dress size?"

Tommy chimes in, "I hear Henry only likes plus women!"

Henry tries to chime in but is in way over his head so all that comes out is, "Very funny."

Tommy, "Thank you."

Spider is the only one that seems to know anything about women's dress sizes saying, "A 10's a pretty small woman."

Henry says, "You're an expert on women's dresses?"

Spider retorts, "Well no, I just know…"

An annoyed Skull continues, "You sexist pigs, lemme finish my story."

Everyone suddenly sits in dead silence looking at Skull.

Henry says, "All right, go on."

Skull slowly tries to return to his story saying, "She walks up to Henry and asks if he wants to dance." Skull grabs Henry around the neck and puts him in a chokehold, "This idiot says, uh, I don't dance."

Tommy laughs and says, "Smooth, Henry, real smooth."

Henry is clearly embarrassed.

Spider has been very quiet. He notices Henry's embarrassment and says to him, "C'mon, let's get some drinks."

Spider and Henry leave.

Zeke says, "Maybe we shouldn't go so hard on them."

Skull looks incredulous.

Zeke says, "Are you kiddin'? Henry's screamin' to be made fun of."

Everyone laughs except Skull who's looking at Henry and Spider over at the bar.

Skull then, confused, says, "Isn't that the woman?"

They all look at the bar but in shock, and with their mouths open, the hot blond from last night is talking to Henry. Tommy stands up to head for the bar. Skull stops him, "No, man, leave him alone. Let's see if he can reel her in tonight. Not too many get a second chance."

Tommy agrees and sits down again.

Meanwhile at the bar things are really heating up. Henry says to the hot blond sitting next to him, "So do you come here often?"

"No, last night was my first night," says the sexy blond.

Her girlfriend taunts him, "She saw you last night and was hoping you'd be here again tonight."

The hot blond embarrassed tries to stop her from speaking further and covers her mouth, "Terry! Shut up!"

Henry smiles. He looks at this drop dead gorgeous woman and says, "I didn't catch your name?"

"Oh I'm sorry. I'm Candice. What's your name?"

Geeky little Henry says, after nervously pushing his glasses further up his nose, "Henry."

Spider is totally enthralled with, Terry, Candice's enticing brunette friend. Spider says, "Could I buy you a drink?"

"No thank you. I've gotta get up early for work tomorrow. C'mon Candice, we should go."

Candice says looking at Henry, "You have a car?"

Henry quickly answers, "Ya."

Terry looks at Henry and obnoxiously says, "Then you should go home."

Candice, now embarrassed, says, "Terry!"

Terry continues unabated, "Uhh Candice I don't know if this is such a good idea. I mean, no offense, Henry."

Henry quickly says, "None taken."

Terry looks long and hard at both of them. She sees Candice appears to have made up her mind. Terry stands up and says, "All right. Have fun kids!" Terry then turns to Spider, "It was nice meeting you."

Terry stands and leaves while Spider stares as her skinny, long legs walk out of his life. Spider then turns to Candice and says, "It was nice meeting you."

Candice says, "Likewise."

As Spider walks away from the bar and toward Skull, Zeke and Tommy, he makes a 'that was hot' look with his hands and face.

The guys all laugh.

Henry then works up the nerve and asks her, "Wanna dance?"

Candice answers, "No."

Henry, disappointed looks down like a pouting little boy and says, "Oh."

Candice takes her index finger and puts it under his chin, lifts it up so they are eye to eye and says, "But we can go back to my place if you want."

Henry practically spits snot out of his nose. But without doing that or literally anything else he nervously says, "Okay."

Henry quickly pays the bartender and the two of them head out of the bar.

A huge cheer goes up from his rat pack of friends as Candice makes a runway model exit on Henry's arm.

***

Candice's condo is down Connecticut Avenue at 2660. Henry helps Candice out of his black, government issued, car. They walk to the lobby past, perfectly manicured, grass and bushes. Henry thought, well this woman clearly has some class. Even though the building looked like it could be 100 years old it has been recently remodeled.

As they step off the elevator Candice kicks her high heels down the hall. She giggles and laughs as they hit a door.

Henry is clearly a bit worried about the noise level, "I hope that's your door."

"Oh it is!"

As she opens the door Henry sees this is clearly not your average old apartment.

"My God, what's this place worth?"

"Oh I just bought it for 7.5," says Candice.

"Million? Seven point five million dollars?" asks a confused Henry.

"Ya," she says in a very sexy manner.

"What do you do?" asks Henry.

"My family owns things. Lots and lots of things," says Candice taking a chilled bottle of Dom Perignon from the fridge. "Here, open this. I'm going to go somewhere for something." With that Candice disappears into one of the four bedrooms.

Henry is ready to have a heart attack as he stands staring in disbelief at this fantasy. He then realizes he's holding a chilled bottle of very expensive champagne and begins frantically looking for a corkscrew. Eventually, he finds one in a drawer then heads to the bedroom where Candice disappeared. He stops and runs back looking for two wine glasses. He settles for two coffee cups and runs to the bedroom.

He enters the bedroom thinking, this alone must be worth a couple of million dollars. It is decked with plush dark woods, white marble and gold and marble inlays in the crown molding.

Candice is in the bathroom and the door is closed. Henry nervously tries to take out the cork with his bare hands. Finally, he has to use his teeth. The cork pops out and makes quite a unique sound (And for $300.00 a bottle for the "Anniversary Collection" it should do something unique!).

Candice, from the bathroom, excitedly says, "All right Henry! I'm almost ready. You have your clothes off yet?"

Henry begins frantically undressing, "Almost. I'm almost there."

Clothes go flying in every direction. He is carrying his service weapon, a holstered Glock 43 which only weighs slightly over 1 pound. But considering Henry is such a "light" weight, it's perfect for him!

He carefully places his Glock by the side of the bed and then puts his suit on top.

Henry throws back the covers and jumps into bed.

He has to get back out of bed as he left the champagne and cups on the other side of the room. He grabs everything and heads back under the covers.

He pours two very tall "glasses" of Dom Perignon into the coffee "cups" and sets one cup on her side of the bed.

He takes a sip from the coffee cup. He likes it so much that he starts drinking from the bottle. After a moment he straightens the seriously messed up sheets.

"Okay, Candy, I'm ready when you are."

Candice walks out in a really hot looking negligée. She sexily walks to the foot of the bed and crawls onto the bed on top of Henry.

Henry is motionless.

Motionless because Henry has passed out.

It could have been that he's a geek and not used to alcohol but that wasn't the reason.

Candice slaps Henry's face, "Henry! Henry!"

Nothing. Henry's out cold.

Candice goes to the corner of the room and retrieves a small concealed camera device and talks to it, "Now what do you want me to do?"

Before she gets an answer Skull, Zeke, Spider and Tommy burst into the room with guns drawn.

Candice freezes.

A totally naked Candice, freezes.

Spider knowingly says, "I thought you were a little bit too hot for Henry to be believed."

Candice says, "What? He just passed out. Look for yourself." Then Candice says disgustedly, "Could I please put something on?"

Skull tosses her a white robe sitting across a chair. She quickly puts on the robe.

Skull walks over to the champagne bottle, picks it up and hands it to Candice. He says, "Drink it."

Zeke sees the tiny camera that she's trying to hide saying, "What's that you're holding?"

Candice then says, "What? This? Oh, it's a camera. A girl can't be too careful in this town." She pushes away the champagne bottle and suddenly gets very defensive, "What is the meaning of you guys breaking into my place like this?"

Zeke says, "Well after you drink that wine, we're gonna go talk with the manager."

Candice says, "I'm calling the manager right now and have you guys arrested..." Candice walks to a phone on her nightstand. She continues talking while not looking at them, "And it's not wine. It's Dom Perignon."

Skull asks, "Are you gonna drink it or not?"

Candice is on the nightstand phone and also grabbing something on the side of the nightstand. She wheels around with a cheap knockoff of a Walther PPK pistol.

Skull laughs, "There are four of us. Who are you gonna shoot first?"

"Whoever comes at me first?"

Zeke says, "Then you're a dead woman."

Candice retorts, "And then so is the first idiot who comes at me."

Skull intently asks, "Who do you work for?"

Spider asks, "Is Henry, okay?"

Candice, "He'll be fine. I work for the FBI. We think Henry might be passing secrets to Russian agents."

Zeke laughs, "Henry?"

Spider sarcastically says, "Well, if that's not the pot calling the kettle black!"

Zeke, who is black, jokingly says, "What'a you, racist?"

Tommy, who is Hispanic, talks like the old, white, racist character, Captain, played by Strother Martin, in *Cool Hand Luke*, "What we have here is a... Mexican standoff."

Zeke's been looking over the tiny camera says, "So do we wait for the cavalry to come in?"

All of a sudden Candice starts grabbing her ear as she waves her PPK revolver around.

All four guys simultaneously point their weapons at Candice.

Skull screams, "Put the weapon down. Now!"

Candice, appears to be in a lot of pain as the gun drops. She continues to scream holding her hands on each side of her head. She drops to her knees right beside her gun. She takes one hand and quickly reaches for the gun.

Skull screams, "Don't do it" and runs toward the gun.

Candice grabs the gun and everyone but Skull fires several bullets into her. She continues to pick up the gun and she fires at Skull, who's the closest to her. Thirty rounds of bullets are emptied into Candice as she falls to the ground, dead.

Everyone freezes.

The next person to move is Skull who checks to see if he's been hit. A bullet went right through his shirt, missed his arm and went out the back side of his sleeve.

Tommy looks at his shirt which was only grazed too.

Zeke looks at the gun saying, "This is a cheap Chinese knockoff of a PPK... luckily, it's notoriously inaccurate!"

Skull nervously says, "Okay, let's get pretty boy here dressed and get outta here."

Spider, the slowest in IQ of the bunch says, "Shouldn't we wait for the FBI?"

Skull, Zeke and Tommy all say in unison, "No!"

Skull ignoring Spider, "He works for the CIA. They'll know where to find us."

Spider not getting it says, "Well, shouldn't we at least tell the front desk?"

Zeke looks at Skull saying, "Where'd you find this guy?"

Skull sarcastically says, "The Pep Boys parking lot... he was looking for food... in a garbage can."

Spider, still not getting it, says, "But if she lives here someone really needs to know about this."

Zeke stares at Spider for a moment in disbelief that he's really that dumb. Finally, Zeke pries the tiny camera Candice is holding in her cold, dead fingers and looking into the lens says, "Whoever, wherever you are, we will find you."

Zeke and Tommy dress the still unconscious Henry.

Spider asks, "You guys really think the FBI would drug someone?"

All look at each other.

Nobody answers.

Skull is still looking at the pistol, "I doubt anyone in the FBI would use a cheap Chinese knockoff with the serial numbers scratched off."

Zeke, "We're not prepared here for a real gunfight."

All look at each other again, then hurriedly drag a half dressed Henry from the room.

8

Melania and The Donald are in bed on Air Force One heading back to D.C. The room is all white, including the satin sheets on the bed. It looks more like a room out of a Vogue cover shoot than the inside of a jet. Melania has decorated this room herself.

Donald has on a pair of reading glasses and is reading the New York Times print edition.

Melania is reading a nice children's book titled, "I've Loved You Since Forever."

Donald mumbles, "Those bastards!"

Melania shakes her head, sees what he's reading and says, "Oh Donald, why do you read that stuff? It makes you so mad."

"These bastards are twisting the facts again. Fake. Fake. Fakers!"

Melania curls up close to him. "I'm worried about you Donald. Why didn't you let your doctor look at you today when you had that terrible headache..."

Donald says, "No time for doctors. I gotta get back to Washington."

Acting very sexy, Melania tries to kiss him on the lips, "Why don't we get some sleep?"

Donald says, "If you want us to get some sleep. That's not the way to do it."

Melania playfully says, "Maybe I don't really want to sleep."

Donald grabs her and rolls her onto her back, "Come here you little vixen. I knew there was a reason I married you!"

She stops him and asks, "So what happened to you today?"

Donald responds, "Dunno. Was weird. "It seemed like I didn't know what I was saying. It was like I couldn't control my words. I wanted to say one thing and the opposite thing actually came out. I'll go back out tomorrow and correct all that."

This seems to satisfy Melania more than "anything" else.

As The Donald continues to kiss her, one of his hands rubs the area where that "thing" was implanted in his head as he looks a bit confused.

9

One of the most beautiful parts of Portland, Oregon is the area around Reed College. I've always loved driving through this part of town. Well, with the exception of one cold, rainy night. I grew up near here and slammed my 1965 Mustang convertible into a telephone pole right in front of the college. I was 16 and the stupid kid in the car with me asked, "How fast can you go around corners?" I was young and stupid too and didn't know that answer. So I had the car up to about 60 miles per hour when I hit a big stack of wet leaves. The car slid off the road and right into a light pole. I flipped the electric lines on to my car and they started sparking as they danced across the steel hood. As we sat there I asked my "friend," "You okay?" He said, "Ya" and started to get out of the car when I yelled, "Stop!"

I didn't know much at 16 but I did know electricity, metal, water and humans don't mix.

The police department, who never wrote me a ticket, told me later that I likely saved my friend's life!

Come to think of it, I don't like this street at all!

But Reed College does have a beautiful campus. A long, plush green, front lawn of the college looks more like Harvard or Yale than a college in Portland. It's a tiny school by university standards. There are only about 1,600 undergrad students.

So you might be asking: So what are two Russians, Jen and I doing here?

I'm getting there — as slow as it may seem. I am getting there.

Alexi and Casmerov seemed to really like Portland a lot more than living in Haines, Alaska. But Alexi did say he liked Haines, Alaska a lot more than Russia! These guys were more like kids in a candy store loving everything they were experiencing. It's really kinda fun to watch.

The Russians stood in a Fred Meyer the other day and couldn't believe the number of different kinds of bread on one aisle. I was enjoying their company — Jen? Not so much. They were living with us since they had no money, no references and were sprung from the most notorious max prison in America!

The FBI, Jen and I used to work for, was supposed to set up Alexi and Casmerov with their own place but their paperwork went "missing" so we got stuck babysitting. Jen's much more paranoid than me. She thinks it's intentional. I doubt it. I know how the government operates. They'll pay billions for something, if the paperwork is in order.

I guess I should tell you that Jen quit working for the FBI after she saw politics became far more important than the law.

The reputation of the FBI has dramatically suffered with all of the Trump, Russian collusion stories. No one I met in Washington, military, non-military, even die hard politicians, wanted to talk about the Trump - Russia collusion.

Politics had become so bad at the FBI that it literally started to depend on how well you were connected in Washington. That connection depended on how important you were. And that depended on whether you were "in" or — were in jail. The drug lowlife would get 20 years in federal lockup while a well connected politician skated. We haven't evolved any further than the feudal system except now the peasants, who work for the king, are trying to take out the king.

The job was easy.

The politics killed us.

I was glad to leave too!

However, life recently had been difficult for us.

I was not home as I was constantly flying all over the world with the SEALs. I told Jen not to quit but she was so done with the FBI that she actually might have burned her bridges on her way out. She told off her boss and said it felt, "really, really good!"

I said, "What if you want your job back?"

Jen said, "I will never go back to the Portland FBI."

"I said, "Never say never."

With my new title as Commander of a SEAL team there was much to be done. Unfortunately, there was too much talking, talking about paperwork, doing paperwork and definitely not enough action.

The guys complained that whether we went on missions or not had become more and more political. This wasn't only with the current administration. This had been going on more and more since I had left the SEALs.

But the guys left those decisions for the politicians to decide.

Me?

I no longer trusted politicians.

Any of them!

Jen is getting anxious for me to ask her to marry her. I want to but haven't found the right time, just yet.

Anyway, we go onto the Reed College campus. We're looking for one of Professor Ruddy's friends, a Russian Professor, Anton Pavlov. We're trying to track down the missing nuke that Ruddy and Katrina recovered off of those Iranian kids.

I'm sure they didn't need to shoot and kill four teens. Publicly, both Russia and the United States pretend there are no nukes walking around the U.S.

Why don't I believe politicians?
They claim all the nuke suitcases have been recovered!
Have they?
Hell no!
No politician will admit a nuke blast went off in Alaska!
Can you imagine what the media would do if they knew there could be "any number" of nuke suitcases wondering around North America?

There is at least one nuke that we know of and our best intelligence believes it's still somewhere in the greater Portland area.

This professor we're looking for is a pretty well known nuclear biologist. This seems suspicious since Reed college doesn't have a nuclear biology program. What's even more suspicious is that Reed College has a working nuclear reactor on campus! Again, it has no nuclear biology or medicine program! Weird. Really, really weird.

We were already sent ID badges. That was nice. I seriously doubt the college is, in any way, involved in this. However, the Russian professor, I'm not so sure.

Alexi's cover name is: Tom Beatty. Casmerov is: Jonathan Stein. They proudly already had their IDs around their necks. It must be a Russian thing. I refuse to be intimidated by rules so I had my badge hidden in my pants pocket. Jen notices and asks, "Where's your badge?"

"Badges? We don't need no stinkin' badges!"

Jen immediately laughs and says, "Treasure of the Sierra Madre. What year was that?"

"1948. John Huston wrote and directed his father, Walter Huston, who won an oscar for his role as…"

Jen interrupts, "… okay, okay! I'm sorry I asked."

It's a really weird thing, how so much information is right at the tip of my tongue. I really do love this new found memory. I used to be terrible at remembering certain things. I had short term memory loss. Which means I could say or do something and literally three seconds later, not remember what I just did or said. Very dangerous. Especially for a Navy SEAL commander.

But not any more!

Suddenly, I hear this weird bird noise above my head. In a tree nearby is a kid dressed all in black and in black face staring at me.

All four of us stand there watching this crazy kid pretend to be some sort of "Birdman." Another student walks up to us and says, "That's Kyle. He's experiencing what it's like to have a black face in a white space."

Jen says truly confused, "What?"

I then say, "Does he know what black face means?"

The kid looks at me with a blank face. We look at each other and continue into the L.E. Griffin Memorial Biology Building.

Over the top of the building is a sign that says:

WELCOME TO SWAMP RAT, OREGON
POPULATION 1,606
(Not including the rats!)

Maybe this story will help put my nonchalant attitude toward the crazy kids here into context. This campus had a low power radio station, KRRC that was started by students in the 1950's. It only had a 10 watt transmitter. I had a 50 watt transmitter on my CB radio (illegal, but that's another story)! I lived less than a mile from Reed growing up but couldn't hear the station half the time! I loved to sneak an old radio under the covers late at night when I was supposed to be going to sleep and listen to old shows of the local Reed legend, Dr. Demento. The good doctor was Reed's "official weirdo of the weirdos."

As we walk I notice a door with a name on it. All it says is: "PROFESSOR NUTT"

Is that a joke?

Maybe, it's Reed College.

And this is Portland… so, probably!

I stop a student walking past me, "Excuse me miss, we're looking for Professor Pavlov."

"He" answers in a very deep voice not caring that I called him a woman, "Right there."

I now realize my mistake and am about to apologize when I realize Jen, "Tom," and "Jonathan" are already walking into the professor's classroom.

I look back to "the guy" who helped me but he's long gone. I mumble in the direction he was last spotted saying, "Thanks."

I catch up and wander into the professor's classroom. It's empty except for the four of us.

I call out, "Professor Pavlov?" There is no answer.

I check my watch. We had an appointment for 2 p.m. It's 2:02.

Jen says, "I'm going to the office to see if…"

A shot rings out just missing my head.

All four of us drop to the floor and pull our guns.

That's right. I gave Alexi and Casmerov guns!

I hope I don't regret that!

Is it legal that two Russian felons have guns?

Probably not!

The Presidential Pardon wasn't clear on that issue.

So I took some liberties and gave these guys guns.

I motion to Alexi. He rolls and exits a second door leading to the main hall.

Jen looks at me. I motion for her to head toward the only other door in the room. This sounds like from where the shot rang out.

As we close in on the door it looks like the shooter has fled. I kick open the door and we are in another classroom. On the far side of the room a door leading to the main hall is slowly closing. Jen and I run for that door. I look around and only now realize Casmerov is nowhere to be seen.

It looks like he might have run out of the wrong door leading to the outside of the building.

As I kick open the hall door I can see a man standing with his hands in the air. A gun is still in his hand.

As Jen and I slowly walk into the hall guns drawn and pointed at the man, I can see Alexi has already stopped the man by standing in the path of the only exit at the end of the hall. Alexi is pointing his Glock at the man.

The man starts to slowly back away from us toward his only exit left. Casmerov comes running from that direction and pulls his gun. He's out of breath as he apparently ran around this entire building.

The man realizes he's cornered. He pauses.

I yell, "Drop it."

The man has a blank stare on his face like he's trying to understand what that meant.

Alexi then says, "бросать пистолет," which in Russian is: "drop the gun."

The man seems to not understand that either. Suddenly he grabs his head and starts screaming in pain. He begins to wildly fire his weapon. All four of us unload at least 20 rounds into him.

He falls immediately to the ground.

I walk up and push the gun away from his cold, dead fingers.

I then check his pockets.

Nothing. No ID. No papers. Nothing.

I look at Alexi first and jokingly say, "Okay now we're even."

Alexi says, "I'd say I'm two, you zero!"

Casmerov is still trying to catch his breath.

Alexi laughs and says, "вам нужен Джек Дэниелс!"

Casmerov barely spits out one word, "Da!"

Jen and I look at Alexi inquisitively.

Alexi says, "I say you need Jack Daniels... he agree."

I think, *Russians!*

Actually, that's pretty good.

They must have fallen in love with "Jack" during those long, cold Alaskan winters.

Casmerov, "So in America, who cleans this up?"

I pull out my phone and disgustedly say, "Oh we have people."

***

A short time later we're sitting in the President of Reed College's office. Thomas Watson is a kind looking man in his 60's. "I don't understand. We've never had anything like this ever happen here. We had a wonderful grad student that defended two woman from some guy on the MAX."

MAX is Portland's light rail system. Some "guy" was harassing two Muslim girls when two guys stepped in. The man pulled a knife and stabbed both of them, killing them. One of them was a student at Reed College.

Jen nudges me as I'm lost in thought: *How could someone do that?*

About ten thousand other things flew past my brain but the only thing that comes out of my mouth is, "Professor Nutt... is that with two Ts?"

The president is taken back. "What? Oh, on the door in biology? Kids are playing a bit of an inside joke on one of our own."

I ask, "Nuts?"

The president sounds very presidential, "I believe we have fun around here. There's nothing illegal about that, is there?"

I smile, "No, sir."

Jen jumps in asking, "Where is Professor Pavlov?"

The president looks me straight in the eye and says, "We haven't seen him all week. We're very worried."

I ask, "Did you report this?"

President Watson quickly fires back, "No. No. He's done this before. So we thought maybe he just wandered off again."

"You need to give a statement to the officers. For now, if we could get a cell phone and address that would be most appreciated."

The president seems to have nothing to hide, "Oh sure. My secretary can give you all of that."

Jen and I stand up to leave. Jen says, "Thank you for your help, sir."

As we leave, the president continues, "If there's anything I can do please don't hesitate to let me know."

I politely answer, "Thank you. We'll be in touch."

Alexi and Casmerov are in the president's waiting room. We leave the administration building and head for our car.

When we arrive at our car I pop the trunk and pull out a military grade geiger counter with a directional finder on it.

I can't believe we're getting some pretty high readings for radiation in a parking lot.

"Look at this," I say to Jen and the Russians.

Alexi says, "You said they have working reactor on campus. Maybe you're picking up that."

Jen who's a nuclear engineer and former Lieutenant Commander of the nuclear powered boomer submarine the USS *Alaska* says, "Maybe in Russia a reactor would have that level of leakage but an American reactor better not be leaking that much radiation." Jennifer, worried, looks around. "No there's a much higher radiation source and it's close. Probably in this parking lot."

We all look around in fear.

Everybody pulls their guns.

I motion for everyone to fan out.

All four of us head for the four corners of the parking lot and then start working our way toward the center.

All of a sudden an old rusted, dark brown, Chevy panel van practically runs over Jen. We all began firing rounds into the van as it speeds away.

10

It's July and it's cloudy but at least it's not raining. Ketchikan, Alaska has a way of raining at any moment and it looks like it might — again. That wouldn't stop the Great Alaskan Lumberjack Show. In the summertime it went on as often as five times a day.

Former Police Chief Robert Stone sits with the Mayor of Ketchikan, Mark Brown. The show hasn't started yet so the two shoot the breeze. Former Chief Stone says, "Well, that's a very generous offer but I'd like to take it easy for a while."

Mayor Mark says, "Well, I hope you'll take this offer seriously. This place has not been the same since you left." The mayor stands.

"You're not staying for the show?" asks Stone.

"No, I've gotta go to the office," says the mayor.

The mayor maneuvers past the wooden benches packed with cruise ship tourists. As soon as the mayor leaves an old friend of Stone's moves in front of an annoyed row of tourists. He sits next to the chief. Stone isn't aware that his friend and bush pilot, Jimmy Thomas (JT), is sitting beside him. Jimmy waits until Stone turns.

JT is in his 90s and still flying!

If that doesn't scare you, nothing will.

A huge smile comes across Stone's face, "Jimmy! How ya doin', man?"

They Alaskan bear hug each other.

Jimmy asks, "So where ya been?"

"Oh here and there. Gettin' in ta trouble," says Stone (which is the understatement of the century!). Stone continues, "How are you, JT?"

"Good. Good, jolly good." replies Jimmy with his Queen's English accent.

JT fell in love with Alaska right after he fought in World War II. He moved here as he said, he felt a "connection with the sky" in Alaska. He also said he felt "closer to God more here than any place on earth."

"What've you been up to?" asks Stone.

"Oh it's crazy 'round here. The place is like an occupied foreign country. The military's using the entire town as a staging area. A whole lot of people we know left for the lower 48."

"I've noticed," replies Stone.

"Ya, nothing's the same 'round here, except for summertime, when all these tourists pay my bills for the rest of the year," says JT happily, as this is the majority of his business.

"You still flyin'?" asks Stone.

"Ya, but if you try to fly west of here they'll yank your pilot's license," says the disgusted Brit.

"Bokan?" Stone asks.

JT responds, "Ya, no one can get near that mountain anymore. The 'hottest' local attraction is at the high school gym. On Wednesday night the homemade Geiger counter club meets."

"Radiation?" Stone asks.

JT says, "Ya, the few that still live here are paranoid. Military says there's nothing to worry 'bout but many locals don't believe them. Are ya gonna move back?"

"Ya," says Stone begrudgingly, "My wife has family here. So it makes more sense. Besides, the rest of the world is crazier than here," says Stone.

"Things are pretty crazy 'round here too," says Jimmy.

Stone then says, "I love this place… and I hate this place! So I hear your new police chief's nuts."

"Well, let's say, there's nuts, fuckin' nuts, then there's Chief Butler!"

"I heard he dressed up like Darth Vader and came to work one day. For Halloween?"

"It was last month! He punched in and started working like it was a normal Monday… except he had on a Darth Vader helmet!"

"Well, that is nuts," says Stone.

"That's not the half of it. Another day they found him in front of the police station riding some kid's tricycle, yelling, "Daddy, come home!"

"Really?" says Stone laughing.

The crowd starts to cheer as a young man dressed in black, obnoxiously takes center stage.

"Who's ready ta have some fun?" says the guy with an over modulated, wireless microphone.

"I'm Chuck Nature. Part time newsman… full time comedian!"

The crowd claps politely as any good cruise ship audience would. He's been "trying" stand-up comedy for some time and has been booed out of every club in Anchorage. He works for ABC TV 14 in Anchorage as a reporter and meteorologist. Chucky has been reviewed as "possibly the worst comedian I've ever seen… living or dead… and the audience last night preferred the latter." Another merciless review, "It helps to order much more than the two drink minimum as quickly as possible!" And those reviews were from his co-workers!

"A tree walks into a bar and asks, Witch way to the bathroom?' Bartender says, I wooden know. I think you'd better leaf. The tree doesn't leaf so the bartender says, You must take me for a sap! So then the tree says, stop barking and pour me a logger."

Chucky is the only one laughing as the tourists stare at him.

"Harold Potter, pilot extraordinaire, who got Alexi and Casmerov away from the U.S. Coast Guard, sits alone on the side of the stage, drinking. He yells, "Get the Russians back. They were funny.""

The crowd laughs at drunk Harry as he slides off his chair and hits the floor.

This gets an even bigger laugh from the crowd.

Chucky nervously tries to laugh at Harry Potter.

Stone leans over to Jimmy, "Is this guy's material all this bad?"

Jimmy answer cheerfully, "Oh no. It gets worse. A lot worse. The locals all hate him. He's from California. He's the only one that's ever thought those lines are funny. The only thing that's actually funny is that he takes his comedy pretty seriously."

Chucky continues his disaster, "An owl walks into a bar and says, "How about you sing me happy birthday?" Bartender says, "Sorry pal, this isn't Hooters.""

This time one large woman in the front row starts laughing. Chucky plays to her, "Thank you ma'am. I'm here all week."

"She quickly says, "Thank God! I'm not!""

Now the audience laughs.

It's never a good sign when the audience is funnier than the "talent."

Backstage two female, muscle bound, loggers are watching Chucky's disaster unfold. One says to the other, "C'mon, before he ruins our show." They both take the stage. Chucky says, "Who wants ta see some real loggers?"

Finally, the audience has something to cheer about 'till they see they're women. The clapping quickly subsides.

A bearded, tough looking, logger sits next to Stone.

Upon seeing the two muscle bound women he mumbles, "Alaska: Where men are men and some of the women are too!"

Stone claps and laughs at this.

11

Mrs. Vasili is baking pies in her old but "tasteful" kitchen. The old farmhouse never smelled so good.

There's a knock at the door. She looks outside and sees a black SUV sitting in front of her house.

She goes to the door and hesitantly opens it. She knows these are likely "G" men but pretends to play stupid. "I don't need any insurance. I don't need any..."

Fred is standing with Jerry. Fred pulls out identification and interrupts, "Excuse me ma'am. We're from the White House and have a few questions."

She tries to close the door when Jerry puts his foot in the way. "We have a warrant. We can do this the easy way or we can do this the hard way."

Mrs. Vasili opens the door disgustedly mumbling, "... thinks he's Rambo..."

Fred motions to the SUV. Two more big looking dudes standing nearby head for the front door. Fred, trying to change the mood, says cheerfully to Mrs. Vasili, "Oh something smells nice."

Mrs. Vasili is walking to the kitchen again mumbling, "Ya, well something in here stinks."

Mrs. Vasili has left the room. The two big dudes walk through the door and Jerry motions for them to search the house.

Somewhere in Paris, Elena hears an alert on her phone. She pulls out her phone and sees the very same camera feeds Fred and Jerry were using to spy on her mom. She says, "God damn it!" Elena hails a cab. She jumps in and speeds off.

Meanwhile Fred and Jerry have followed Mrs. Vasili to her kitchen. Fred very innocently asks, "When was the last time your daughter contacted you?"

Mrs. Vasili quickly answers, "Sometime before you people murdered my husband."

Fred and Jerry look at each other. They hear something break in the other room.

This upsets Mrs. Vasili and she heads in the direction of the breaking glass. "That better have not been what I think it was."

Fred stops her and, annoyed, says, "I'm sorry Mrs. Vasili. Jerry, go see what the hell that was."

Jerry quickly leaves the room.

Fred continues, "This will go much quicker if you're honest with us."

Mrs. Vasili stops and looks as if she might cooperate. She sits and starts to cry. Fred has no idea how to react. Mrs. Vasili says, "My family. You wiped out my entire family and now you want me to tell you where my only living daughter is? Even if I knew I'd never tell you."

Fred seems sympathetic, "I understand your pain…"

"You don't understand!"

Fred stops because, it's true, he doesn't understand squat.

Jerry finally enters the room and shakes his head to Fred meaning they found nothing.

Fred looks back at Mrs. Vasili who's staring at the floor. Fred says, "Okay, we're going to go now. I'm going to set my card here. If you change your mind please call me."

Jerry pipes up, "Please send a bill to that address and we'll pay for the vase we broke."

Fred and Jerry look at Mrs. Vasili who sits motionless. They both leave.

They meet the other two guys standing at the front door. All four hop into the SUV and drive away.

Mrs. Vasili stares as the floor when her oven starts smoking. She shrieks and jumps to her feet. She grabs some oven mitts and flings open the oven door.

Smoke pours out as she grabs her blackened pies. She tosses them into the trash one by one.

When all of this is done she stands in the middle of the smoke like General Patton. She looks toward the SUV's kicking up dust heading away from her farm. She says, "Time to take out the trash!"

12

Monaco, a city state, on the French Riviera is filled with the wealthiest of the wealthiest. The Grand Prix races right through the streets of Monte Carlo. I thought the Long Beach, California Grand Prix was something. But it was nothing compared to the Grand Prix in this tiny but very rich city state.

Elena's people have taken over the entire Villa La Vigie in beautiful Monte Carlo, France. Elena managed to steal several billion dollars from unsuspecting banks.

She spent some of it to take over the NSA's Utah Data Center (*JD II*). The problem was: her money was no longer able to be hidden in bitcoin, litecoin, ethereum, zcash, dash and ripple.

Her anonymity began to evaporate as she was forced to transact her "anonymous" money on big, centralized exchanges that collected detailed user data — and then provided it to government investigators. No matter how well Elena hid who she was, someone was able to snoop around her assets.

She also had to worry about criminals. A Russian "banker" had already stolen about 100 million from her — that's right — 100 million dollars in bitcoin alone!

There were lots of people looking for Elena.

It was only a matter of time before they found her, and her money, or what was left of it.

Elena is having a problem getting to her cash without drawing attention to herself. Her business people spent months laundering bitcoin through legitimate businesses throughout the world. This included many construction companies who were rebuilding what Elena had recently destroyed!

Nice scam, if you can get it.

Cities, ships, airports, and famous sites are all being rebuilt, in part, by Elena's companies. Adding insult to injury, she was actually making a nice profit! It's nice to have the money to hire the best and the brightest. These guys had no idea who their real boss was.[4]

All they knew is that they worked for a multi-billionaire recluse. Word was, "If you thought Howard Hughes was strange, you've never met this guy!"

That was the line all "her" people were told to spread.

Elena pulls up in a sparkling new, black, Rolls Royce SUV. You wouldn't know it from looking at this thing that the base price is $325,000.00!

Her bodyguards hustle to the car. Elena casually steps out of the car looking very elegant in an Oscar de la Renta Fishnet Embroidered Gown.

Elena enters the lobby of this magnificent villa that sits on a cliff overlooking some of the most expensive real estate and private yachts collected anywhere in the world.

She continues down some stairs to the basement.

This facility would make a James Bond villain very jealous.

The rock walls and cool salt air make this place a perfect place to hide from the world. The floor of the tunnel is smooth black granite.

She actually imported this granite from mines in India.

It's weird because it's shiny like you think you'd slip and slide. Instead you could walk across this in cotton socks and not feel like your slipping around at all.

Elena walks past many scientists working feverishly in front of twenty banks of servers, similar to the Utah Data Base and the DARPA stage in Virginia.

It's amazing how few questions people ask when they're being paid extremely well.

She walks aggressively to a scientist, Doctor Franz Gebhardt. He is an imposing man. He is tall and slender with chiseled cheekbones. He looks more like a Greek god than a scientist.

"So when are we operational with Denning and Trump?"

"Deep brain stimulation is not an exact science. Not at all exact."

"Yet. You mean deep brain stimulation is not an exact science yet? Correct?"

The "good" doctor is a very nervous and a repetitive person who speaks very quickly and abruptly, "Of course. Of course. We're almost there. I promise. I promise."

Elena impatiently asks, "So what's the holdup?"

The doctor responds, "The specially built DNA strands are not attaching to their specific neuron receptors in the brain. We're having problems with heating our nanoparticles that are instead attaching to the wrong…"

"All right Einstein, how long?" asks an impatient Elena.

"It could be a few hours, days, or weeks."

"We don't have weeks. You have 24 hours!"

The scientist who looks twice the size of Elena quickly answers, "Oh sure, sure."

Elena looks at him suspiciously then heads for the stairs.

Upstairs, a group of men wait for her in the library. Beautiful, but dark, African woods accent the room. Black cherry and black maple give this library a look that exudes money and class.

This tall room is covered with books from floor to ceiling.

The irony is: It's all for show. Elena has never cracked a book since she was in Russian elementary school. Since then she's only used laptops and tablets. It's no surprise she graduated from NYU with a computer science degree. So these books are ancient history. But this room does make an impressive place to meet.

If you want to hide from an angry, poor, destitute world and you have lots of money, this is the place you'd most want to be.

In Monaco.

And in this villa.

I could go around the table and name all of her well-dressed henchmen but it would do no good. The average person would not recognize one name. However in business, finance, internet, corporate governance, and security, these men are the titans behind the titans of the planet.

Elena storms in and shuts the tall, black, cherry, doors.

"All right, somebody start talking."

The youngest in the room, a kid no more than in his late 20's, speaks, "U.S. agents left your mother's house without finding anything. Our ghost protocol system is currently being rebuilt. It will take some time before its operational again as the…"

Elena cuts him off and asks, "What did she do after the CIA guys left?"

The kid now becomes much more hesitant to answer, "Well she… she burned some pies and then started…"

"Started what?"

"She started crying."

Elena screams, "I want all those people dead. You hear me? Dead!"

"Yes ma'am."

"And where's Denning?"

"In D.C. When they extract the device from our D.C. operative it will lead Denning to Paris. We're repeating the suggestion to Denning's brain that he wishes he could find you."

"Excellent! Grant him his wish!"

13

I'm sitting in a doctor's office at an "undisclosed location" with Henry. This CIA place is known as "The Intelligence and Investigation Laboratory - Lancashire."

Insiders refer to this place as "ILL" as pretty much the only things that come out of this place either has made or can make people "ill."

Usually, anything nuke, biological or chemical (NBC) can be tested at the FBI labs.

This medical laboratory is state of the art. Even the FBI doesn't have clearance to these highly sensitive materials.

This is one of those cases.

I haven't told Henry about this thing in my head yet.

I'm playing with the doctor's Newton cradle. You know those metal hanging balls that swing back and forth to hit each other. They transfer the same amount of energy from one set across to the other when they swing and hit the others. When one set of balls hit the others the first set of balls stop, transfer their energy and propel the exact same number of balls into the air.

Anyway, I'm playing with these when I notice I'm really annoying Henry.

"What?"

"Do you really have to do that?"

"What do you want me to do?"

Dr. Allan enters his office. He's an ordinary looking man in a white lab coat. The doctor is holding a small baggie. Inside the baggie is a small, round, metal disk. It's about the size of a quarter.

"Well, we've pulled this out of the decedent who is, weirdly enough, not yet been identified. Want more weird?"

"Please," I say.

"We have no idea what this is. We've run this through battery after battery of tests. I can tell you many, many things about this device but what I cannot tell you is how it works. I might as well have found this on Mars. And if I had found this on Mars, I'd of guessed this came from some very advanced alien civilization because all of the pieces combined in here should not work as they, apparently, do.

"So what are you saying, doctor?"

"I'm saying that whoever or whatever implanted this device in the decedent has such advanced knowledge of neurobiology and neuroscience and several other areas like quantum mechanics that I would really, really like to speak with them."

"Anything else?"

"Yes. The chip was actually manufactured by a tiny company in Paris."

"What?" I ask with suspicion.

"That's right. As strange as it may seem. This chip has no other identifying marks except for the stamp on the back of the chip. It's almost as if someone was shouting from a rooftop, it's me! Come get me!"

Henry and I look at each other knowing what Paris means.

We stand and shake the doctor's hand.

"Thank you doctor."

Henry chimes in, "Yes, thank you doctor."

The doctor's final words to me are ominous, "Be careful."

We walk out of the office and I say to Henry, "Jen won't be happy with me but pack your bags. We're goin' ta Paris!"

Henry says, "I can't. I have to find out on this end who's behind all of this."

I look carefully at Henry and realize he's right.

"Be careful," I say and then think: *What a stupid comment?*

Henry seems to notice. He smiles and says, "You too!"

14

Diary of Olga Kasparov

As anchor of Russian TV-12 I have always towed party line. But because of this, I always have exclusive interviews with people in power, like president. Last president's fate did not end well. As I sit opposite most powerful man in Russia today, I'm very nervous.

President Putin is not paying any attention to me but distracted by his own assistant that's briefing him. I'm relieved that I've been told I can ask president "anything" I want. I'm suspicious of this, as I know my TV station is controlled by the government.

My stage manager shouts to me, "мы зайдем через 5 секунд," which translates we're going in 5 seconds.

Mr. Putin's assistant rushes off camera and I look directly into teleprompter located directly above the camera.

Stage manager says, "пять, четыре, три..."

I pause until I see the stage manager quickly make a fist as he moves his hand from the front of the teleprompter.

"Good evening I'm Olga Kasparov and this is Russia 12 Today."
Dramatic Russian music and a cool graphic briefly takes over the screen.

"I'm privileged to be sitting here with the President of the Russian Federation, President Putin."

I reach over and shake his hand.

"Good to be here Miss Kasparov," he replies.

"This has been a trying time for Russia and the world," I say. "Russia was mercilessly attacked without provocation. There has not been this level of attack since Hitler's Germany mercilessly killed twenty million Russians in 1939."

The president solemnly responds, "It's been a trying time once again for the Russian people. But we are survivors. No matter what."

"Many people believe the Americans were behind this attack on Moscow. Can you confirm that?" I ask.

"At this point we cannot confirm the Americans ordered this attack. What we can confirm is that some of the servers which assisted this attack were run by American intelligence."

"So what are you saying?" I ask.

The president responds, "I'm not saying anything other than what I know. I will say that we have a number of assets in the United States helping to get to the bottom of this. In fact, two highly decorated Russian Naval Officers helped save millions of lives. How were they repaid? They were sent to a supermax prison in Colorado."

I feel confident in asking a tough question, "Some reporters in the United States are claiming that there are one or more Russian nuclear suitcases somewhere in the United States. Is this true?"

The president becomes somewhat evasive. "We take very seriously accusations like that. We believe there were rogue elements of both governments conspiring to start a nuclear war. Their intentions were to blame all on the governments of Russia and the United States. They had one purpose in mind: to take over the military and political systems of the U.S. and Russia. Again, we're fully cooperating with the U.S. government to find the perpetrators."

I press him on the sources of these attacks, "So do you believe the secret society of The Snakes were behind these attacks?"

President Putin confidently answers. "They certainly had a hand in this. That is all I will say about them for now."

I then ask, "Forgive me, I have to ask you this as well: Western media have been pounding on this for months, Did you try and affect the outcome of the American elections?"

"Preposterous! You think some Russians sitting on a computer in Penza could affect the votes of 120 million Americans? If so, I'd like these people to show me how! I would like them to do that for my next election."

I laugh out loud. That really was a good line. And Penza, as Russians know, is one of the poorest regions in all of Russia. I continue, "Now, due to all the American hysteria, I also must ask: Did you collude or in any way do anything to help Donald Trump get elected?"

The president does not like this question at all. But he answers saying, "Mr. Trump ordered the bombing of 200 Russians in Syria. All of them were killed by U.S. bombs. He put sanctions on several of our businessmen and their businesses. Finally, he is actively trying to stop a multi-billion dollar pipeline between us and Germany. If I helped him in any way, I'm now really sorry."

I smile. This man is actually quite funny.

The president continues, "Democrats in the United States thought they had won the election. Their egos were hurt, so they made up this fantasy because the truth is too hard for some to accept. Republicans are no better. They claim we helped Mrs. Clinton by writing a fake dossier. Yet they provide no evidence Russians were involved. A former British spy made up this fantasy."

I'm not sure that's entirely true. I really want to ask more questions on this subject as the president likely knows more than he is saying. However, for the sake of easing very tense relations between Russia and the United States, I move on to lighter subjects.

"So I understand you have a beautiful, new girlfriend? Is this true?"

"A gentleman never talks about such private matters," Putin replies with a slight smile.

I really wanted to ask more political questions but, instead, I meandered into nonsense and fluff for the better part of the hour.

When we were done and the cameras were off Mr. Putin pulled me close and said, "You did wonderful. I will come back here any time you wish."

What charmer the man is.

15

As my plane lands into the fog at Charles de Gaulle Airport, France, I'm careful not to talk to anyone on the flight. I was once told by an NBA referee friend, Greg Willard, to be careful if some young, beautiful woman flirts with you. You never know who they really are. One NBA referee went to jail because he was accused of helping fix NBA games for mobsters.

Greg said, "When I get on a flight and someone wants to get chatty seated next to me and they ask: What do you do for a living? I tell them... I sell toilet paper. That always shuts them up!"

If I don't want to talk with someone I turn back and forth between CNN and FOX News on the TV in front of me. Whichever one seems to annoy them the most, that's the station I leave on for the entire flight!

As I disembark I think I might have picked up a tail. It was pretty easy to spot. The guy was mirroring every one of my moves.

Bad spycraft.

As I bend down to take a drink of water at a drinking fountain, I no longer see the tail. I look around carefully. This new brain implant can help me scan everyone and look into their background in seconds. None of the people I'm scanning even remotely would set off warning bells.

He must've realized I spotted him, as this guy's nowhere in sight. I, again, carefully look over the area and even though the terminal's pretty crowded this guy appears to be long gone.

As I walk to the front, I've already summoned an Uber.

This chip thing is really cool, really cool 'till someone sets it off and turns me into a murderous zombie.

I'd like to rent something really nice but the last car I rented in Paris I could've outrun!

I didn't tell anyone except Jen where I was going as I can't trust anyone. All I need is for someone to tip off Elena.

Little did I know, Elena already knew – and was waiting for me!

16

Several unwashed, rough looking Teamsters are quickly laying cable. Lighting technicians are working on focusing spotlights.

The Oval Office of the White House is an amazing room. It exudes beauty and class. The office sits right next to the Rose Garden. There are three large south facing windows right behind the president's desk. There is a beautiful fireplace at the north end of the room.

Donald Trump sits behind his desk going over some papers.

He has a makeup person and a hairstylist pampering him.

Several aides rush around the room making sure everything's in order. One of the aides looks over some papers then rushes out of the room. He runs into Mike Pompeo, Secretary of State and former Director of the CIA. "Oh sorry, sir," says the flustered aide. He bounces off Pompeo like he's a ping pong ball.

Dan Coats, Director of National Intelligence, walks into the room right behind Mike saying, "You know what this is all about?"

Mike answers, "I have no idea but these impromptu press conferences always worry me."

"Ya, me too, especially the way he's been acting lately."

"Did he ever get those headaches checked?"

Dan says, "Are you kidding? Melania says he won't even take an aspirin for them."

Mike shakes his head.

"Do we dare interrupt him?" asks Dan.

Mike says, "We better. Who knows what he'll say if we don't."

Dan replies, "Who knows what he'll say if we do!"

They walk to Mogul. The Donald looks up saying, "Hi Mike. Hi Dan."

Both formally shake his hand and say, "Mr. President."

Trump then says, "I think you guys will love this. I've made a major breakthrough, maybe the biggest in history. Just wait 'till you hear this beauty!"

Dan, worried, says, "Don't you want to run this by us before making any public announcement?"

Trump answers, "Are you kidding? This can't wait."

Mike says, "Mr. President, I would caution you to…"

"Ya, I know you guys would, that's why I'm not telling ya anythin'."

Trump sits down again behind his desk as Mike and Dan, worried, look at Trump and then at each other.

Trump sits at his desk, clearing his throat. He looks up saying, "All right boys, tell me when…"

An assistant director now walks up to the president, "I'll give you a warning and then…"

Trump interrupts, "I know how this works, son. I'm a TV star. Just point and I go!"

The assistant spins around in disgust and rolls his eyes at everyone standing behind the cameras.

Again, Mike and Dan give another concerned look to each other.

The assistant director checks with his crew then spins around and points at Trump who's not looking.

The assistant looks to the director for help.

The director says, "All right Mr. President we're ready when you are."

Mr. Trump is not paying any attention but is writing something.

Director and assistant director now look at each other. The director walks to the president saying, "Mr. President, we're ready."

"Ya, ya, okay," says the president. He looks up and starts talking, "Hello America."

The director jumps in, "Wo! We're not on yet Mr. President."

The President stops and is upset, "Well when you people get your act together, tell me." He goes back to writing something on a notepad.

"Mr. President, we're ready."

Mr. Trump then says, "Well, now, I'm not. You're just going to have to wait."

The director is now upset but stands there in disgust trying to decide what to do next. After a long uncomfortable moment the director turns and motions to go live.

"Mr. President, we're going to go live so whenever you're ready, you're on," says the director.

Mr. Trump continues to write something without acknowledging he heard the director.

Director nervously, and now live, says, "Mr. President?"

Still nothing.

"Mr. President?"

Annoyed and not looking up says, "What?"

We're on!

"We are?"

Yes!

"Oh, well why didn't you say so. Good evening, America and people of planet earth."

Everyone in the room stares at the president in disbelief.

"I just want to say how proud I am of all you people. The whites, the blacks, the Asians and all the rest of you are now getting along just beautifully. And thanks to my presidency, things will only get better. A lot better. I'm announcing something I've been secretly working on for a long time... peace for our planet. I'm calling this: Peace for Planet Earth." Trump looks to his room. "Sound good to you people?"

No one moves a muscle but stares back at the president. "Okay, good. The first big step in this venture will be to make countries who are not friends, to be friends. Russia and the United States today are thought of as mortal enemies. This shouldn't be true. Russia should be our friend."

As the president drones on Mike and Dan are waving their hands to get the President's attention.

Trump is not paying any attention so Mike and Dan walk closer to the back of the camera.

"I'm announcing today a joint plan for the Russian Federal Assembly and our Congress to work together. The plan will be to combine our great empires. I want to call it: U.S.S.R... The United States of Soviet Republics. That's just a working name I came up with..."

Dan and Mike have gotten the director to pull the plug.

In a Washington D.C. bar two lonely drunks are watching Trump drone on.

"What'd he just say?"

"I hate him."

"Me too."

"Wanna fight?"

"Okay."

The bartender steps in, "Go outside, you idiots." The bartender goes back to watching the President in the Oval Office.

Back at the White House, Trump is still talking in the background, not knowing the plug's been pulled. Everyone in the room is either on the phone, or talking with someone whose phone is going off in their hand. Every phone in the room is now beeping or ringing.

All of a sudden as the President is rambling on, he begins to put a hand up to his head.

"I'm sorry ladies and gentlemen, I have some sort of ..."

President Trump then starts shaking his head saying, "No... no... no. I won't say that."

Then, out of nowhere, the president asks, "Where's my football?"

The "football" is in reference to the suitcase that contains the nuclear codes. Only the president of the United States can order a nuclear attack. No one can stop him.

Before any order can be processed by the military, the president must be positively identified using a special code issued on a plastic card, nicknamed the "biscuit." Only the president can order the release of nuclear weapons. However, the order must be verified by the Secretary of Defense, who fortunately is not in this room.

The verification process deals solely with verifying that the order came from the actual President. The Secretary of Defense has no veto power and must comply with the president's order.

This obviously is a weakness in the system and is now being exploited by someone or some group.

Once all the codes have been verified, the military would issue attack orders to the proper units. These orders are given and then re-verified for authenticity. The President has the single authority to initiate a nuclear attack since the Secretary of Defense is required to verify the order, but cannot legally veto it.

Everyone in the room is aware of this and stands in stunned silence.

All talking, writing, or doing anything, for that matter has ceased.

When this chip was put in my head a year ago, I was ordered to kill Jen. I couldn't do it.

President Trump's sits there, frozen, like there are too many conflicting ideas in his brain at once.

The president stares at the camera while massaging his head and that thing on top called hair.

17

As I pull up to a small Paris warehouse I calculate: what are the chances this is a setup? Statistically the number is very high. I've left a text message for Jen saying exactly where I am. She went back home to Portland, Oregon. At least she understands: if I don't do it, who will?

Henry had pulled up this area for me on a CIA Reaper drone. The CIA was not told by Henry anything about my mission as we no longer trust anybody. The building looks to be abandoned. I still feel it's better to go in without the cavalry. Elena would likely kill a lot of people.

She obviously wants to see how this thing in my head is doing so I'm taking a big chance.

That thought would not turn out to be one of my better ideas. Little did I understand, at this time, that Elena's people can manipulate thoughts so well that you can't tell the difference between yours and hers.

It feels like Portland in Paris today. It's cloudy and raining as I step out of my bright red Renault Clio.

Nothing like looking inconspicuous in a neon red car.

By the way, the Uber driver was drunk. I drove him home and walked to a car rental office for this thing that screams, "Look at me!"

The building looks abandoned, like in the drone files. I walk to the front door but it's locked. There are no signs of life anywhere. I try to peer in some dirty, old windows next to the front door.

The place is empty.

This looks very suspicious.

A chip that defies all known physics was pulled out of an assassin. It was made at this abandoned manufacturing facility. I had looked up the name and the company. It's no longer in business and hadn't been for over a decade.

Again, weird, very weird.

I walk around back.

As I make my way around the corner of the building two large dudes' Uzi submachine guns are stuck into my head and chest. I could take these guys down but there are two more dudes with two more Uzis standing not far off.

I slowly put my hands into the air. The guys pat me down and remove my Glock 22 .40 caliber pistol. I'm thinking, *I could really use my team 'bout now.*

These guys really like their Uzis.

Everybody but me has one!

A black SUV door opens.

Out steps a woman with a scarf and a super large pair of Louis Vuitton sunglasses. I can only assume it's Elena. As she nears and pulls off her black framed sunglasses I can see the scars I put on her face with that shotgun blast.

Elena stops near me and casually says, "Hello, John."

I answer slightly disgusted, "Hello, Elena."

"Well, now that we've gotten that out of the way, where's your team?"

"I thought I'd have a better chance of finding you if we were low profile."

Elena hands me an 12.9 inch iPad pro. There is a script that is open on the screen.

"Read the last line," says Elena.

I can't believe my eyes. Everything I was saying, word for word, was on this page. The last line says, "I thought I'd have a better chance of finding you if we were low profile." My greatest fear has come upon me. I have now become a zombie robot for the world's most dangerous woman.

I say to her, "Just like at the Eiffel Tower?"

She smiles and repeats my words as I said them, "Just like at the Eiffel Tower."

As we walk to the SUV's I think:

Is there any use in fighting her or even talking to myself?

Apparently, she has the rest of my life already planned out.

Another fine mess you've gotten yourself into JD.

***

We're only minutes out of the Charles de Gaulle Airport. We're flying in Elena's private Gulfstream G650 jet. Elena said we're going to Monte Carlo on the French Riviera. At a speed of about 800 miles per hour, in this $65 million jet, we'll be there in well under an hour.

As soon as thoughts pop into my head Elena looks over to me.

Can she read my thoughts?

Is she playing me?

I can't tell the difference between her thoughts and my thoughts.

Humanity is doomed!

These are a few of the million thoughts that flood my mind when a large thug walks to me with a tray of food like a stewardess. He looks impatient and as if to say: I can't stand here all day.

I shake my head in a disgusted fashion when Elena walks toward us. She grabs a sandwich and takes a bite saying, "I'm not gonna poison you. I need you. "C'mon, have something."

I am really hungry.

God! I'm like a dog.

All I can think about is food, sex and —

I suddenly blurt out, "I have to use the bathroom."

Elena points in the direction of the cockpit and says, "Sure. You don't mind if he goes with you, do you?"

I sarcastically say, "Brutus and me in an airplane bathroom? Together?"

Elena looks at me with disgust.

Elena looks at "Brutus" and says, "Go with him."

This dumb hunk of flesh says, "So do I go in with him?"

Elena and I stare at him.

Finally, I say, "I really think you should shoot him first."

I walk off to the bathroom. I close and lock the door loudly behind me.

Elena is still staring at Dumbo. He still looks confused.

Elena turns, shakes her head and returns to her oversized, white, Italian leather seat.

Dumbo continues to stand, frozen in place, staring at the bathroom door.

Elena mumbles to herself, "Shoot him first. That's funny."

I look around the tiny bathroom to see if there's anything I could use.

Nothing.

I check my pockets and they've taken everything.

I then put my hand in the trash and feel around.

"Eww!"

Then I touch something that's cold, wet and sticky.

I'm not sure what it is so I pull it out. It's a metal pen. I unscrew it and now I have two weapons, one for each hand. I take a paper towel and wipe off the cold, wet, snot.

I put each half in each front pocket.

These might come in handy later.

I hope Elena doesn't know what I'm thinking or I'm screwed!

I step out of the bathroom and everyone looks at me except for Elena. Elena's casually reading a magazine. I can't read her body language at all.

Maybe she knows. Maybe she doesn't. It doesn't matter. I've gotta get this thing outta my head before she forces me to do something horrible.

***

We are airborne again in three helicopters after landing at the Nice Côte d'Azur Airport in the south of France. I have no chance to escape. The helicopters were following the beautiful French Riviera coastline south by southeast.

I'm sitting right next to Elena.

I could probably pull out my metal pen and stab her in the throat right now.

What would that get me?

She'd be dead but so would I.

No, I've gotta find out what Elena's up to.

The helicopters land on a helipad build over the Mediterranean Sea in Monaco. We are met at the helipad by 9 brand new black, Range

Rover SUVs. These vehicles may be the last stand for the passenger diesel engine. They are nice inside but a 6 cylinder diesel engine in an SUV?

Elena is in black leather and in Gianvito Rossi pumps.

She blends right into the black leather seats.

We're briefly on Avenue Princesse Grace. I remember seeing the beautiful princess, Grace Kelly, in Rear Window (1954) and To Catch a Thief (1955). I remember thinking:

This is the most beautiful woman I've ever seen in my life.

This is before I met Jen, of course.

Apparently, that's what the Prince of Monaco thought as well. She was whisked away from Hollywood by Prince Rainier in 1956. They quickly married and lived right here in Monte Carlo like a modern day fairytale.

I've always wondered if her death was some sort of message that some very bad people were trying to send the prince. Rumors were, her brake lines were cut, but that was never proven since the palace never allowed experts to examine the car. Experts did say the British Rover 3500 had a dual, fail safe, brake system which makes it "impossible" for the brakes to fail. There were no skid marks or attempts to brake as the car plunged off a 100 foot cliff.

Call me suspicious because this town is loaded with billionaires, some who made their billions honestly, but others, not so much.

Elena, clearly, is in the "not so much" category.

We pull up to the Villa La Vigie. It's sits on the beautiful Point de la Veille, overlooking Monte Carlo. The point faces the Monte Carlo Bay Casino and was the scene of a painful moment from my past.

I proposed to a woman at this point not so long ago.

Oh my God!

Is she planning on proposing to me or has she programed me for some suicide mission?

Elena has been quietly sitting beside me in the black leather seats. She leans over to me and whispers, "You're very perceptive, JD."

My heart fell further than the day at the Eiffel Tower when I realized Elena could read my mind.

I could probably get those pen halves out of my pocket in case I needed to stab someone in the neck.

Elena then says tauntingly, "You really don't want to kill me, JD. The party's just gettin' started."

She holds out her hand. I begrudgingly pull the two pieces of metal from my pockets and slap them into her hand.

"Oh ouch!" says Elena, sarcastically looking over the empty metal pen halves. "But these are so dull. I doubt you could have punctured my carotid artery."

I sarcastically say, "Oh let's try it."

Elena, without batting an eye, says, "Okay."

Sitting nearby is the big, ugly, thug from the plane. He whips out an Uzi and points it at me.

I tell Elena, "Well, if you get your goon to put away his toys…"

Elena looks over to Dumbo and after a disgusted pause he puts his Uzi back in his jacket.

Elena grabs my hand, puts a pen half into my open palm. She then closes my fist and pulls my clenched fist to her neck.

She dares me, angrily yelling, "Go ahead do it, just do it!"

I look at her soulless eyes and there is nothing in there.

"How did such wonderful parents get stuck with you?"

"I dunno, just lucky I guess," responds a sarcastic Elena.

Elena then says only in my thoughts,

I hope you can see that a big part of me really loves you.

I answer out loud, "I feel sorry for you Elena, really, really sorry."

You don't see what I see yet but you will.

I say, "I seriously doubt that!"

Then I subliminally say to her:

That wasn't in your little script, was it?

Elena ignores my thought.

Did she hear it? I don't know. This is making me crazy.

We pull up to the front of her Villa.

It's absolutely gorgeous. This place must be worth...

Elena says, "It was 172.6 million U.S. dollars but to me it's priceless."

She's really freaking me out.

It's a horrible thing to force someone to know your every thought and deep dark secret.

It's not right.

Elena then says to me without saying a word, *I think when you get to know me better you'll change your mind.*

Dumbo, her all brawn no brains security guard, has been staring at us. He says, "Wo! That was really, really weird man. Really weird."

Watching thoughts communicated silently to another person and seeing them silently react must be really weird. But no different than Henry watching Jen and me.

When two people think alike it's as if they are one person.

Elena smiles at me.

Believe it or not, I think I smiled back.

Elena's fleet of Range Rovers pull into her compound.

She mumbles something to her goon who obviously doesn't understand what she's saying. Elena then says to her driver, "Where's Tony and Frederik?"

I become aware that her driver and Elena are worried, very worried.

She says to our driver, "Go see."

The driver of the car opens his door. He walks in front of our SUV and talks on his earpiece to the other drivers. One by one, all eight of Elena's drivers cautiously walk into her villa.

The huge oak front door is opened. After an eternity passes and no one walks back outside Elena tells Dumbo, "Stay here with him." She points to me.

Guess our love affair is over.

Elena motions to more of her men to follow her into the villa.

Another eternity passes.

I look at jumbo prawn and he is staring at the back of the front seat. I still have one of those metal pen halves in my palm. I now realize that my palm is sweaty as I'm thinking of sticking this pen in Dumbo's neck.

Did Elena hear what I thought?

I don't know.

But the weirdest thoughts came rushing into my brain.

Help! John, help! Get in here now!

I say out loud, "Elena?"

She now screams in my ear, "Yes, John, help! Now!"

I say to Dumbo, "Elena is calling for me!"

Dumbo says, "What?"

I start to get out of the car when the big, dumb, oaf pulls me back saying, "We wait!"

I say, "You wait. I'm goin' in."

I don't know what inspired me but I ripped away from his Kung Fu grip and headed for the villa.

Dumbo yells, "Stop or I'll... Stop!"

I ignore him and, amazingly enough, he didn't drop me. Guess he isn't such an idiot after all.

I want to get behind the heavy iron doors as quickly as possible, as I knew one direct hit from an Uzi and I would be seeing Jesus.

I flew through the doors. The entry and living room is larger than a lobby in most office buildings!

However, it's empty.

The white Italian marble floor and huge marble columns are breathtaking.

John, help, they're taking us to the basement. Come quickly. Can you hear me?

I then say out loud, "I hear you."

Elena then says in my thoughts, *You don't have to speak out loud. Just think it.*

"Okay… oh sorry," I say again out loud.

Are you messing with me?

Elena, in my head, says, *No! Come to the basement through the door in the kitchen.*

Now!

I run to the kitchen without "thinking."

This place has two of everything. Two Viking stoves, two Sub Zero refrigerators and wine closets, and 4, count them, 4 microwaves. Most restaurants would die to have half this kitchen!

It's amazing what dirty money can buy!

Uh, I didn't mean that Elena.

There's no answer in my head.

I finally find the open door and assume this must be where they're headed.

This looks to be a cave, hued out of solid, black, rock.

I can hear men talking.

"My men have already taken control of this compound."

I can't see who's talking but he has a Russian accent.

I suddenly turn to my SEAL training. This is like having a SEAL team in your ear, only better.

Elena?

Yes.

What do you want me to do?

They're looking for you now.

Who?

Admiral Victor Perchinkov.

That's the guy that assassinated Russian President, Ivan Mironovich. Everyone in Russia is looking for him. How he's managed to escape every intelligence agency in the world is beyond comprehension. There is only one way that's possible, he had help.

You must leave now.

Get out. Get out now.

I try not to think. That's impossible.

I'm not leaving.

What?

I'm not leaving.

A long pause ensues between Elena's brain and mine.

Suppressed shots ring out. Elena's men are being assassinated. I peer around a corner and see one of them.

It's Dumbo.

How did he get captured so fast?

I look at him lying face down and actually feel kinda sorry for him.

In Russian, Perchinkov is barking orders. I speak some Russian and know they're looking for me and a scientist. Perchinkov's men fan out as Elena is shoved into the room. I see Elena standing in front of Perchinkov.

Perchinkov asks, "So where is he?"

Elena doesn't answer.

"Where is Doctor Gebhardt?" asks Perchinkov.

Perchinkov puts a Russian PSM pistol to her head.

Perchinkov then says as he points the gun into the middle of Elena's forehead, "All right then, where is Denning?"

Elena calmly says, "I don't know."

I'm gonna have to walk out there.

Elena quickly puts her thought into my mind, *No!*

As I begin to walk, I raise my hands in the air saying, "Don't shoot. Don't shoot."

Every gun in the room moves toward me.

Elena silently says to me, *You shouldn't have done that. Now, we're all dead.*

I had no choice, they'd of killed us all.

It's clear Perchinkov has no idea that Elena and I are communicating with each other.

Perchinkov says, "Well, well, well. If it isn't the great John Denning. So nice to see you again. Monte Carlo is much warmer than G North."

"Pleasure's all mine," I say with some sarcasm. G North is the term for the geographic North Pole. This is where a very important nuclear submarine exchange occurred between Russia and the United States (*JD I*). That was the last time we saw each other.

Perchinkov looks to Elena and adds to my sarcasm, "And thank you Elena for bringing him to me." Perchinkov continues, "I hear you have something implanted in your head that gives you an amazing memory. May I test you?"

I don't have to show off but I say with some morbid sarcasm, "What would you like to know?"

Perchinkov asks, "So who was the first Tzar of Russia?"

I quickly respond, "Ivan the third. The Muscovite ruler was first recognized as an emperor by Maximilian I, the emperor of the Holy Roman Empire in 1514. However, the first Russian ruler to be formally crowned as the 'Tsar of all Rus' or 'Tsar of all Russias' was Ivan IV, until then known as Grand Prince of all Rus'."

Perchinkov claps his hands suspiciously asking, "Do you love Russian history?"

I disgustedly say, "I hate history."

Perchinkov then adds, "I love history. That chip is so wasted on you. I must have Doctor Gebhardt put that chip in me."

I look at Elena with a considerable amount of worry.

Dumbo, still laying face down, lifts up his head to look at us.

Perchinkov knocks it into the concrete floor.

Perchinkov's men walk in with Elena's head scientist, Doctor Gebhardt, who doesn't look too happy.

Perchinkov looks pleased as he walks toward the doctor saying, "So this is the famous **Doctor** Franz Gebhardt?"

Franz doesn't acknowledge Perchinkov's words.

"Doctor Gebhardt, would you be so kind?" says Perchinkov as he walks all of them to a robot arm attached to a medical chair. Perchinkov continues, "Now, I understand that you've developed deep brain stimulation techniques and implants that are more advanced than anyone in the world, is that true?"

Gebhardt looks at Elena who nods to go ahead and tell him.

Doctor Gebhardt says, "Yes, that's true."

"Well, I've already seen your work in action with this prime specimen," says Perchinkov as he points to me.

I'm now some sort of lab rat to be experimented on?

Elena answers in my thoughts, *I'll never let them do that to you, JD.*

Please explain how you made this work," says Perchinkov.

The doctor is hesitant but slowly speaks, "We implant specially built DNA strands configured to you so your body accepts them as your own. Then we heat nanoparticles which are released by this chip," he says as he puts his hand in his pocket. All Uzi's train on him.

Perchinkov motions for them to put their guns to low ready and they do.

He slowly pulls a tiny round disk that looks like a watch battery from his white lab jacket. This disk looks identical to the chip implanted in my head.

The doctor continues, "After the implantation of the chip, the nanoparticles are released and attach to specific neurons in the brain and communicate with the data on the chip. The chip in turn communicates back and forth with us."

Perchinkov says, "Sounds simple!"

Gebhardt replies, "Quite the contrary. There are millions of hours of research before formulating the exact process. It's like the computer. If you have one single connection on the motherboard that's bad your entire computer stops. Billions of nanoparticles must all work in perfect synchronization with billions of brain cells. You see the brain makes connections through repeated stimulation to the motor cortex areas of your brain. Our chip can tell us whether blood flowing to your brain is oxygenated or not, meaning we know when your brain is tired. We direct blood there so you continue even when tired. Another process is called neuroplasticity. Stimulating the areas with our information makes people think our thoughts are their thoughts. Repeated stimulation makes our thoughts become more important than their thoughts."

I interrupt, "God gave us free will."

Gebhardt confidently says, "There is no God."

I confidently say, "I'm no scientist but if you believe, given enough time, a rock created Beethoven, then you've got rocks for brains!"

Perchinkov, "I'm not sure we'll solve the meaning of life today with a rocks argument."

I answer, "Oh I think we could. I'll put you both in Leavenworth. There you can discuss all the properties of rocks, all while you make big rocks into little ones."

Perchinkov ignores me, "I want the good doctor to play God." He points to one of his men saying, "Do it to him."

Gebhardt stutters, "Well, it's not that simple. First we have to…"

Perchinkov puts a gun to Gebhardt's head. Gebhardt says, "We can prep him but I can't do it until we take DNA and brain samples.

Perchinkov puts the gun down saying, "Well then do it!"

Gebhardt walks away with Perchinkov's soldier and two others.

Perchinkov then turns to Elena and me, "Okay, now what do I do with you people?"

18

The Ketchikan, Alaska airport is on an island across from the city. Stone has decided to take his family out of the "radiation zone" for a little vacation to Seattle.

Some "experts" say there are no radiation levels above what they were before the "incident." Most experts will not admit there was an incident.

Many people here do not trust the government or anything the so called experts say, especially when the experts only fly in for a few hours.

Alaska Airlines flies several nonstop flights daily to and from Seattle.

As Stone boards the plane he says to his wife, "Are you all excited?"

His wife looks at him and sarcastically says, "Oh sure, you?"

"Ya, this will be great!" says Stone with childlike excitement. He totally misreads her boredom.

"I know and the price was so cheap too! We're gonna have some fun. The giant Ferris Wheel down by the dock, Pike Street Fish Market, The Space Needle! We're doin' it all." says an excited Stone.

His wife smiles knowing she really has made him happy.

His two, twenty something boys, are in tow. Their "husky," Alaskan physiques make you realize the winters in Ketchikan really must be pretty boring.

***

It's a beautiful evening sunset in Seattle, Washington.

A hit from the old brown van that escaped Reed College was spotted by the Seattle P.D. They didn't move in. The Seattle Police Department tracked the van to downtown. The police told Jen three guys, one fitting the Russian professor's description, had all climbed into a black Cadillac SUV.

Jen, Alexi and Casmerov pull away from the multi-story building at Sea-Tac Airport. There must have been about 10,000 rental cars in this building and the Russians pick a sub — sub compact Chevy Spark? A tiny little thing that barely fits Casmerov's six foot four inch frame. Casmerov has to sprawl across the entire back seat of the car so that he can fit. He's also holding his carry on like it has gold inside. Truth is: all the luggage wouldn't fit in the back of this little sardine can.

Jen, who's driving, looks in the rearview mirror at Casmerov and says, "All the cars in that place and you guy picked this?"

Alexi, stone faced, says, "It only had 11 miles. Never been in brand new car."

Jen doesn't believe him saying, "Oh come on."

Casmerov chimes in, "True."

"They don't have new cars in Russia?"

Alexi answers, "Of course but on pay we make? Never."

Casmerov disgustedly says, "Don't let him fool you. He came from wealthy family. Probably never been in car this small in life."

Alexi is not happy, so he pretends to ignore the comment.

Jen pulls over to the side of the road.

Alexi says, "What you doing?"

Jen hands Alexi the keys, "I'm letting you drive."

It's like two kids in high school driving by themselves for the first time.

Alexi runs around and jumps behind the wheel.

He starts laughing as he hits the gas. Without looking he pulls into traffic as a big rig lays on the horn. Alexi rolls down his window and waves at the big rig that quickly rolls past them in the next lane.

Jen said hanging on to the roof, "It's more likely that we get killed by you than by a nuke blast."

Alexi tries to catch up to the big rig that's directly ahead of them.

Alexi swerves around car after car.

Jen yells at him, "Watch out!"

Alexi ignores her and continues to swerve across all of the lanes on the interstate.

Alexi finally stays in the number one lane and accelerates.

Alexi impressed, "Oh, lots of power for tiny American car."

Jen shakes her head then checks her phone

Jen says, "The SUV just pulled into the Space Needle's parking lot."

Jen checks other messages and looks worried.

Alexi sees this and asks, "What's wrong?"

Jen says, "Haven't heard from John in 24 hours. I think something's wrong."

Alexi says, "As soon as we take care of this, maybe you should call your people."

"My people?"

"Yes. Don't you have people that can check on him?"

"Yes, but they won't."

Alexi asks, "Why not?"

"That's not the way things work with U.S. intelligence agencies, especially when it's not one of their own," replies Jennifer.

Alexi adds, "He should've taken Henry."

They pull up to valet parking for the Seattle Space Needle.

A kid, who couldn't be over 18 runs to the car. Jen shows a badge. It's the kid's first week on the job and acts disappointed that he can't drive the car.

Casmerov is having a big problem climbing out of the back of their sardine can. Jen tries to ignore him saying, "All right, we don't want to spook these people. We know what the professor looks like. We don't move in until we know for sure who's involved in this, okay?"

Alexi holds his thumb and index finger up to make a perfect circle. Then making fun of Jen he slowly says, "Oookaaay!"

Jen looks at Alexi with disgust and mumbles, "I shoulda gone ta France with John."

To ascend to the top of the Space Needle there are three elevators taking you over 500 feet into the air.

It's nighttime as they exit one of the elevators. There's a tour taking place. The three look at each other and pretend to be part of the tour.

The tour guide is this annoying young woman with a annoyingly high pitched, California valley girl voice with a name tag that says Debbie, "Okay people, we're walking, we're walking." She begins motioning to Jen, Alexi and Casmerov to get closer to the rest of the group saying, "Now stay with our group. You don't wanna get lost."

Thank God!

She's clueless!

Debbie annoyingly speaks valley girl, "As you can see we're all standing on glass."

Jen looks down and her heart sinks. The entire floor of the restaurant is glass!

"This floor is like part of the 100 million dollar renovation. There are like 37 tons of glass and like 12 motors that make us like spin all around... like we're in a flying saucer flying through space (Finally! A proper use of the word "like.")"

Alexi and Casmerov stare at each other unimpressed. Jen told me that they were far more impressed with their Chevy rental car than they were with 'Space Saucer.'

The room is filled with tables of people eating dinner. The Space Needle is one of the priciest places in town. The 'Space Saucer' is currently filled, mostly, with tourists. As our motley crew walk around the Sky City Restaurant, there seems to be a few well-dressed business types, but mostly tourists. No one fits the professor's description. According to TripAdvisor.com it has five stars with over 3,000 reviews. But at around 50 dollars per entré, it better be!

Wait!

Three men sit by the window at a table overlooking downtown Seattle. One looks to be Professor Pavlov.

The tour guide drones on, "This entire floor will turn 360 degrees in like 40 minutes. It could go faster but we don't want the 'Space Needle' to like fly off into space!" Debbie laughs at her own bad joke.

Jen gives a deadpan glare to Debbie.

Alexi and Camerov are doing the identical stare in Debbie's direction. They look as if, this person's an idiot.

Jen, Alexi and Casmerov follow the tour near to the table where the three men are sitting.

Alexi and Casmerov put hands on their guns. Jen shakes her head and looks around to see if anyone else nearby might be part of this plot. As Jen, Alexi and Casmerov near the table, they recognize Russian Professor, Anton Pavlov. As they walk by the table one of the men has a gun under the table pointed at Pavlov. The other man has a briefcase. Is that the nuke? Jen isn't sure. She doesn't want to tip off these guys as they might set off the nuke right here. If that's a nuke, they'd all be toast, not to mention much of downtown Seattle.

She looks at Casmerov who pulls out a small handheld device which registers no radiation in the air.

Casmerov shakes his head no. Jen quietly leans to Alexi and Casmerov saying, "If it's lined with lead, the nuke still could be in there. That lead would be really hard to lift. We'll know when we see 'em lift it."

A nuclear airburst over Seattle could render widespread exposure to radiation. This would also shut down electricity and communications for weeks or months.

There is a rule called the 7:10 rule. It's not really a "rule" but more of a very general guideline. So the 7:10 "guideline" means that for every 7-fold increase in time after a nuclear detonation, there is a 10-fold decrease in the exposure rate. This means the radiation after the detonation of a nuclear weapon would dissipate very quickly or — so "they" say!

However, the psychological effects of knowing you live near a recent nuclear explosion would be devastating.

Further, the amount of physical repair work necessary to build back infrastructure would be devastating as well.

Ever try and get anything done in a head to toe NBC hazmat suit?

Jen is worried the terrorists might be planning to set off the explosion right here and right now for maximum damage.
All three continue walking past the terrorists. They stop and look at the tour guide and her group. Jen, Alexi and Casmerov are able to duck on the other side of the crowd so they can't be seen by the terrorists.

Jen walks to a bartender and whispers something in his ear. He immediately leaves.

Jen walks back to Alexi who is casually looking over a wine list.

Alexi tells Bartender #2, "I'll have the Seattle 73!"

Bartender #2 disgustedly says, "Uh, ya, that's over in the Sky View Observatory." The Bartender #2 takes the wine list trying to figure out what Alexi was reading.

Alexi had read something online about a famous Seattle drink.

Jen says slowly and forcefully, "You're in wrong building."

Alexi says, "Good joke, no?"

Jen upset, "No. No, not really."

Jen looks over to an empty table and says, "Where'd they go?"

Alexi, disappointed, responds, "I turn back for just second… they all go down elevator but C-Man with them… I think."

"'C-Man' with them, you think?" Jen has so much to say but there's no time.

Alexi says, "C-Man stole a car."

Jen says, "Stole a car? Should I be worried?"

Alexi, "Not at all. Casmerov do it all time in Moscow."

Jen, exasperated, finally asks, "Well, did you at least see if the briefcase was heavy?"

Alexi, "Did not see."

Jen angrily says, "Well, if you weren't reading wine lists…"

Jen stomps toward the elevator.

Alexi casually shrugs his shoulders to the bartender and follows Jen to the elevator.

The elevator door opens.

A Seattle police officer is with the first bartender as they exit the elevator.

Jen shows the officer a piece of paper, "This is a PPD directly from…"

The police officer grabs the paper and knows exactly what a PPD is. They are Presidential Policy Directives and can be public, private, secret, or Top Secret. This one has the seal of the president on the paper and stamped: TOP SECRET!

The officer says into his mic on his left shoulder, "10-45, repeat, 10-45! This is not a drill. Three males dark suits. One has a black Samsonite briefcase chained to his wrist."

The next words on the officer's radio blurt out, "They're leaving the parking lot."

Jen, Alexi step into elevator with the Seattle Police Officer and the first bartender.

The bartender stands there staring at them before he realizes they all want him to leave.

"Oh right," the bartender steps off elevator. The bartender tries to talk into the closing doors, "Should I leave the Needle? Should I leave Seattle?"

There's no answer from anyone as the door slams shut.

After an uncomfortable pause, the officer says, "I never thought I'd go out like this."

Jen and Alexi look at each other.

Alexi's phone rings. He quickly answers it, "Go for A-dog... Go C-man... uh huh... uh huh. All right call you in 5." Alexi hangs up and tells us, "C-man's trackin' 'em. Heading West on Broad. Black Cadillac SUV."

Jen and the police officer stare at Alexi without any expression. Jen finally says, "A-Dog?"

Alexi says matter of fact, "Ya, A-Dog."

The elevator door opens and they quickly exit.

Several police cars sit in front of a black GMC Seattle Bomb Squad truck in the valet parking area at the base of the Space Needle. They're facing the street and all look ready to roll.

Jen says to the officer, "Think these guys have any experience in disarming a nuke?"

The officer confidently answers, "I'm sure. Let's ask."

Jen, Alexi and the officer walk up to the driver's door of the bomb squad truck.

The officer asks, "You guys have experience disarming nukes, right?"

The Seattle PD officer quickly and confidently responds, "No. None whatsoever."

Jen is already on her phone saying, "We're at the Space Needle. What's the ETA on NBC Group 3?" Jen is waiting a very long time for the answer. "Uh huh, okay, thanks." She hangs up the phone.

The bomb squad officer asks, "So what'd they say?"

Jen has a grave look on her face, "We're on our own."

The Seattle PD officer asks, "You need an escort?"

Jen answers, "No, the lower the profile, the better… for now."

The Seattle PD officer then says, "Okay, I've texted you all our numbers including air assets, if you need them."

Jen says, "Thank you."

Jen and Alexi take off running. They tear past a valet kid whose voice cracks when he nervously asks, "Parking ticket please?"

The kid now realizes they are with the police and raises a hand and waves to them, "Oh, okay, never mind." However, Jen and Alexi are long gone and the kid does this as more of a clueless realization to himself.

Jen and Alexi jump in their little red Chevy Spark, turning right onto Broad Street.

Alexi's on the phone again, "Okay, C-Man, where are you?"

Jen mumbles in disgust, "C-Man… whitest foreigners in America... think they got rap swag."

Alexi says, "You know S.W.A.G now means 'Secretly We Are Gay', right?

Jen didn't know that, so ignores him.

"C-Man" has followed the black Cadillac SUV on a tour of downtown. They finally have stopped near Pier 55. Jen and Alexi drive past the Pike Place Fish Market. Alexi says, "Boy, I would really like to stop and try some of their famous clam chowder."

Jen stares at him for a moment before she runs over a curb on the pier and her attention is drawn back to the chase.

Jen and Alexi fly their Chevy onto Pier 55. They finally spot the car that apparently Casmerov stole.

Jen radios Seattle PD and tells them to NOT put out an APB (All Points Bulletin) for the stolen "C-man" car.

"A-Dog's" phone rings and he says, "Go for A-Dog. Ya, ya… K… Dog out." A-Dog hangs up the phone.

Casmerov comes running around the corner toward our car pointing toward the pier.

Jen guns it (if you can "gun it" in a subcompact). They race up to Casmerov.

Casmerov shouts, "We're losing them."

Jen yells, "Get in back."

Casmerov opens the hatch and dives into the back as Jen hit the gas. The three drive the rental car over another curb and head further onto the pier. The black Cadillac SUV is nowhere in sight.

"Where'd they go?" I ask.

"Pier 55," says Casmerov.

So Jen heads onto the pier. She sees nothing but a large dinner cruise ship loaded with people pulling away from the dock.

"Maybe they're on the dinner cruise," says a very worried Jen. "Looks like you were made 'C-Man'."

Casmerov looks stumped as to what she means.

"Made. Seen. Found out. Spotted," Jen then says.

Alexi disgustedly says, "глупый глупый идиот!"

Roughly translated he called Casmerov a, "dumb, stupid, idiot!"

Alexi's still mumbling, "Son of bitch, shit."

Jen's phone rings and she answers it, "Ya, ya, okay. All three got out?… Where's the SUV? Good job. We're headed there now." Jen disconnects her phone.

Jen hits the gas and Casmerov flies out of sight. Jen flies over another curb. The little Chevy Spark takes it like a champ.

Casmerov, not so much.

This makes Alexi smile as he looks into the back seat.

"You okee dokee?" asks Alexi.

One long leg and a cheap Nike sneaker is the only sign of life as C-Man tries to sit up again.

As he gets up Jen swerves to miss a large delivery truck.

"And back down he goes," laughs Alexi.

Alexi sounds as if he's Howard Cosell announcing a boxing match, "And down goes Frazier."

Jen asks, "You're too young to know Howard Cosell."

Alexi simply says, "YouTube."

Jen looks twice at him as she runs a red light.

Alexi doesn't seem to mind this insane driving at all.

Jen is sweating.

"Is that sveat (sweat)?" asks Alexi.

Jen angrily says, "You try driving like this!"

"Do it all time in Moscow traffic. Much vorse (worse)," says Alexi with a deadpan stare.

Jen looks at him to see if he's kidding or not.

She can't tell.

No one can.

He's Russian!

Casmerov finally sits up in the seat.

All three calmly stare down cars and trucks honking at them.

They continue to stare while brakes screech and cars crash.

After an interminably long pause, Alexi asks, "So, where we go?"

Jen screams as she almost is hit by a city bus head on, "Where ARE we GOING? Didn't anybody teach you morons how to conjugate verbs?"

After another interminably long pause Alexi, deadpan, says, "No."

Alexi mumbles to Casmerov, "Barking Chihuahuas can never be controlled. You ignore hysterical barking because you love them."

Casmerov looks as if he understands and nods a serious approval.

Jen ignores both of them.

After what seems to be forever, Jen pulls the tiny Chevy up to the Columbia Seafirst Center.

Upon seeing Jen, there are already no less than six police cars that come screeching up to the front of the tallest building in the state of Washington. The Columbia Seafirst Center has a SkyView Observatory on the 73rd floor.

Jen yells to the officers who are running toward her, "Set up a perimeter of at least 3 blocks. Try to get everyone out of the area."

The officers acknowledge and begin speaking on their two ways attached to their epaulet on their left shoulders.

Seattle Police Officers scatter in every direction.

Jen, Alexi and Casmerov run up the steps of the 76 story building. They race past the glass front doors.

They get their pick of two elevators for the 70 second ride.

Jen, A-Dog, and C-man push the elevator door panel. An elevator immediately opens. They practically stop each other from moving as each tries to beat the others.

The elevator song playing all the way to the 73rd floor is: Summer Somba by Walter Wanderley.

All three stare at the front of the elevator as the horrid, yet somehow cool music, plays on...

... and on ...

... and on ...

All three notice 71, 72...

They pull their guns. Then have to wait as the time between 72... and 73 seems to take far, far more time than all the other floors.

Enough time, in fact, for them to give disgusted looks to each other several times as they wait impatiently to save Seattle.

The music!

My God!

Will it ever stop?

Finally!

The three are relieved of their pain as the door finally opens. The crowd begins laughing at something they cannot see.

Jen peeks around the corner and lowers her gun.

She looks back to Alexi and Casmerov who still have their guns at high ready.

Jen lowers her weapon to low ready and hides it behind herself.

She motions to Alexi and Casmerov to do the same and they do. They split up as they round the elevator bank toward the crowd.

Unfortunately for all, there's a comedian "trying" to do standup. It's Alaska's very own Chuck Nature. He jokes, "I'd say what a TREE T (treat) it is to be here but you might think I'm talkin' 'bout all the trees out there! Can anyone 'fathom' how much water is out there?"

No reaction from the bored crowd.

"So the name's Chuck Nature... I'm on the 73rd floor. I know the elevator operator here on a first name basis. When I get on the elevator in the lobby he now asks me, Up Chuck?"

Since there is no elevator operator there is silence from the audience. The tourists continue to stare at 'Numb' Chucks.

Former Chief Robert Stone has been mingling with his family and only now realizes that Chucky is from Ketchikan.

Stone disgustedly says, "I can't catch a break!"

His wife and two sons look very bored as if they could care less about this entire vacation. Tony Stone is very quiet. Stone's other son is very impatient. He weighs 300 pounds and is a bit agitated. He asks, "Can we go home now pops'"

Stone ignores the question.

Jen spots the professor and the two guys with the nuclear suitcase first. Casmerov suspiciously closes in, looking around, Jen realizes he might tip them off. Jen pulls her gun and aims for the terrorist, standing, holding the handle of a very heavy suitcase resting on a chair.

She now notices two wires sticking from the large, black case. They are precariously close to one another and presumably could trigger the nuke.

She nods to Alexi who's on the other side of several tourists. Alexi looks and acknowledges the dangerous situation and begins to close on them.

Casmerov is approaching these guys from their back. Jen tries to get Casmerov's attention trying to say no. Casmerov doesn't see her silent instructions as he nears the suitcase.

Stone now sees Casmerov and yells, "Russians!"

Stone knows these are Russians because their submarine was surrendered to him. These guys had an All Points Bulletin (APB) put out on them when they escaped from JD and his SEALs in Alaska.

Apparently, Stone didn't see the retraction or the presidential pardon.

Stone charges Casmerov and takes him to the ground.

Alexi charges the nuke and the terrorist sees him coming. The terrorist puts the wires together but nothing happens. Alexi then takes the terrorist holding the nuke to the ground in one dramatic flying leap that would've made Russian dancer Mikhail Baryshnikov proud.

The heavy nuke 'briefcase' attached to the terrorist's wrist ends up on top of the terrorist's chest.

As the terrorist struggles to put the wires together Alexi punches him in the face. One blow and the terrorist is out cold.

Meanwhile, Professor **Anton Pavlov** puts his hands in the air as Jen points her gun at the remaining threat yelling, "FBI! On the ground."

The second terrorist reaches for something, presumably a weapon. Jen drops him with one shot to the heart.

Jen then screams, "Everybody on the ground!"

Most are too scared to scream, frozen in place, but finally drop to the floor.

One poor old woman is standing, shaking.

Jen looks about and sees no other threat.

She puts her gun away and walks to the poor, elderly woman.

She grabs the woman by the shoulder and calmly says, "It's okay. It's all over now."

Jen looks around and sees Alexi looking up from the ground.

Alexi sarcastically says to Jen, "You told everyone 'on the ground'... I'm already on ground. Can I get up?"

Jen ignores what must be more bad Russian sarcasm. Jennifer rolls her eyes (which is the treatment I get).

Seattle police swarm into the room in numbers nearly equaling the tourists.

The professor nervously says to Jen as she walks to him pointing a gun to his midsection, "They kidnapped me. Made me try and set off the nuke. I made sure it won't work. I'm not with them. I'm a Professor at Reed College and..."

Jen holsters her gun, interrupting him, "We know Professor Pavlov... I believe you."

He seems instantly much more relieved.

The head of the Seattle bomb squad unit, Captain Steve Johnson, arrives. He's a tall, handsome man in short sleeves, shorts and looks more like a tourist, "Thank you for your work here, agent...?"

Jen answers, "No problem. And it's former agent. It's my day off too... I quit!"

Captain Johnson looks at his own attire and sarcastically says, "How could you tell?" He then seriously says, "Thanks for not quitting today."

A guy in a full bomb suit waddles up to Steve.

Steve says, "You might as well take all of that off. Won't do you no good anyway."

The officer cannot be seen as a huge helmet covers his face. He then slowly waddles away. His body language appears to be happy that he won't be dying today.

The professor opens the nuke and after some examination shakes his head in a slightly disgusted fashion.

The Seattle police instruct the tourists, "All right people. Everyone calmly walk to the elevators and..."

Alexi looks at the crowd quietly filing out of the room and mumbles, "There are too many pussies in America."

Fortunately, nobody in America heard his comment.

Some tourists appear a bit disappointed that the show's over. The police show — not the Chucky show. All are escorted to the emergency exit by Seattle's finest. Chuck Nature disappears as if he's a tiny chicken under a herd of cattle.

Was he stampeded?

We'll never know.

All we know is this crowd hated Chucky and his horrid comedy act.

Jen calmly leans to the professor who's sitting on the floor, "What's the problem?"

The professor says, "The Russians don't build things the way that you should."

Captain Johnson hears the professor, "Aren't you Russian? So what da ya need?"

Professor Pavlov ignores the Russian comment and says, I need a pig lined, lead coffin. You guys have that I hope?"

The bomb squad captain calmly and with some disdain looks to an officer and asks, "Where'd Tim go?"

"He's in the lobby. We're sending him and his team up here with a lead coffin now."

Jen has pulled her Geiger Counter out and says, "I'm still not getting any serious radiation readings."

The professor quickly answers, "It's actually a clever design with the radiation core being shielded with a combination of lead and tungsten to make detection very hard."

Jen asks, "So why did I get readings on this in the Reed College parking lot but not here?"

The professor answers, "Maybe there's more than one radiation source. More than one nuke."

This was not the answer Jennifer wants to hear as that realization hits her.

Tim waddles up with his full bomb gear on and a, pig lined, large, black coffin on a four wheel hand cart. The professor nods and Jerry approaches the bomb. He carefully places the bomb in the black box and shuts the lid. The lead is so solid it makes a large thud like nothing else you'd ever hear in everyday life.

As the police leave with the bomb, Stone walks to Jen saying, "Of all the gin joints in the world... I'd say it's good to see you but whenever I do very bad things always seem to happen."

Jen smiles and answers, "Ya sorry chief. So I hear your gonna get your old job as chief of police back?"

Stone answers, "Ya, the guy they hired is f*ing nuts! So where's JD?"

Alexi and Casmerov have been standing there quietly. Casmerov says, "Of all the gin joints in the world... that's from Casablanca with Humphrey Bogart, isn't it?"

Jen quickly answers, "Well done! You know your American movies. YouTube?"

Casmerov proudly answers, "Da!"

Jen remembers to check her phone. She looks very worried saying, "He hasn't checked in. He told me to start worrying if he didn't check in by now."

Stone, "Where is he?"

Jen answers, "Paris."

Stone quickly answers, What are we waitin' for? Let's go find him."

Alexi chimes in, "Ya, what are we waitin' for. Let's find him."

Jen smiles at the dedication of these men.

Jen asks Stone, "What about your wife and sons?"

Stone answers, "They hate vacationing with me. They'll be happier back in Alaska."

Jen smiles, knowing Stone was arrested multiple times by police in Paris while trying to vacation.

She looks around and Alexi is at the bar drinking.

Jen walks up, "What are you doing?"

Alexi says to the bartender, "Seattle 73's for everybody!"

The bartender says "They're $19.00 each. Who's payin'?"

Captain Johnson walks up, "Send the bill to the mayor." Johnson continues, "Waters all around for my guys."

Everyone clinks glasses.

However, the celebration was a bit premature.

19

The Situation Room at the White House is crowded but an eerie somber silence fills the room.

Vice President Mike Pence, and all 15 members of the president's cabinet: The Secretaries of Agriculture, Commerce, Defense, Education, Energy, Health and Human Services, Homeland Security, Housing and Urban Development, Interior, Labor, State, Transportation, Treasury, and Veterans Affairs, and the Attorney General are quietly seated.

In addition, the White House Chief of Staff and several other departments are present. Mike Pence stands saying, "It doesn't give me any comfort to do this but I know this is something that has to be done. Only fifteen of you will be able to cast this vote. I trust you'll all do the right thing. Any questions? No? All right then all in favor of removing the President from power raise your hand."

Seven hands shoot up immediately. Several cabinet members sheepishly look around. One more cabinet member (to be left nameless) slowly raises his hand.

All right, I see eight people in favor. All opposed?

Seven hands shoot up immediately. Pence continues, "All right I see seven opposed. The I's have it. Now you know the president will likely protest this. So this will go to Congress and two/thirds will likely have to decide as I'm sure Mogul will object. We must alert them that Mogul is acting unstable and wants, apparently, to launch nuclear weapons without any provocation."

No one wants to utter a word. It's like a funeral. In a way it is. A funeral for the president.

A tiny staffer at the back of the room raises his hand, "And who will be alerting them?"

Pence without hesitation says, "Why, you will because you're the chief of staff's secretary."

The kid looks very nervous and worried, "Thank you."

"Any other questions?" asks the Vice President.

The room continues to feel icy cold.

A commotion is heard in the hall.

President Trump barges into the room joking, "What? There's a cabinet meeting and I wasn't invited? What the hell?" The president looks about the room and sees something is gravely wrong.

"What?"

Nothing but silence.

"All right, I need the nuclear football. Who knows where it is?"

Again, nothing but stone cold silence.

"What is it with all you people? Kelly?" the president looks for John Kelly, his Chief of Staff.

John Kelly appears at the back of the room saying, "Yes, Mr. President?"

"Do you know where my football is? I have Q Clearance and I want my football!" says the president sounding like a small child.

John Kelly, pauses, then says, "Mr. President, I think you should know, we've taken a vote and the majority of us agreed based on the 25th

Amendment to the United States Constitution to have you relieved of command."

An angry Donald Trump heads for John Kelly, "What? How did you vote?"

"I can't vote," says Kelly.

Trump then looks at the nearest sitting cabinet member, "Well, how did you vote?"

The terrified cabinet member doesn't want to answer.

Trump then stomps toward the former Marine Corps General saying, "All right Kelly, I thought I could trust you but it's now clear that..."

Trump grabs his head and winces in pain. He bends over as the pain is very intense.

An aid opens the doors and yells to the president's Secret Service detail. Two agents rush to the president looking worried. One says, "What happened?"

Kelly steps forward, "We were just discussing a very volatile subject when he started holding his head."

The president is still bent over mumbling, "No I won't do that."

Kelly and the other agent grab each side of the president under his arms and drag him out of the room. The second agent is on his earpiece, "Mogul is down, repeat, Mogul is down. We need a medivac to the south lawn ASAP."

The room returns to its morbid funeral feeling.

Mike Pence then speaks, "All right we need..." looking at General Kelly's secretary, "... for you to transmit our vote, in writing, to Congress. Tell them we have a priority one situation and that details will follow. While they're convening we all need to get over to the hill and tell them what just happened in person. Questions?"

No one says a word.

"All right then, let's get to it."

Everyone, still stunned, leaves the room.

Fred and Jerry, former NSA guys who now work in the White House, have been hiding in the back corner of the room. They look at each other. Fred says, "I think we better look for another job."

20

Cities across the world have cleaned up the devastation from Elena's evil ways. The Statue of Liberty is surrounded by scaffolding and looks to be nearly rebuilt.

In London, a group of tourists snap pictures on the Westminster Bridge. Big Ben and the Palace of Westminster look to be nearly repaired as well.

Westminster houses both the House of Commons and the House of Lords which, combined, is the British Parliament.

A blond haired, blue eyed, young man calmly drives a large truck across the Westminster Bridge. As he nears tourists snapping selfies, he swerves into them, running some down. The driver doesn't seem to be upset at all. In fact, he's whistling happily as he casually murders people.

He scratches the side of his head revealing a new scar. He accelerates his truck toward the crash bollards and balustrades in front of the Houses of Parliament.

Two London Metropolitan Police Officers are on patrol. They see the maniac heading right for them. The Bobbies, now finally armed with

Beretta pistols, pull and empty their weapons into his windshield. He swerves and crashes into a bollard barely missing both officers.

They reload their weapons as they slowly approach the vehicle. The driver is already long gone. Several bullets have hit this man in his head and torso.

A crowd of tourists with cameras slowly encroach the crime scene snapping pictures. One obnoxious young man, with a selfie stick, takes a snap standing right in front of the car. The Bobbies now yell, "All right move along. It's over."

The kid gets in one more shot of himself and the dead body before the Bobbies walk toward him. The kid runs away.

The crowd now slowly pushes back. One woman sees the kid and pulls out her phone mumbling, "Wish I caught video of that."

Interesting how the Brits named their police "Bobbies." The British home minister, Sir Robert Peel (1778-1850), created London's first organized police force. Before Peel's 1829 reforms, public order had been maintained by a few night watchmen, local constables and red-coat-wearing army soldiers, had been deployed primarily to rough up anyone disloyal to the King.

London's Metropolitan Police were headquartered on a short street called Scotland Yard. Peel sought to create a professional law enforcement unit that was as accountable to everyday citizens as well as to the ruling classes.

When Peel's opponents complained that the creation of the new police force would restrict personal liberties, Peel responded, "I want to teach people that liberty does not consist in having your house robbed by organized gangs of thieves, and in leaving the principal streets of London in the nightly possession of drunken women and vagabonds."

"Peeler's Bobbies" became so successful that many American cities soon began to copy the idea of an organized police force to protect the innocent.

Initially Bobbies only carried the famous whistle and nightstick. Today, about ninety percent of Bobbies still don't carry firearms. However, in sensitive places, like Parliament they do. In this case these armed Bobbies likely saved many lives today, including their own.

But who was behind this attack?
Elena?
The U.S.?
Perchinkov?
The Snakes?
Did someone else have this technology now?

These were all questions that needed to be answered. Unfortunately for me, I had no answers but I did continue to worry about one thing: *Am I the next suicide bomber?*

Guess I should've let Jen's doc friend pull this thing out of my head!

21

Doctor Sam Mustafa sits at his desk in Alexandria, Virginia doing paperwork when his secretary enters the room. She is holding a huge stack of files. She hates her job and is not afraid to share that fact with anyone and everyone, including her boss.

She carelessly sets the stack of papers on her bosses desk. Her boss totally ignores her as he feverishly looks through a file for something.

His phone rings and he answers, "Hello." There is a long pause as he looks very concerned saying, "I'll be right over."

The good doctor stands and impatiently waits for his slowly moving secretary to move out of his way.

Eventually, she moves and he nervously makes his way out the door.

Doctor Mustafa hurries to Walter Jones' office, the head of this Top Secret DARPA facility. Jones was a former lieutenant colonel in the Marines and seems clearly like a fish out of water. He hates his job but the pay is good! If there are three things Walter believes in: it's punctuality, speed and efficiency.

As the doctor enters the room, Jones immediately looks up from his paperwork. Jones says, "Please, sit doctor."

Jones opens a large, flat screen television on the wall and points a remote toward it. As he hits play a picture of a dead woman is shown on a morgue table. This is the woman from the D.C. hotel blown away by Henry's friends. "Did you know this woman had one of our chips in her head?" asks Jones.

"No, no… It wasn't ours…" says a flustered Mustafa.

Jones then shows the British Parliament building in London. A security camera picked up the terrorist car racing toward the Parliament before being shot and killed by London Police. "This happened only two hours ago," says Jones.

A picture of the descendent terrorist is shown.

"A chip was pulled out of this man's head too," says Jones, clearly getting more and more upset.

"Impossible," replies the doctor, "This technology is so advanced we've only used it in prototypes but not in the field."

Jones is not convinced, "Well someone has gone operational. Is it possible the Russians or Chinese have developed this… thing?"

"Anything's possible… however, it's highly unlikely," replies the worried doctor.

"Unlikely? I'd say we're way past unlikely, is some non-government rogue doing this?" asks Jones.

"Highly, highly unlikely," responds the doctor.

So that brings it back to this building. "Could anyone in this building have done this?"

"Impossible!" scoffs Mustafa.

"I would know about it. Each one of those chips has a unique signature and a pattern that can be traced but it will take some time."

"How long?" asks Jones.

"In a couple of days we should have some preliminary…"

Jones interrupts, "You got 24 hours, dismissed."

Mustafa wants to continue his thought but the lieutenant colonel clearly is sending the signal that the conversation is over. Mustafa receives the message loud and clear, stands and leaves without saying another word.

22

    I sit, sipping a martini, watching Perchinkov play tennis with a short, horrible, pasty white Russian kid. I'm surrounded by two probably former Spetsnaz (Russian Special Forces) types. With their black suits, they could easily pass for Sicilian Mafia thugs. I say "thugs" as many Sicilians didn't like the flare ups of mob turf wars that murdered many innocent family members.

    Except these guys had one huge difference: Their white, pasty, skin clearly shows they aren't Sicilian. The Russians stand out like sore thumbs.

    The Villa La Vigie overlooks the beautiful city of Monte Carlo.

    If you do a Google search you will see there's a small bay between us and the Monte Carlo Bay Casino. This tiny body of water separating us would soon turn out to be very important.

    Perchinkov hits a backhand down his opponents line and the kid misses the return. Perchinkov acts as if he just won Wimbledon. His thugs next to me clap as if they're paying fans. This whole charade is becoming annoying.

    Perchinkov walks to me and cheerfully says, "Walk with me."

    Do I have a choice?

Of course not!

So I follow the former head of the Russian military.

He takes me to a hospital surgery room. The room is white with a surgical chair in the middle. A team of doctors and nurses parts and Doctor Franz Gebhardt takes off his surgical mask in front of an operating table.

Some poor man is laying on the table with a clear scar on the side of his head like mine. He's been implanted with one of those chips too. The man slowly wakes.

Perchinkov immediately takes over asking, "Andre' how do you feel?"

"Fine, I feel fine," replies Andre'.

Perchinkov enthusiastically replies, "I saw the whole thing. That was quick and painless. Imagine an army of men who will do anything upon command. That's been the goal of every general, admiral or king for thousands of years. Loyalty, to death."

I'm not so impressed.

Robot loyalty is not loyalty at all but rather slavery. The opposite of freedom.

The man on the table suddenly sits up and looks directly at me saying, "Ahh, but freedom isn't any good if you have nothing. With this chip we can now have everything our heart desires."

So this big jerk can read my thoughts?

"Yes I can," replies the big jerk.

"I'd rather have nothing and have true freedom than have what you call everything and be controlled by someone, never knowing when that someone will decide that today may be the day that you die."

Perchinkov says, "Ahh but many would trade that freedom for the knowledge you now have, Denning."

I have to look twice as these ideas appear to be making Andre' flinch. He's frozen like me when I was commanded to kill Jen. I don't think his brain has the answer. Maybe he has a thousand answers and can't decide which one to pick.

Perchinkov looks worried saying, "What's wrong with him?"

"Nothing!" a nervous Doctor Gebhardt replies. "He needs some time to adjust to the new wealth of information he now has at his fingertips."

"Nothing like having the world at your fingertips with no sense of right and wrong, huh?" I sarcastically add.

Doctor Gebhardt examines the patient with a small pen to the eyes. He engages me with some verbal banter, "You Americans all think you're God's gift to the world."

I reply, "Well, we did save your kraut kissing asses from the Nazis!"

Gebhardt says, "I have some German in me but I'm Belgian."

I verbally go on the attack, "Okay, then, you waffle-eating, kraut kissing, Belgian bastard!"

Gebhardt is very defensive, "But I have some French blood too."

I have no idea why I'm doing this at this point. I've insulted half of Europe and most of my ancestors. Remember, when I get nervous I start verbally joking. These jokes might have gone a bit too far as I then say, "The French are nothing but small, snail, cheese eating, croissant licking frogs who, when war comes, go down faster than a whore on the titanic."

Perchinkov is not amused with our conversation.

Gebhardt ignores me.

I'm glad.

At this point, I'm ignoring myself.

Gebhardt has been busy performing a PERRL test. He's making sure the patient's Pupils are Equal, Round and Reactive to Light. The pupil is the black part of your eye and he's making sure the pupils are reacting normally. When a person becomes comatose the eye reacts abnormally to light. So he is examining the pupils to see if the pupils are the same size. When a light is shining on the pupil does it react to that light and constrict like you'd expect?

Apparently it did.

Doctor Gebhardt says, "Patient appears normal." The doctor then shouts a bit too loud to the patient saying, "Can you hear me okay?"

The patient looks at him as if he's crazy and sarcastically shouts back, "Yes, thank you."

Doctor Gebhardt then backs way off, "Okay, okay. Good. Good."

Perchinkov's patience is wearing thin, "All right. I want no flaws. When can we mass produce?"

"Very, very soon… soon." replies the genocidal doctor.

Perchinkov replies, "Let's make it sooner than that. Much sooner." Perchinkov then has a light bulb go off in his head saying, "I want you to put the next chip in me."

The worried doctor starts to object, "I really don't think…" when Perchinkov interrupts saying, "Don't think, do. Put it in my head now."

The doctor looks to an assistant saying, "Do we have his DNA results?"

The assistant nods.

The doctor knows better than to say no. He looks at Perchinkov and says, "Right away… right away." The doctor motions to get rid of the last guinea pig in the surgery chair and then invites Perchinkov to sit down, "Please, please, sit."

Perchinkov's like a little kid. He almost runs and quickly climbs into the chair. Everyone, including me, stares at Perchinkov. The former Russian admiral looks at me and says, "Get rid of him. All right, let's do this."

23

President Trump is asleep in a private hospital bed, a rare sight to see. Mike Pompeo and Melania Trump talk nearby.

Melania says, "It was crazy. He was saying he wanted war with the world and that Putin was his friend. I've seen him say some strange things but never anything like that."

A medical doctor pushes open the private door to the president's room and is holding one of those quarter like disks. "This is what we extracted from the president's head," says a worried doctor.

"What is it?" asks Mike Pompeo.

"We're running tests. We're not exactly sure yet but inside this device is an electromagnetic chip that's truly extraordinary. This might have been able to send some sort of commands to control the president," says the doctor.

"Well, that would be the first time in history that anything was able to control Donald," says Melania only half joking.

"The CIA and FBI are already fighting to take possession of this device," says the doctor. "I'm giving it to whoever shows first!"

Donald starts to move his head and then attempts to get up. All three run to him. The doctor says, "Easy. Don't try to get up. You've had surgery."

Donald says, "Really? Well I hope they were all Republicans." No one laughs. That doesn't stop him, "C'mon, lighten up. That joke worked for Reagan."

No one wants to say the obvious. Donald seems to enjoy all the attention anyway.

The president continues to swing his feet out of bed, "All right, get my clothes. I've got things to do. Places to go. People to bomb."

Mike says to the doctor quietly, "I thought you said you took that thing out of his head."

The doctor says, "We did!"

24

InterPol (The International Criminal Police Organization) had spotted Elena and JD at the Charles de Gaulle Airport in France on cameras.

No matter how smart you are in evading the law sooner or later some stupid little thing trips up even the most sophisticated criminal. As technologically savvy as Elena and her men were, apparently none of them were aware of the recent move to prevent terrorism. The police had installed security cameras at the private jet hanger from where they had departed.

Jen, Stone, Alexi and Casmerov had already spoken with police officers at the Nice Côte d'Azur International Airport. They were shown footage of the three helicopters that picked up Elena and me. Our flight plans had us heading for Italy but radar showed us landing in Monaco before going on to Italy.

The local police then said something astonishing, "The Monaco police will not cooperate without evidence of a crime."

Monaco is a tiny city-state on the French Riviera and has its own prince and princess. The entire country is only .78 of one square mile but has more money per square foot than any other country on the face of the earth. The only city-state smaller in the world is Vatican City.

But the big difference is: This place is richer! Far, far richer.

The Vatican might argue it has "priceless treasures" but Monaco can argue its "priceless treasures" are in banks owned by the living.

Monaco is a beautiful city where Gucci, Dior, Rolex, Tag Heuer, and hundreds of other high end adverts litter the streets like graffiti in most Western inner cities. There are more high end shops in closer proximity to each other in Monte Carlo than in Beverly Hills, California.

There are no income taxes in Monaco, nor in its city, Monte Carlo. Because of this much of the wealth of the world have a second or third or fiftieth home, boat and car parked here.

They say when the Formula 1 or the yacht show is in town there are about $5 billion in yachts sitting in Monaco's three tiny harbors. There's more money in pleasure craft sitting here than most ports of the world transporting commercial goods.

Monte Carlo is also the most densely populated city in the world and certainly the wealthiest per square mile. So the local police do not want to "disturb" the money parked and spent here, so long as you don't draw too much attention, of an illegal nature, to yourself.

Monaco does cooperate with Interpol and other police agencies but only to a point and again that point is: You better not disturb all of the money parked here.

There's one policeman for every 70 residents and more closed-circuit security cameras per square foot in public than any place on earth.

This place is basically Disneyland for billionaires.

The biggest event in all of Monaco is the Formula 1 Grand Prix. You know those tiny race cars with huge tires. They tear up and down the streets of Monte Carlo once a year. The event draws many thousands from all over the world who come to drink, gamble and pay as much as one million dollars for one day on one balcony to sit and watch one race. What do you get for one million? Well, you get a front row seat in a high rise above the starting line and all the champagne you can drink.

What a deal!

Could I invite a friend?

That better be one special friend!

Jen, Stone, Alexi and Casmerov flew into the Nice airport. Then they took the train to the Monaco station. Apparently, there was an argument at the car rental lot.

The train and the station are sleek and modern. The station is built under a mountain.

"I feel like I'm in a James Bond movie," said Jen as the train pulls into the station.

They are met by the head of the Monaco Police who says, "My name is Robert Ovwà. I am the Dérector of Police. How can we assist?"

Although Ovwà is looking at Stone, Jen speaks up after showing a picture of Elena and JD, "Have you seen these two?"

"That depends."

"On what?"

"On what your purpose is with them?"

"Well, the man on the right is my lover and the woman on the left wants to blow up the world. Good enough?"

"Good enough," says Ovwà. "Follow me."

Jen and company walk to the front of the station where two black Mercedes S cars await. In front and behind are tiny little white Fiats that simply say: "POLICE."

While they walk to the cars in silence Stone breaks the ice saying, "So you're the director of Police. I like that title. I was once the Police Chief in Ketchikan, Alaska."

The snotty Frenchman says with attitude, "How neece."

Stone is not sure if he's been insulted or not.

He has.

So Stone decides to go all the way, "Doesn't your name, Au revoir, mean something in French?"

Even Jen, Alexi and Casmerov who've been totally silent now think a million words as they look at Stone and roll their eyes.

Ovwà says, "Yes, I believe the American comedian, Steve Martin, said it best when he said, 'those French have a word for everything!'"

Stone doesn't get the joke and says, "Boy, ain't that the truth."

All step into the very nice, black, Mercedes S Class sedans. Ovwà says to Jen, "We know where they are. What we don't know is what they're up to. All we really know is that they have a lot of people at the Villa la Vigie."

The cars go about one block and stop. The doors open.

"Okay we're here," says Ovwà.

Casmerov mumbles, "Boy this really is a small town."

Alexi, "Could've walked."

Jen is more suspicious looking around, "Where are we?"

Ovwà, "Please step inside."

Jen, Stone, Alexi and Casmerov all follow about 10 police officers armed to the teeth inside a building.

The inside of this building is a modern looking police station — a very modern looking police station.

There are large white marble pillars and marble floors. In fact, this looks nothing like a police station but more like the Taj Mahal.

Ovwà heads them into a large room at the back of the station. It looks more like a military command center than anything you'd find in a police station.

The room is filled with numerous monitors with another 15 men watching large, flat screens. On a wall at the back of the room are even larger flat screen, wall monitors which everyone in the room can see.

The monitors have drone shot footage of all 10 of the black Range Rovers pulling up to the Villa la Vigie several days ago. Then the monitors cut to much larger numbers of drone shots with men in troop transports pulling up to the Villa.

Ovwà says, "The second video you're now watching happened several days prior to the Range Rovers arrival. We know these men are loyal to the Russian fugitive and former Admiral Perchinkov. We also know that your 'boyfriend' came in with the woman we've identified as G2 or Elena. They appear to be held against their will. What we don't know is what the hell's going on in there?"

Jen says, "I believe they are going to try and force my 'boyfriend' to kill someone against his will. He has a device implanted in his head that might trigger this Navy SEAL to do something terrible."

Ovwà begins speaking nervously in French to his men. One man stands and says, "Watch this."

The Monaco police put on the largest screen a video of a billionaire being abducted from his huge yacht and stuffed in a small car. When the billionaire's men try and come after the small car, gunshots fire toward the yacht and the men retreat back onto the yacht.

"This was taken by our security cameras yesterday," says Ovwà.

"Why haven't you…" Jen stops herself as she is watching Perchinkov's men from the drone footage on another screen continue to unload crates from the Range Rovers.

Jen continues, "… I assume those are crates of weapons and you don't want to assault the compound?"

Ovwà says, "Correct."

Jen says, "Don't you people have any gun control laws?"

Ovwà then says, "Gun control?… The tighter my grip, the better my gun control!"

Another Police officer says, "Yes, if there's a gun in the room, I want to be in control of it."

Jen sarcastically asks, "Do you people have any laws or do you just do Clint Eastwood impressions?

A third officer with a thick French accent says excitedly, "Clint Eastwood. Dirty Harry! Bang! Bang!"

After Jen looks about the room in a disgusted fashion she then asks Ovwà, "So what's your plan?"

Ovwà quickly says, "We wait."

Jen can't believe what she's hearing, "For what?"

Ovwà says, "The Commandement des Opérations Spéciales will arrive within the hour."

Jen quickly says, "French Special Forces?"

Ovwà gets snotty again, "Oui!"

Jen says, "Do the Americans know?"

Ovwà responds, "Oui."

Jen pauses waiting for a more thorough answer and when none comes says, "...And?"

Ovwà says, "And they have no ships or planes that can get here for at least 24 hours."

Jen walks out of the room. Stone, Alexi and Casmerov look at one another and follow.

Jen is pacing in front of the police station, clearly upset.

Stone, Alexi and Casmerov exit the station and are not sure what to do next.

Alexi is silently chosen as the one to speak with Jen. Alexi carefully approaches.

Jen says, "We've gotta get that thing out of his head before they force him to do something horrible."

Alexi, trying to blend, simply says, "Oui."

Jen looks with pursed lips at Alexi who simply shrugs his shoulders.

25

The French Special Forces have been delayed several hours. Although no one would say exactly what was the delay, apparently, it had something to do with a wardrobe mishap (only the French!)!

Jen and company, still worried about me, were convinced by Ovwa' to kill some time at the casino.

I'm being turned into a human time bomb and my friends are turning into tourists?

Little did they know what really happened to me!

So the Monaco police drop my friends in front of this beautiful Casino. It was built in 1863 with an idea from French stage actress, Princess Caroline for some different kinds of entertainment. Over the years as the casino became a huge money maker, more and more upgrades and extravagant fixtures littered the premises.

Today, the front is "littered" with Ferraris, Bentleys, and Rolls-Royces. When I went to the casino, I wondered if most of these cars were really owned by the Société des bains de mer de Monaco, a public company, which owns the casino. Although Monaco is littered with expensive cars, I've always wondered if this is a publicity stunt to entice tourists and gamblers. The public company is primarily owned by the royal family but they distribute money the casino makes to each of Monaco's 38,000 citizens.

My kinda country!

Gambling by residents of Monaco is strictly forbidden. The idea is that they want foreigners to lose their money inside and then give their take to the locals. I'm not much of a gambler so I'd like to be a citizen! It's much tougher for a man to become a citizen than a woman. All a woman needs to do is to marry a Monégasque man.

How sexist!

I think when this is all over I shall appeal directly to the prince.

I once told Jen about the interior of the casino but clearly didn't give her proper instructions. To get inside men must not be wearing shorts. Women must be wearing dresses. Although on the day that I was there, this seemed to be more of a guideline rather than a strict rule.

You can only go into the "actual" gambling areas if you promise not to take pictures. Men must also have on a suit and tie (again, this was not enforced on the day I was in attendance). In addition, it currently costs €17,00 (That's roughly $17.00… not $17,000 as I first thought! Europeans use a comma where we Americans use a period.).

The first time I went inside was before 2pm in the afternoon. After a metal detecting wand gave me the once over I was "allowed" to enter the lobby. Another security guard stopped me from entering one of the two actual gambling parlors. When asked, he said you can go in for free but not for another five minutes.

I said, "Really? Five minutes?"

He said, slightly embarrassed, "Yes." Then he immediately looked at another security guard giving him the eye.

I looked at his likely boss then back to him and I suddenly understood and nodded to the guard, okay.

After five minutes a line of people had gathered at this all important entrance to the gambling rooms. The inside of the gambling parlor, from what I could see, looked absolutely stunning. The chandeliers in there alone must be worth millions. The ceiling, with rich inlays of gold and other precious stones, metals and rare carved woods, really is a site to behold. If you're interested in saving €17,00 you can simply Google the pictures.

Anyway, at 2pm some women started to slip by the security officer. He stopped one woman and in a very bad British accent I said, "'Tis alright, darling," I look at the officer and proudly say, "She's British." The woman looks at me and says, "Really?" I said, "No." However, this was long enough for the guard to take his eyes off of the woman and to slip past his massive body. Now the security officer was overwhelmed and a flood of old people made a bum rush for the double doors. We made it another 20 feet.

At that time more security officers stopped us and said, "Tickets, please."

I said, "At 2pm I was told we could go into the casino. The man said, "You are now in the casino but to go any further you must have a ticket. I looked at all the old British women who were gathering and I screamed, "Do it for England!" then charged the poor man.

He was overwhelmed and we all were able to see this beautiful room without any further restrictions. That is until about 50 security staff (most of these guys were armed) showed up. I said, "The man said..." then I realized all I was doing is getting some poor guy in trouble. "Oh, never mind." With that I walked out the door.

Jen, Stone, Alexi and Casmerov paid their €17,00 and still only saw as much as I did.

The fact that this casino was built in 1863 and the site of James Bond adventures really does give this place street cred, especially with the old folks.

Just then, three bullet resistant, armored trucks pull up to the front of the casino. Out jumps Ovwà with a French Special Forces Commander.

Jen, Stone, Alexi and Casmerov are walking down the steps of the casino.

Ovwà makes the motion to get in the back of the bright yellow truck. Jen asks, "Where are the SEALs?"

Ovwà says, "They are still a few hours away. Commander Pierre Killy is confident his team can assault with a minimum of casualties."

Jen says, "Pierre? Killy? Minimum? What if the minimum is you 'killy' JD? That's not minimum!"

They begin speaking to each other in French and eventually the Commander chuckles and laughs presumably because Ovwà told him Jen and I are in a relationship.

"It's not because he's my boyfriend. The SEALs would go in and hit Perchinkov before anyone knew they were there. Can your team do that?"

The French commander puts his nose in the air slightly saying, "Not to worry. Why don't you go do some shopping or something while we work."

"All you needed to add to that was… little lady and you'd sound like a real sexist pig, you French swine!"

This did not go over so well with the commander. He begins shouting to Ovwà. They all hop into the armored vehicles without Jen, Stone, Alexi and Casmerov and leave.

They are all standing in the street looking dumbfounded.

"Well, what do we do now, soldier?" Alexi asks Jen.

Jen doesn't say a word.

Stone doesn't say a word.

Casmerov is, once again, playing on his phone.

At the Café de Paris in Casino Square nearby I'm casually watching them while sipping a very good, but very expensive, cappuccino.

Now you may be asking yourself, wasn't I captured by Perchinkov's people?

Well, you need the rest of the story.

Let's say the two Russians who tried to kill me, fortunately for me, were not as well trained.

A very knowledgeable man is seated at my table discussing local politics with me, "He was a gambler, a drunkard, and profligate in every way. He's squandered our country's precious resources with wine, women and song."

I ask, "So just over there…" I point toward the Fairmont Hotel, "is the famous hairpin curve on the Formula 1 track?"

"Yes, you see these red and white checkered paint marks on the side of the street?" the man asks.

I quickly answer, "Yes."

"Well, that's the Formula 1 course. You can follow it all over town," the man says.

"Thank you. I wondered what the red and white checkered pavement meant."

"When ya get to the bend in the road ya want to carefully take your car using the classic S pattern past the pool and then accelerate hard 'till you hit the Mediterranean," the man says.

This was my first clue that the guy I was listening to wasn't playing with a full deck. I ask, "What did you say your name was?"

The man quickly answers, "Lord Sandwich, Lord of all Sandwiches."

Well now I know I'm listening to a nut.

The nut continues, "That's where my family made our fortune… sandwiches. Subway, McDonald's, Burger King. You've heard of them, right?"

I'm afraid to answer but I do, "Right."

Unfortunately Lord Sandwich continues, "I invented the sandwich, so I wouldn't have to leave the gambling table."

Some guys yell, "There he is!" and start running toward me. I want to get up and start running when the nut at my table quickly stands and says, "Gotta run!"

He takes off running as men in white coats, I can only assume from a local mental hospital, give chase.

Clearly the man wasn't all there — but he was really interesting.

Somehow the man is able to jump into the driver's seat of a Rolls parked in front of the casino and speed off.

"What the..." Jen now spots me and comes running toward me.

As Jen arrives I thought she'd be happy to see me. Instead, she slaps me and then starts hitting me. I have to grab her hands to stop her attack. Nobody in our motley crew wants to get near either of us.

"What are you doing... how did you..." asks Jen not completing a single sentence.

I try and very, very calmly answer, "Remember, I have a chip imbedded in my head. It's easy to tap all of the police systems. I knew exactly where you were and what you were doing. The French Special Forces team took only slightly longer to hack and..."

Jen interrupts, "That means Elena knows what we're doing right now too."

I say, "Not to worry. Elena's been captured. The guy we worry about is..."

Stone interrupts, "It's good to see you John."

"Good to see you, chief," I say.

"Chief? Please call me Robert. Chief sounds too Indian," says Stone, again sounding a bit racist.

Alexi jumps in to the conversation, "Jen says you were being held by Elena. How did you get away?"

I quickly answer, "Elena's not our biggest problem. Perchinkov is."

This finally gets Casmerov from looking at his phone, "Admiral Perchinkov?"

"Yes," I say.

Alexi chimes in, "That bastard!"

I begin to walk away, "C'mon. We gotta go to Norway."

Everyone is dumbfounded.

Jen asks, "Norway, what's in Norway?"

I stop and quickly respond, "Perchinkov and probably the biggest danger the planet's ever faced."

Jen asks me, "What about Ovwà and the French Special Forces?"

"They can handle any of Perchinkov's men still at the Villa."

As we try and leave the cafe all sorts of horns begin honking and a parade of Porsches, Ferraris and other beautiful cars round the tiny square in front of the casino.

Trailing them, being pulled by a truck, is a Formula 1 (F1) race car. It has Red Bull stickers all over the beautiful, low profile vehicle.

Out of a 2018 Porsche 911 GT2 RS steps Daniel Joseph Ricciardo. That Porsche alone is worth over $350,000.00 but it's his Formula 1 car that intrigues me and worth millions more. A Formula 1 team can cost over $300 million dollars a year. That's why they need sponsors.

A crowd of tourists, attracted to Daniel like bees to honey, begin gathering around him and his multi-million dollar machine. The F1 is truly a sight to see. The super low profile and super wide tires make this vehicle stand out from all the other very expensive machinery now parked in front of the casino.

There are at least 20 Monaco police officers who have marched in precision alongside of these vehicles and are keeping a huge crowd at bay.

One obnoxious American yells out, "Gentlemen, start your engines!"

Daniel, also called "Riccardo" is from Australia. His father was born in Sicily but moved to Australia when he was seven. Riccardo has three F1 wins and 10 podiums to date.

Riccardo walks over to the flatbed upon which his shiny red F1 sits. Several guys put down planks behind the flatbed. Riccardo hops into the driver's seat and starts the car.

The crowd politely claps as most have never probably seen an F1 up close.

Great! How do we get out of this place quickly?

As I start to walk, a suppressed round goes into a coffee cup right where I was standing.

Another round quickly shoots a police whistle out of the mouth of an officer nearby.

I dive under a table.

Jen, Alexi and Casmerov quickly follow while Stone is still foolishly, standing nearby, staring at the F1 car. Apparently, with all the clapping and F1 engine racing, Stone didn't hear the shot ring out.

I grab Stone's leg and pull him under a table.

Another round chips off the side of the wooden table inches from my head.

I yell, "Get down."

Only now do people nearby begin to scream and panic.

The police officer, missing his whistle, is trying to herd people to safety without much success.

The Monaco police look in the direction of the screaming crowd not realizing a sniper is shooting from a window nearby. The suppressed rounds ring from a third story window in the Hotel de Paris. The hotel sits across from the "grassy knoll" and us. Ricardo's F1 car sits between us and the sniper.

I now see two black suited goons closing in on us from the casino which is our only real escape route.

We're trapped!

These are Perchinkov's men. I recognized them from when I hit them over the head to get out of the Villa. They don't look too happy. One has a bandage on his nose. The other a black eye.

156

I ask Jen, "Give me your gun."

She says, "The Monaco police took our guns when we arrived."

I disgustedly say, "Great!"

Jumping to my feet, I dive over the outdoor restaurant's two foot high decorative concrete.

Beautiful! Thinks my stupid brain now running hundreds of miles per second.

I then yell, "I'm drawing fire."

Jen yells, "What?"

I start to yell again when a series of sniper rounds ping the concrete very near my feet. I find myself bobbing and weaving as the shots continue.

I am forced to run directly toward Riccardo and his F1 racer. His is talking politely with the crowd as he holds his racing helmet.

I know you see this coming!

I grab Ricardo's racing helmet which he's holding under his arm. I put it on, jump in the car that's running and, after grinding a gear, burn rubber.

Riccardo seems so shocked that he didn't even put up a fight.

Lucky for him or we'd probably both have been shot.

A Rolls Royce rear window is shot out directly in front of me and I'm forced to take the first right. A bright red Ferrari 250 GT SWB California pulls directly behind me and it's on! Several tiny Monaco police cars make it about a block before they give up.

We leave them in our dust!

I take the next right again and without knowing it, I've been on the F1 race course and am heading for the infamous 180 degree hairpin turn. I have to brake hard to avoid going directly onto the Fairmont Hotel's roof! If I hadn't hit the brakes I felt like I would have flown directly over the four story Fairmont. The next stop would have been the Mediterranean Sea! Crazy 'Lord Sandwich' was right.

As I round the hairpin, I accelerate leaving a 15 million dollar Ferrari in the dust.

It then hits me, *I hope everyone else is okay. I better circle back.*

Circle back was the appropriate word but it would be over two miles to get "back" after going all the way around the entire "circle." How is that possible you say when you're only two blocks away? Well, I'll try and answer your question while I drive a car going well over 200 MPH!

I could walk back to them but there's a small mountain now between us.

I'm gonna have to drive to them.

By the way, a professional race car driver can lap this entire two mile course in just over one minute!

But I'm not a professional race car driver.

If I'm still alive I'll bet I can do it in under two!

Those times won't get me into the next Monaco F1 event but might be enough to keep me alive.

I take another right skidding toward a guard rail. This flimsy little metal railing is the only thing between me and the Mediterranean.

I manage to correct the slide and then head for — a tunnel?

I see the Fairmont Hotel directly above me as I speed into a tunnel under the hotel!

Only in Monaco would a hotel be built directly over a Formula 1 race track!

The Ferrari has now caught up with me as we accelerate through the tunnel.

It seems to be two miles long all by itself.

Fortunately, the police seem to have gotten the word out and have pulled traffic to the side. I'm trying to figure out why they aren't stopping me when the thought crosses my mind: The F1 race is tomorrow and everyone in town appears to really be enjoying two, really nice, cars race.

My theory is backed up, when, as we reach the other side of the tunnel, people are out of their cars. As we zoom past them they all begin clapping and yelling things.

At least that's what I think they were doing. I had 00.08 of a second to hear and see that!

I'm slapped back to reality when I sideswipe a Bentley.

Great!

That'll cost me about a million dollars!

Uh oh!

I'm not able to make a 90 degree turn and stay on the F1 course. Instead, I head into another tunnel under where I arrived, Prince Rainier's Castle.

Inside the tunnel I learn this is only wide enough for one car and it's one way!

Guess which way I'm going?

THE WRONG WAY!

I can't see what kind of car is coming at me. What I can see, and can see very well, are two very large headlights shining at my head.

I drive onto a tiny curb and literally onto the side of the tunnel wall. Fortunately, I have very wide and very soft tires as the sides of the tunnel are carved out of bumpy rock.

My life flashes in front of me (along with a car headlight that's seems inches from my face!)!

As I bump along the wall all I can think about is: *Why is Jennifer so mad at me!*

Don't know how I did it but I passed the very expensive Rolls literally on the side of the tunnel wall. Guess it's good to have super wide tires but I'm not sure they were ever intended for that.

As I make my way out of the tunnel, a large parked bus forces me to swerve right. *Apparently, I can only drive to the right in this car.*

I see a sign that said Avenue Albert II.

Like that helped.

Good job JD.

Shut up!

I crash through an outdoor cappuccino stand. As patrons go running I yell out, "Sorry! Sorry!" I hear a loud crash behind me and am hoping that's the 15 million dollar Ferrari that hit the bus.

I'm literally in a shopping mall and the street is nowhere in sight.

I look back toward the tunnel.

The Ferrari is still after me.

Hundreds of police in this town, where's one when you really need one?

I'm not looking where I'm driving but I drive into a shopping mall that's built, you guessed it, right into the side of this mountain, still under the Prince's castle.

What a town!

I love Monaco and I feel like I've seen most of the city in two minutes flat!

I'm racing through this mall and pass some very exclusive shops.

I really like the look of those sunglasses!

What am I talking about?

I truly have gone mad.

As I'm shopping in my F1 racer I see the red Ferrari on the other side of the mall.

What the...

How did he?...

I'm going down one side of the two sided mall while the Ferrari goes down the opposite side. There's other shops in between us so this buys me a little bit of time.

Maybe you'd like to do some more shopping?

Idiot!

I race, if you can call it that, outside and put the F1 into a 180 degree spin to avoid some tourists.

Directly in front of me is an escalator, going up.

I can see the Ferrari is trapped in some clothes racks in the mall but will soon see me.

I decide the escalator is my only route of escape.

I may have to bail from the car.

It's gonna be tight.

I wedge "my" F1 race car at a 45 degree angle onto an escalator going up.

As I reach the top of the escalator the wide tires on the passenger side simply roll right off the handrail.

The problem is: now there is nowhere to go.

Trapped!

Trapped like a rat in a maze… but if I've gotta be in some maze somewhere in the world this is the maze where I wanna be trapped.

The Ferrari comes flying out one floor below me going in the opposite direction. He doesn't see me, I don't think.

Two huge double glass doors open. The sign above them says, S.A.S. LE PRINCE DE MONICO.

I see two guys motioning me to drive the F1 inside the double, all glass, doors. What choice do I have? I quickly drive inside the building. My "pit crew" quickly close the large elephant doors behind me.

Inside my mouth drops open—

Rolls Royce's, Bentley's, F1's, and many, many old models of cars I've never seen before dot the inside of this— car museum?

Several guys run up to the car. One turns off the engine while four others push the car to an empty spot on the exhibit floor.

A sign on the exhibit floor in front of this empty spot says, "DANIEL RICCARDIO F1 - SPONSOR: RED BULL (2018). I guess I accidentally delivered Daniel's F1 to his next stop: Prince Rainier's car museum!

My pit crew is motioning me to get out of the car and take off the helmet.

I gladly do.

I'm like a little kid in a candy store. A 1903 DE DION BOUTON, a 2013 LOTUS F1 via HISPANO SUIZA, ROLLS ROYCE, LINCOLN, FACEL VEGA, DELAGE, DELAHAYE, PACKARD, HUMBER, NAPIER, FERRARI, MASERATI, LAMBORGHINI, ALFA ROMEO, and LEXUS dot the interior of this place. The cars in here are clearly priceless and worth millions more than the F1 I was just driving.

As I walk around I'm truly, maybe for the first time in my life, speechless. And for me, that's something.

The beauty, the elegance, the, dare I say it, Grace, of these cars brings back memories from movies all throughout my childhood.

I was living in this Oregon cult with my mother, two brothers and one sister. My sister and I used to love to watch old black and white movies. We were only allowed to watch a movie once a week and with the prior approval of the cult leader, of course!

I remember imagining that I was rich and chauffeured about in the back of this old Rolls.

I look around and nobody is paying any attention to me.

Did the guys think I was part of Daniel Joseph Ricciardo's F1 team?

Were they helping me escape from assassins?

This chip in my head is making me crazy thinking about all sorts of thoughts.

I've checked out of reality!

Where is Jen?

Alexi?

I've gotta get back to them.

But I also suddenly have millions of thoughts of my childhood.

I didn't know 'till later that Doctor Gebhardt was doing all he could in manipulating my thoughts to distract me.

I cross the golden rope and open the door of the old Rolls. Now this feels like a car!

Solid steel doors.

It's a tank.

I'll bet this vehicle could push anyone right out of the way!

I hop into the back seat.

The smell of "new" leather in this very, very old Rolls makes me wonder about the guys building this car in England. They were probably some poor schlubs who were wondering: Who has this much money? I can barely feed my 5 kids!

I'm confused.

I should be worried about Jen and my team but instead I'm momentarily sucked back to my childhood and all the wonderful memories of my sister. My thoughts almost immediately then go to memories of her suicide. Suicide because she was forced by her "pro-life" mother and "pro-life" cult leader to have a quiet abortion so as not to "embarrass" them because she refused to marry the polygamous cult "god," Rudy. The leader had this flock of gullible women surrounding him.

I'm sorry to say my mother and my sister were very gullible.

At least two women in the cult were pregnant at all times.

They had this motto, "Souls of great light are waiting to be born, have one."

I'm sure you say that to all the girls!

Because of all this, my sister had a forced abortion and then jumped off the highest bridge in Portland (381 feet) to her death.

Her body washed up on shore miles down the Willamette River several weeks later.

How I wish I could've been there.

Every time I see her in my mind I literally shout out loud, "Don't do it! I love you!"

But it's always too late.

She keeps falling and falling and falling and I jump after her.

I'm falling and falling and falling.

I usually wake up in a cold sweat.

I've had that recurring nightmare almost every week for the last 20 years.

I sat there staring at the back of the black leather seat for eons.

Those eons probably were, in real time, about one minute.

Thugs in black suits walk through the front door. A little man tries to stop them and is immediately shot in the head.

This snaps me back to reality.

I'm having a hard time moving.

Something in the back of my head tells me I've gotta get to Jennifer.

I'm frozen!

Just like when I was ordered to kill Jennifer last year.

I struggle with myself for a few key seconds but have figured out how to push certain thoughts aside.

The thugs walk to, for lack of better words, my pit crew, who stand there.

I'm thinking of a way out.

There is only one, past the thugs in black with guns.

My pit crew pretends they don't know anything.

One of them has a pistol pointed right at his head.

I still feel like I can't move when another innocent man is shot in the head.

This seems to push this thought forward — Jen!

I struggle but slowly move to open the door. Just then my eye catches something shiny reflecting off the museum's bright lights.

It's a key!

It's in the ignition!

You see where I'm going here now, don't you?

I roll into the front seat and grab the ignition key.

I turn over the old Royce's engine.

It's starts on the first attempt!

These guys must start and tune up these cars regularly — or thank God, at least this one.

I hit the gas and head for the murderers.

They look so shocked that the fools stand in the way of "my" oncoming old "Rolly" that appears to weigh 50 tons.

I knock all four thugs like pinballs at a bowling alley.

Steeeerike!

Direct hit!

My pit crew has already scattered.

And Perchinkov's men begin firing at "my" old Rolls.

Their bullets don't even break my back windshield.

Boy!

They don't make 'em like they used to.

I crash through the large, glass, elephant doors and more thugs await me outside. However, they're the lookouts and don't have guns drawn. I knock one of them over the side of the escalator as the others draw their guns.

This time I don't take the escalator.

I drive right over the side.

My Rolly rips through the beautiful three foot concrete rail like it wasn't even there.

I'm flying.

I wonder what's below?

Guess I should've asked that question BEFORE I went airborne.

It's always nice to have a plan.

I had none.

None other than — get away!

Get away now!

I crash onto a table with cups of what appear to be cappuccino.

I hit another table with the front bumper.

Fortunately, there were no people sitting at the tables.

I'm not sure what it was but the table acted like a catapult for a cup of something.

A coffee cup flies into the air and then lands directly onto my windshield blocking my vision with something brown. I can only assume it's coffee.

I put the wipers on — eventually — finding the switch was nearly impossible.

These wipers are terrible. Replace them at once, Wadsworth!

My hand collects some of the brown stuff and, I don't know why, but I taste it while I swerve toward the tunnel.

Coffee?

Yep.

Cream and...

Sugar.

And something else I can't quite place.

Hazelnut!

I'd bet my life on it.

(Although that might be a poor choice of words right about now!)

As I race back through the tunnel I'm looking for my headlights.

Why, even today, is it still not easy to find where headlights are on a car?

I look up and here is this tiny little thing coming at me.

Behind me is the red Ferrari again.

"I can't stop. Move!" I scream.

The little car stops and hits reverse.

He's driving backwards at the same speed I'm driving forward.

The problem is, the Ferrari is gaining on me so I quickly help the little guy along.

I helped him a bit too much.

His little white Fiat shoots out of the tunnel like a cannon ball out of an old cannon.

The little car goes airborne and into the Mediterranean.

This Rolls is great!

I wonder if I could keep it?

I wouldn't need a tank to move people out of my way.

Just my Rolly!

As I whiz past the poor man's part of the harbor (Yachts here go for only 100 million and below) I look to see a Vogue type of photo shoot. A woman in a bikini is pretending to sun herself on a rail while a photographer snaps pictures.

Wow!

Isn't she beautiful!

The next thing I remember is that I'm airborne — again.

It's one second of pure exhilaration and silence — and then splash!

Am I in the Mediterranean?

No!

Where am I?

All I know is that I'm sinking. I'm sinking into water and sinking fast in a car that will take me to the bottom. Princess Grace shot her first film with Cary Grant in less time than I took to get out of the Rolls.

I'm in a swimming pool at the beginning of the F1 course.

The crash into the pool was deafening.

I put up a wake of water so high into the air that it drenches about 50 people sunbathing on one side of the pool.

Meanwhile on the "dry side" a pretty girl is sunbathing. She takes wireless headphones out of her ears and, not seeing my Rolls Royce sinking, says to her girlfriend, "Did you say something?"

A tourist from China has summoned a waiter near the edge of the pool saying, "Waiter, waiter, there's a car in my pool."

A tall, skinny, French waiter who thinks he's a world famous "insult" waiter at Lindy's in New York City, says in a most condescending manner, "There's also a hole in your head but you don't see me complaining."

The Chinese man obviously does not understand what this pretty good comedian said. He stares blankly at the waiter as the waiter continues, "Is there anything else that neither of us can change?"

The Chinese businessman then rudely says, "Well, should you not alert someone?

The Frenchman says, "It appears the media has already beeeen a-lerted." The waiter continues bent over staring closely at the man as his tall finger points to a helicopter above. After a dramatic, and for no apparent reason, pause, the Frenchman says, "Now, will there beeee anything else?"

The Chinese man then angrily says, "Yes, yes, for what I'm paying here, get it out of my pool!

Without missing a beat the rude, waiter says, "I'll fetch the pool boy at once." The waiter looks around, aimlessly, and in a very snotty fashion yells, "Renaldo? Renaldo?" as he claps his hands twice he continues, "Chop chop!"

The very handsomely chiseled body of Renaldo in a speedo, comes running out with a 20 foot leaf skimmer on a pole.

Our snotty French waiter turns up his nose at the Chinese man and loudly announces, "And now, I leaf!"

His exit alone should have won him an Oscar.

About 10 police officers converge on me as the red Ferrari slowly pulls away. It gets about 10 feet before a squadron of tiny, white, police cars surround it like a pack of wolves slowly moving in for the kill.

The Monaco police might appear to be in tiny cars but those tiny cars, all apparently, carry some very heavy firepower. Several police officers pull out, fully automatic, *M16* machine guns and point it at the Ferrari.

The guys in the Ferrari very wisely and very, very slowly put their hands and pistols in the air.

Meanwhile, I'm standing on the side of the Stade Natique Ranier III pool dripping wet.

The "priceless" F1 car of David Riccardio might have been saved by the museum but an even more priceless Rolls lets out one last bubbling glug as it sits in its watery grave at the bottom of the pool.

Oh I'm goin' to jail.

Again!

And when I get out this time I'll be working for Prince — whatever the hell his name is — for forever.

As I stare at the Rolls at the bottom of the pool I somehow hear Titanic music playing in my mind.

I'll never be able to afford to pay the prince for those ridiculously large, whitewall, tires on Titanic II.

As the crowd disburses I continue to stand, dripping wet, while I look about.

It's such a nice town, I hope I'll be doing my jail time here.

A local runs up to me and says, "That was the prince's priceless Rolls!"

I very, very, slowly answer with my best Peter Sellers accent, "Not... any... more!"

Jen, Alexi, Casmerov and Stone come running toward me with Ovwà bringing up the rear.

The first thing I notice is that none of the Monaco police have their guns out.

If I was in charge of this place I would have taken me down by any means necessary.

I'm really glad I'm not in charge of this place.

For the first time I notice Police Chief Stone.

Wow! Stone's in better shape than he was in Alaska. He's not even huffing and puffing any more.

"Stone! I'm impressed. Have you lost weight?" I ask.

Stone answers, "Ya! Chasing you all over the world... I lost 20 pounds!"

I smile, "Congrats!"

Stone beams with pride.

This outdoor pool is near the starting line for the Monaco Grand Prix.

I see a sign that says: F1 and another that says: FU!

I foolishly ask, "What's FU?"

A Monaco police officer says, "The cheap seats. In FU you can only hear the race!"

Jen points to the water — the real water. The Mediterranean. Four Special Warfare Combatant Crafts with SEALs are full speed inbound.

Skull is on the lead boat. As he steps off the craft, he walks up the steps laughing, "We've been watching the drone feed." Skull points to a drone above. "Nice job, Mario. A perfect 10!" Skull looks at the Rolls sitting at the bottom of the prince's pool.

 Alexi wants in on the jokes, "I sign you up for next race!"

I smile at these guys.

Skull then says, "Okay Flipper, get in the boat."

I look around to Ovwà to be sure I'm not going to be arrested, shot and hanged. Ovwà simply says, "Au revoir" as he calmly waves goodbye.

I don't care what they say, I kinda like the French, at least the French in Monaco.

All of us climb into these sleek, light, special warfare crafts and are off to the *USS Gravely*, a guided missile destroyer, sitting in the harbor nearby.

26

President Trump is back at work in the Oval Office. He's chatting it up with the Prime Minister of Canada, "All right tell ya what, Trudy, you drop all your dairy tariffs on us and I'll drop all my steel tariffs on you, deal?... Well, you tell your people that's my final offer. If they can't do it tell them to go suck maple syrup where the sun don't shine... which is everywhere in Canada! Bye, Bu-bye!"

The Donald slams the phone down on his desk.

Mike Pompeo and Melania are standing in the doorway at the other end of the room.

"Well, I'd say he's back to normal, wouldn't you?"

Melania smiles but says nothing.

Fred and Jerry walk into the room carelessly brushing Melania on each side of her lovely pink Chiffon dress.

Fred casually says, "Oh sorry."

Only then does Jerry say, "Sorry."

They walk up to the Donald who is busy writing something. They look at each other trying to decide who's gonna interrupt him. Neither have enough guts so they both stand there.

And stand there.

And stand there.

Finally The Donald says, "I heard you were looking for other jobs while working for me. Well, let me just say to you both two words: You are fired. Wait, that's three... You're fired. There, that's two. Bye. Bu-bye."

Both Fred and Jerry again stand there.

And stand there.

Until they both look at each other and slowly walk out the door.

Melania looks at Mike and says, "Oh ya, he's back to 'his' normal."

Several members of the Joint Chiefs of Staff enter.

This looks serious.

Donald finally looks up, "What?"

Mike starts, "Mr. President we have reason to believe that Elena and maybe people inside one of our most secret labs developed that thing that was in your head. That chip can control a person's actions, thoughts and emotions from afar."

The Donald is daydreaming, "Afar. That's funny."

All look to each other, very worried.

"Mr. President, we need an Executive Order to by any means necessary stop these chips from spreading."

"For your eyes only, Mr. President."

The Donald is clearly confused by this terminology and say, "What?"

A file is placed in front of the president. On it is stamped "TOP SECRET" and "COMPARTMENTALIZED."

Also, the title of the file is: "*ZERO HOUR.*"

"Zero Hour? What's this?" asks The Donald.

Mike speaks up, "It's the code name and plan of how we get rid of these brain chips."

Donald opens and kinda looks at the stack of papers. "Sounds good ta me. Where do I sign?"

"Don't you wanna know the plan first?"

"No, not really. Is Denning and that girl helping us?"

"Jennifer Tavana? Yes, sir. We have them enroute to Norway now."

"Norway now? Is that a country?"

"Norway, is, yes sir."

"What about Norway now?"

An unnamed cabinet member whispers at back of Oval Office to another, "Are we sure they took that chip out of his head?"

The Donald then blurts out, "Okay authorize all forces to do whatever they have to. If that means drop a nuke on Norway, do it! Don't ask me, just do it!"

All stand in silence as the president signs the 'Zero Hour' Executive Order.

Another cabinet member whispers at the back of the room, "Glad I didn't take that ambassadorship to Norway."

27

Some poor kid that's only 20 something is sitting at Peterson Air Force Base in Colorado in front of his monitor. The room is filled with about 100 monitors. A floor to ceiling monitor covers the entire wall at the front of the room.

This Air Force base monitors all air traffic in North America and is the air defense command center for any possible 'situation' by air. In today's environment, this would include terrorism.

A phone rings and the kid answers it, bored out of his mind, "Uh huh. Ya."

The kid casually, pulls up radar on his monitor and quickly springs into action. "Thanks." He hangs up the phone and pushes a button which turns the monitors on the giant wall into one giant monitor of the Seattle area.

The kid now speaks into his headset, "Get the general in here. Now!"

The kid mumbles to himself, "... and on my day off too!"

General Norton walks into the room and over to the kid followed by an assistant.

"I'm here. What's up?"

"Looks like someone's hijacked a plane out of Seattle, sir."

"Do we have confirmation?"

"Yes both the control tower and Alaska Airlines, sir. It's one of their planes."

"Are we sure it's a hijacking?"

"We're not sure of anything except there are no passengers."

"Not a one?"

"Far as we can tell, only one pilot, who works for the airline, sir."

"So how do we know it's a hijacking?"

They look at the big screen and it looks like the guy is doing circles in the sky.

"What the hell's he doing?" Asks the general.

"Don't know, sir."

The general asks, "Is this a diversion for something bigger?"

The poor kid in front of him quickly responds, "I don't know sir, listen…"

The kid then puts on the speaker system this,

> "Hijacker: … Hey, you think if
> I land this successfully
> (inaudible) would give me a job
> as a pilot?
> Controller: … You know I
> think they would give you a job
> doing anything if you can pull
> this off.
> Hijacker: … Yeeeeahhh right!
> Nah I'm a white guy… (audio
> cuts)."[5]

General Norton, "Scramble the closest air assets."

Another airman speaks up, "That would be Oregon, sir."

General rips off his headset and throws it. "What? God damn it! The entire state of Washington doesn't have one God damn fighter jet?"

The first kid quickly responds, "Apparently not, sir."

"How far out are those air assets?" asks the furious general.

"Portland, Oregon. It's over 100 miles away. They'll be there in 12 minutes, sir."

The annoyed general says, "Great! This thing may be over in two."

A third person now speaks up, "They're already in the air. Missiles in range in about 9 minutes, sir."

The general seems pleased, "Good! Get them on the horn."

Another kid nearby monitoring says, "Each F15 has 4 missiles locked, and loaded sir."

"So if the commies attack Seattle tonight, I have to scramble some Air National Guard idiots from Oregon?"

A cocky Oregon Air National Guard pilot speaks over the sound system, "Your two idiots from Oregon locked and loaded within range of target in... shortly. Awaiting your command, general, sir."

General is not embarrassed at all, "Good job boys, that was record time! Stand-by... we're tryin' ta get confirmation." The general looks at the first kid, "We need to find out if this guy's nuts or somethin' else is a goin' on!" The general now starts pacing.

Another airman says, "He's doing loops again, sir."

The general says, "What? Impossible. In a commercial plane? We better shoot this guy down before he takes somethin' like a ship or a building out."

The kid, now worried, "I think my parents are in the Space Needle right now. Here, listen, to this guy now, sir." The kid puts the crazy hijacker on the sound system again:

> "Controller: ... Apparently a grounds
> crewman with Horizon, I guess. And

uh, right now he's just flying around,
and just he needs some help
controlling his aircraft.
Hijacker: ... Nah, I mean, I don't need
that much help. I've played some
video games before.
Controller: ... If you could, could you
start a left-hand turn, and we'll take
you down to the southeast, please?
Hijacker: "... This is probably like jail
time for life, huh? I mean, I would
hope it is, for a guy like me.
Controller: ... Well ... we're not going
to worry or think about that. But
could you start a left-hand turn,
please?
Hijacker: ... I don't want to hurt no
one. I just want you to whisper sweet
nothings in my ear... I've got a lot of
people that care about me, and it's
going to disappoint them to hear that
I did this. I would like to apologize to
each and every one of them. Just a
broken guy, got a few screws loose, I
guess. Never really knew it until now."[6]

"Aww hell," The general says, "I'm gonna hav'ta shoot this stupid,
mother fucker down, aren't I? Get the F-15's back on the horn."

"They're already live, sir."

"This is General Norton at NORAD. Are your weapons locked on
target?"

The Oregon pilot quickly responds, "Yes, sir. Locked, cocked and ready 'ta rock... sir."

"General rolls his eyes and pushes a mute button, "Cocky 'lil SOB ain't he?"

The airman kid finally realizes the general doesn't really want any response. The kid ignores the general.

The general then takes his hand off the mute button and says to the pilot, "Hold tight son, we're tryin' 'ta wake the president."

General puts hand on mute button again, "I'm not gonna be the first 'some' bitch ta shoot down a commercial airliner in U.S. airspace. Let that crazy 'some' bitch Trump shoot it down."

Suddenly popping up on a floor to ceiling screen is an extreme close up of President Trump in his pajamas and in bed, "Good evening, general."

The general is taken off guard not sure if he was heard or not, "Oh, uhh, good evening, Mr. President."

"So what crazy thing does this 'crazy some bitch' have ta okay now?"

The general, realizing the president heard him seems undeterred because of the severity of the situation. The general responds, "It appears that some nut has hijacked a commercial airliner. We just need the go ahead to shoot him down if he looks to threaten LLP."

A confused president responds, "LLP?"

"Life, Limb, or Property, sir."

"It's your call general, your call."

"Well sir, I don't want to be the one blamed for shooting down a passenger jet in American airspace."

"Whatever you do, just blame me! Everyone else will anyway."

The general pauses, realizing the president has lifted a huge burden from his shoulders. With the utmost of respect the general replies, "Thank you, sir. I won't let you down."

Trump immediately responds, "Ya, ya, whatever." Immediately, the gigantic screen goes dark.

The general stares at the screen for a moment then says, "Put the OAGs back on the horn."

"Go ahead, sir," says the airman.

"OAG 1 and OAG 2, target is over water with nothing below. You're clear to engage. Splash the bogie, I repeat you're clear to engage."

"Copy that general, engaging now."

The general sees the plane totally disappear on the huge screen.

"Did you already fire your weapons?"

"Yes, sir. Four birds are flyin', I repeat four birds are away."

"Damn it!" replies the General. "I'd bet my retirement… that plane already crashed."

Another young airman says, "Multiple reports are coming in that the bogie crashed, sir."

"Where did it go down?" asks the general.

Another airman says, "Looks like a deserted island somewhere near…"

"So we didn't shoot it down?"

"No sir. Missiles will splash nearby."

"Thank God," says the general as he scratches the back of his head.

"Did anybody see our missiles?" asks the general.

OAG1 answers, "I doubt it, sir. Area looks pretty deserted. I can report visually, sir, one bogie splashed."

The general says, "We got reports it crashed on a deserted island."

"Bogie is no longer a threat, sir," replies the pilot.

"OAG1, OAG2, good job. Return to base, boys."

"Base would be the Portland International Airport… sir."

The general sounds like President Trump and says, "Whatever."

28

<u>Diary of Olga Kasparov</u>

I'm sitting in my little tiny television office in downtown Moscow when Vladimir Putin walks through my door.

I stand flustered.

He smiles, "Sit, sit, please, sit."

I do as I'm told and after an uncomfortable silence I ask, "So what brings you to my office, Mr. President?"

Putin says, "I need for you to do me a favor."

"Anything, Mr. President," I reply.

"Trump is killing our oil business. I need you to put out this story," says Mr. Putin as he hands me a file of papers.

I look them over and it shows how the United States is doing so much fracking that it's now become the world's largest seller of crude oil to the world and undercutting Russian prices.

"Okay, is this true?" I ask.

Putin stands saying, "Of course." He smiles and starts to leave. He stops and looks at my head, "You don't have one of those implant things do you?"

"What?" I chuckle, "No, God, no!"

"Good. People are getting very paranoid around here. Apparently, the American media has made us all a little crazy. I think all American media have been implanted with the zombie chip. The Americans are blaming us for those head implants. The world truly has gone mad but I always want you to be my mishka," says Putin as he wheels out the door.

Now mishka can mean two things to a Russian: 1). A unisex person or 2). A sweet, cuddly, teddy bear. At my age I may not be the most beautiful Russian girl any more but I'm hoping he meant the latter.

I look over the papers and it looks to be filled with all sorts of slight exaggerations of how great the Russian oil program is and how the U.S. will soon run out of oil.

Why did he choose me?

I really wanted to ask him about those nuclear suitcases that might still be on the loose. But I was more curious as to why he chose this way to communicate this oil information. Maybe he wanted to see me.

Olga, don't flatter yourself!

29

An FBI assault team of over 20 members enters the DARPA laboratory in Alexandria, Virginia. These guys are all decked in black and have fully automatic weapons locked and loaded. I would not want to be sitting in the lobby. They traverse the front door in teams of three.

Right behind them is Henry with another team of "suits."

Three guys manning the lobby desk start to pull their revolvers when they see 20 fully automatic weapons point at them.

Henry walks in and casually says, "If you value your lives, I wouldn't move a muscle."

The three rent a cop looking guys stand frozen not moving a muscle.

Henry motions one team to disarm the rent a cops while the teams hit the stairs.

Henry and his suits, meanwhile, take the elevators to the top floor. These are the executive offices of the DARPA supervisors.

Henry walks toward the older receptionist for Mustafa who has on a really nice pair of Bose 35 pro, over ear, headphones. The poor, older woman has no idea that an FBI assault team is right behind her. She is singing a very bad version of Aretha Franklin's 'Respect,' "R-E-S-P-E-C-T tell me what it means to me... sock it to me, sock it to..."

Henry takes off her headphones.

"Where's Mustafa?" asks Henry pointing his Glock at her heart.

The poor, old woman is ready to have a heart attack.

"Where did he go?" asks Henry.

"I... I think he's out of the country. Norway... maybe." says the terrified woman as an FBI assault team stands next to her.

Henry motions to the team leader to head down the hall. Henry gets on the phone saying, "Mustafa's headed to Norway."

I say, "Thanks, Henry. I'd say the pieces are falling into place."

Henry says, "I'll secure this lab and call you if I have anything else."

I say, "Thanks Henry."

I'm in a "Top Secret" part of the ship. The "War Room" on the *USS Gravely*. I'm surrounded by my SEAL team and an entire room of Naval support officers.

I say, "Okay boys, we have the green light to take this place down by any means necessary. The problem is that this place was designed by NATO to withstand a direct nuclear hit. So the element of surprise will be critical."

I pull up a map on the clear, see through glass.

"This tunnel area here under the water is maybe our only way in without alerting everyone inside."

"Satellite intelligence suggests that there are three Typhoon class subs under this rock. *TK-20* just left the facility and looks to be running for the polar ice cap. We have the *USS Bullhead* sitting waiting to sink her. Problem is, that's the only asset we have close enough right now to take her out."

Another Naval officer walks into the room and whispers in my ear, "We have a problem, sir."

I excuse myself and leave the room.

In the hall the officer says, "*TK-20* has started evasive maneuvers. It looks like she knows we're watching her."

"How is that possible?" I ask.

"Above my pay grade, sir," replies the officer.

"... unless..." I'm thinking as a thousand thoughts go through my brain. "We need to shut down all satellite uplinks ASAP. We need to shut down all comm systems. They've cracked our encrypted systems and are watching us."

"That's impossible," the confused officer, however, sees I'm deadly serious and continues with a simple, "Yes, sir."

We head back to the comm room.

I burst into the darkened room filled only with computer screens and people watching them. "Anyone have a Gmail account?" I ask as everyone looks at me as if I'm nuts. "I know this sounds crazy but these people have a way of tapping our encrypted systems and are likely monitoring all of ours. Who has a Gmail account they use all the time?"

Everyone in the room raises their hand.

"Wow, this is a great ad for Google. Hope they pay me," I say as one guy laughs.

I look at him and say, "Thank you. I'm on every night at 11pm in the Main Room with a 2 drink minimum."

The one guy who laughed says, "The alcohol in the drinks are derived from fuel on board."

I look at the guy and say, "Are you in the act?"

"No, sir"

"Then don't add material."

"Yes, sir."

I then muse, "And never use the word derived in the punch line of a joke."

"Yes, sir," replies the sailor and salutes as if just gave the command to attack Normandy.

I salute the sailor, "All right then, carry on." I continue, "I want everyone to compose some sort of sincere sounding rubbish then add the largest, pictures, videos, and other garbage files you can find and send it all to CENTCOM, your girlfriends, family and anyone else in your contact list. Hopefully, the boys at CENTCOM will figure out what we're doing."

I pull up and sit by the guy who's joke I trashed, "I need for you to let me finish composing your email."

"Yes, sir." responds the very polite young man.

"By the way, your joke had a funny idea it's just that the delivery needs some work."

"Yes, sir."

"And please stop saying sir. Commander will be fine."

The guy's not sure what to do.

"Now that was a joke, son," I say.

The guy kinda laughs.

"Seriously, John or Denning is fine."

"Yes, sir... John ... Denning," replies the poor, now very nervous, comm guy.

I smile as I have now finished my text to the Pentagon.

"All right everybody, I want to send all of these files at the same time. Everybody ready to push send."

One woman, still typing, says, "Wait! I'm sending a message to my mom."

"All right, darling, no hurry, just the fate of the world now rests in you and your mother's hands."

The woman now realizes what's going on and says, "Oh, right. Okay, I'm ready."

"Okay, is everybody ready?"

Everyone watches me as their hands are on their laptops.

"Gentlemen, start your engines," I say.

Everybody in the room looks around.

"That means… hit entre'!" I say like a French chef.

Everyone gets it and simultaneously hits their keyboard send button.

"All right I asked CENTCOM to shut down all satellite comm links. I gave them a code when they boot back up to access. Hopefully it will take Perchinkov's people some time to realize what we just did."

The officer that came and got me, says looking at a darkened screen, "Looks like CENTCOM got the message already sir. They're shutting down the satellite systems."

"That was fast," I mumble. "I hope they only shut down the military stuff or we're gonna have planes and ships crashing all over the world," I say, worried.

In the room we now hear, "You've got mail!" from an old America Online application.

I walk over to where that came from and see a naked picture.

"Is that your girlfriend sailor?" I ask.

The kid says, "I wish! It's from CENTCOM. I'm unscrambling the imbedded text."

Another kid laughs, "In... bedded! That's funny."

Everyone looks at the kid.

The women in the room shake their heads in disgust.

"CENTCOM is telling us their systems are not only being hacked but some of their software is being destroyed by a virus."

"Elena!" I mumble, "Perchinkov can't do that."

The officer then looks at me, "Wha'd a we do now?"

I look at him and calmly say, "We wait." Then it hit me, "Oh no!" I begin feverishly typing on the "insult" kid's keyboard and hit send saying, "I hope this gets to our sub in time."

It wouldn't.

30

The submarine base at Olavsvern, Norway was built by NATO during the Cold War. Genius politicians, in their wisdom, sold the base to several groups for pennies on the dollar. The government leases out parts of the base to a Russian group which turns out to be a front for The Snakes and Perchinkov's people.

Ølinesstein Isø told the Barents Daily News that "the owner uses the facility as he wants and the military has neither the authority to impose restrictions on its use, or authority to control civilian or military vessels that may have permission to go there. Any suspicious activities is a matter for the police and judicial authorities and not our concern."

Spoken like a true bureaucrat: "Not my job, man!"

It's nice to have a CIA officer like Henry feeding you intel on what's really going on in this place.

As I sit in a bunk in an officer's cabin aboard the *USS Gravely* I think:

I wonder how badly the Pentagon has already been infected by Snakes. Maybe my "foolproof" idea's not so foolproof.

I've been reassured that only troops, materials and subs have gone into this "abandoned" base. Except for *TK-20*, nothing's gone out yet. I'd bet my life (and I soon may be doing just that) that this is their manufacturing facility and their distribution point. I already know Perchinkov's here. I overheard his men talking just before I escaped from the villa in Monaco.

Plus, Henry's confirmed this.

The puzzling question is: Why is Elena helping him?

If any one of these massive subs is able to get away, God only knows how many of these chips and people, with chips in them could be carried to any place on earth.

We're in big trouble if we don't make it in time.

I pray we're not too late.

A knock on the door.

"Entré!" I say with a pompous French accent. In pops Jen and she doesn't look happy.

"I'm sorry, what's up?" I apologize before she says anything. I don't know why I'm apologizing but it looks like I should be apologizing. I'd try to continue to explain this but you've gotta be in a serious relationship with a very passionate woman to understand.

Jen says, "You still haven't explained why you didn't call when you got away from Elena."

"I'm sorry. What do you want me to say?" I say truly confused.

"The planet is going to hell, you don't call, I think your dead, the next time I see you you're sipping cappuccino in front of the Casino - Monte Carlo." Jennifer angrily then says, "What I want you to say is that, everything's going to be all right, all right?"

So I say, "Everything's going to be all right, all right?"

I must've said this slightly sarcastically as Jen, with anger, stomps out of the room.

Nice job, JD! You ticked her off even more.

Way ta go genius!

Thank you.

Shut up!

I really do need to get this thing out of my head.

Now I'm sitting feeling somewhat depressed and guilty when there's another knock. I don't try that again. I say straight up, "Come in."

It's Alexi and Casmerov.

Again, they're like kids. Since these guys were second and third in command of the largest class of nuclear submarine ever built, a Typhoon, they're fascinated by this ship.

"Did you know this ship is exactly the same length as our *TK-20*?" Alexi excitedly asks.

"I think *TK-20* is longer but in any case, don't get too excited. We may have to sink your boat."

"Boat?" Casmerov is offended, "You call *TK-20* a boat?"

"He doesn't say much but when he does he certainly has an opinion, doesn't he?" I say looking at Casmerov.

Alexi ignores both of us and excitedly continues, "This Arleigh Burke-class destroyer has over 100 missiles on board."

"Ya, don't believe everything the guys in the mess hall say. That's why it's called the mess hall. It's where people mess with you," I say thinking I'm funny.

Both Alexi and Casmerov look at me as if I'm serious and they've been taken.

"I'm kidding. I'm kidding. What am I going to do with you guys?" I say.

They both look at each, shrug their shoulders and simultaneously say, "Ve don't know."

Ignoring that unintelligible reaction, I move on continuing to make fun of them, "So why you here?"

They don't seem to notice my sarcasm, "Ve vant to tell you about huge vulnerability in *TK-20*," says Alexi.

"So you want to help sink your own boat," I say with suspicion.

"Stop calling it boat!" says Casmerov.

"Okay, okay, I'm sorry, shoot," I say.

Casmerov dead pans, "Never say shoot to a Russian."

Alexi smiles, "Russia taught spies in Cold War, if you're in trouble always remember training: Ready? Shoot! Aim."

Casmerov and I don't laugh so Alexi moves on, "Although the caterpillar drive is nearly silent there is a small very identifiable wake that's put out by this drive. If you follow directly in that wake she won't even know you're there."

I say with more suspicion, "Most subs are like this."

Alexi answers, "Ah but because it's so quiet, the propeller is massive. This massive cone of water puts out a huge tunnel that if another sub can ride in it, that sub will never be seen by any Typhoon class sub. I was on maneuvers when we discovered this. Sea trials brought this out but nothing was ever done. And since the drives are so quiet Admiral Perchinkov never gave it another thought. This problem is huge but was never corrected."

"And why are you telling me this?" I ask.

Alexi says, "I am now American. I have been pardoned by your great President Trump and I want to be citizen. My father was worth billions. He went to one of his convenience stores one day, went out back to take out trash and was murdered by professional hit. He said he wouldn't pay money "for protection" to Silovik clan any longer. They murdered him in a gutter like common criminal. I was just boy. I went out to see noise was and all I could see was this red stream of blood running out of my father's head into drain. A small boy, should never see such a sight, especially his own father. Silovik ran most of business operations in Russia and you either were with them or you were squeezed out. My family paid money to Silovik all these years for legitimate businesses. I don't want any part of this. I'd rather live as poor American in an inner city than rich man in Russia."

I'm not sure whether to venture into this or not but wander in anyway, "Most of our cities are not any better. We have drug dealers in most neighborhoods."

"Well, at least government in America is not out to kill you," says Alexi.

"I don't know. It depends. Today, I wouldn't trust an American politician any more than I'd trust a Russian politician. Old American joke, how can you tell if a politician is lying?"

Casmerov starts paying attention as Alexi says, "I don't know."

"His lips are moving."

Both Alexi and Casmerov get this and start laughing uncontrollably. Alexi says, "Now that good joke. Work anywhere in world."

I smile and say, "Yes, I suppose so."

I stand and say, "We've gotta tell CENTCOM and the subs about our little secret."

Alexi and Casmerov eagerly follow me out the door.

Again, it would be too late.

31

TK-20, the massive sub used to smuggle nuclear materials unnoticed into Alaska, is submerged and heading for the polar ice cap. Presumably this Typhoon class submarine could then go anywhere in the world undetected. She is doing this so she can lose any other sub that might be following. Apparently, she knows there is only one American asset in her area right now.

Submarines use active and passive pinging to find what's around them. When they don't want to be detected they only use passive. Active is the sound you hear when you're watching an old World War II movie and you hear that loud "ping." That active ping is never used in combat ops as it immediately gives away your exact position.

Under-ice ops requires a sub crew to plan meticulously and navigate very carefully. There must be aboard very sophisticated ice-mapping sonar. Massive ice keels can protrude down a couple hundred feet so you must be aware of what is around you at all times. If not, these huge protrusions could puncture and sink your "boat."

It's an eerie feeling looking around *TK-20*. All the crew seem to be manning their stations. The inside of this sub is very modern and the work of billions of rubles. It's the work of 40 years of Cold War machinations. Russian scientists worked very hard to see if they could produce a state of the art submarine, larger than anything ever built.

A super quiet nuclear powered engine and propeller was the brainchild of my good friend, **Captain Valentin Vasili, Commanding** officer of the *Severstal,* better known to the West as *TK-20.*

I really miss you, captain!

What's weird about this sleek looking, monitor filled, command center is that the crew seems to be acting a bit robotic. There is absolute silence. No one is speaking to another. They all go about doing their jobs.

All of a sudden everyone freezes in place as if to be listening to something. There is nothing that is spoken aloud. After a moment they resume their jobs.

Everyone on board this ship has been implanted with a chip. They are receiving signals directly from Admiral Perchinkov. If you had a dream crew that would die for you, this is it. Everyone aboard has multiplied their brain power by thousands and thousands. They can execute a command quickly and without hesitation.

If they were told to jump, without question, they'd say how high?

The 20 something missile silos on a normal boomer sub, known as Sherwood Forest to American crews, has been replaced by, what looks to be a large warehouse.

On a sub?

Yep.

This new design was to be able to drive supplies directly into the front cone of this massive sub.

These subs were built to smuggle supplies, unnoticed, into Alaskan waters. Their "Top Secret" mission, *AK-239*, was to build a nuclear reactor at Bokan Mountain, Alaska.

Those days are long past.

With a new president in Russia, Putin, wouldn't stand for such craziness.

So Perchinkov's people implanted chips in Russian sailors and they stole these Typhoon subs from Russia.

How could Perchinkov have done this?

He was on the run.

And he acted like he didn't even know much about these chips.

Do The Snakes have their own chip operation that no one knows about?

These were all questions that needed to be answered.

And answered quickly.

One sailor drops a box. It opens and thousands of chips fall out. The sailor robotically begins picking up his opened box. The other "robots" don't look like they heard or even care. The sailor quickly puts all the chips into the box and throws it on a pile. There are probably over a thousand boxes of brain chips on this one sub.

Meanwhile the *USS Bullhead*, a Los Angeles fast attack submarine, is heading for disaster. She has been ordered to find *TK-20* and sink her.

The *USS Alaska* was ordered out of the area as, although it has some torpedoes, it's primarily a ballistic missile sub used for targeting fixed locations, with its massive nuclear payload. Those warheads were designed to take out as many as 200 fixed targets. The *USS Alaska's* massive weight would put it at a huge disadvantage in fighting a lighter, quicker sub.

Or so I thought.

Aboard the *USS Bullhead* the commander has been given the last coordinates of *TK-20*. The President of the United States has already given the Executive Order in Operation Zero Hour to take out *TK-20*.

The captain of the *USS Bullhead*, Sean O'Conner, is in the warfare room and his crew is already at battle station readiness. The captain asks, "Do we still have ears on target?"

The lead sonar operator says, "Aye captain. We're at 4,000 yards and closing bearing one niner zero."

O' Conner says, "Good. Weapons? Do we have a solution?"

The chief weapons officer says, "Almost, sir."

O' Conner asks torpedo room, "Are we ready to fire?"

Torpedo room says, "Tubes one and two are ready in all respects, the outer doors are open."

The Chief, the commander's second in command, says, "Are we launching counter measures?"

O' Conner makes another fatal mistake saying, "They don't know we're here."

The Chief says, "Do we know that for sure? Do we take that chance?"

O' Conner says, "If we launch countermeasures they'll see us. I don't want them to know we're here. So no countermeasure launch, yet."

The Chief, hesitantly says, "Yes, sir." He repeats the command, "Do not, I repeat do not launch countermeasures."

Weapons assistant repeats the command, "We are not launching any countermeasures, sir."

O' Conner then says, "Keep our depth identical to target."

The sub driver says, "Aye, target depth is niner eight seven feet. Keep follow depth is 987 feet."

Weapons now says, "We have a solution, sir."

O' Conner says, "Good. Tube one primary. Tube two backup."

Weapons says, "Weapons ready, sir."

O' Conner says, "Final bearing and shoot."

Weapons says, "Fire. Tube one. Fire. Tube two."

O' Conner then says, "Give me an able point."

Sonar says, "Able point bearing 185. Terminal homing on target."

Weapons says, "Loss of wire."

There is this eerie moment when no one says a word.

No one appears to breathe.

Sonar says, "Contact one hit. Contact two hit. Both hit sir."

A cheer goes up from the crew but they were a bit premature.

Sonar says, "I'm getting the *TK-20* signature now directly behind us sir. It appears we've hit one of their decoys, sir. Two torpedoes from them away bearing…"

The captain doesn't wait to hear, "Countermeasures now. Evasive hard starboard. All ahead full."

Sub driver, "Aye, evasive hard starboard. All ahead full."

Weapons says, "We just launched countermeasures starboard."

The commander says, "Shit! Torpedo range."

Sonar, "One thousand yards and closing fast, sir."

O' Conner says, "Evasive hard port… now!" He says this in a bit of a panic as he clearly has steered his boat right into the same path as his countermeasures. Meaning the torpedoes will likely lock on his boat now no matter what he does.

Sonar, "500 yards and closing, sir. Two torpedoes. Keep follow path is on us, sir."

We can literally see sweat coming off the commander's forehead as his second in command looks at him.

Second in command, the Chief, ignores his boss and says to his crew, "It's been my honor and pleasure to serve with all of you. I know I will see all of you in the next life. Godspeed, ladies and gentlemen, Godspeed to all."

O' Conner looks at him and yells, "Relieve this man of his command immediately!"

Everyone in the room stares at the commander.

Sonar says, "100 yards and closing. Brace for impact. Brace. Brace…"

Those were the last words anyone aboard the *USS Bullhead* would ever hear on planet earth.

Both torpedoes ripped through the sub and in an instant blew two holes in her. One made a direct hit in the torpedo room that instantly exploded many of the torpedoes aboard. The explosion was so huge it took a bubble of water and debris 987 feet to the surface.

Water and debris lifted surface ice several feet into the air.

It was probably lucky that it was a direct hit as all 143 officers and enlisted personnel died in an instant.

No suffering.

No pain.

No nothing.

This would be the first American ship to be sunk by an enemy since 1945 when the original *USS Bullhead* met a similar fate by a torpedo dropped from a Japanese plane.

***

I stand in the war room shaking my head.

"Perchinkov knew we were coming," I say responding to a red monitor of the Polar Ice cap area with a big red X through the *USS Bullhead*.

The monitor shows *TK-20* turning and heading toward the Bering Strait and Alaska.

"How is it we're seeing this in real time? Weren't all our comm systems shut down?" I ask.

The comm guy speaks up, "CENTCOM used your coded message to encode this behind all sorts of gibberish. I think it's working," says the kid who's probably no more than 20 years old.

"How do you know," I ask suspiciously.

No one answers.

Well, that's not reassuring at all.

I see another dot sitting off the coast of Alaska and ask, "What's this?"

Everyone looks at everyone else. No one seems to know.

"Well, it has its signature identifying info turned off. Is it ours?" I say with concern.

Casmerov, who's been playing with his phone again, suddenly pays attention.

"I'd bet that's a U.S. sub," he says with the confidence of a general.

"Why?" I ask.

"Because when we came to Alaska to deliver supplies to Bokan Mountain We noticed your Navy had affixed a listening device running parallel to those fiber optic lines."

(AKORN - That's the superfast Alaska-Oregon Fiber Network running from Florence, Oregon to Homer, Alaska.)

"They probably did that to disguise the electronic signature put out by the submarine's listening devices."

"So?" I say.

"So, I told our Russian commanders at the time and they had us tap those lines to be able to see and/or confuse any American Naval presence in Alaska." Casmerov says. "Is it possible Putin's has told Russian Naval forces to broadcast this data to us as Perchinkov will only worry about what Americans are doing? He might not think his old Russian military might help Americans."

"Wow! That was a long way to go for such a complicated analysis. Only a Russian would think like that."

I stare at Casmerov who boldly stares back.

Then I stare at Alexi who is being just as bold.

Only then do I think maybe these guys aren't so crazy after all.

"Anybody else concur with this madness?"

Everyone in the war room suddenly has a case of dry mouth. Nobody says a word.

"Nobody?" I ask.

Nobody looks to be breathing.

"Have you all had the brain implants too?" I ask.

Everyone then quickly begins talking and defending themselves — all at once.

"Okay people we can't all talk at once. Well, we can but nobody will know what anybody else just said, except maybe me but I don't want to try that right now."

Alexi has been watching the red Alaska monitor this whole time. He walks closer to it and says, "I think that's the *USS Alaska*."

"Why do you say that?"

"Because that thing's the size of a boomer. She'll park for weeks or months and only move to return to port in Kings Bay, Georgia. Last we saw she was heading in this direction from the Bering Strait, right?"

"How do you know this?"

"We study American sub movements. It's part of our training. The *Alaska* goes all over the world, parks and sits. But when she sits you see that little flash of light right…" Alexi's waiting to show us all something very, very tiny. He continues as he excitedly points, "There. Right there. Did you see that?"

One of the sonar guys chimes in, "I saw it. The boomers need to exhaust stale air every few minutes. Our heat signature equipment can pick this up. It can tell the difference between water temperature and the temperature of air being exhausted. This is Top, Top Secret. We didn't think anyone else in the world knew about this."

"So how do you know about it?" I sarcastically ask.

"I've been trained to watch for this. Only a handful of people in the U.S. Navy know about this," the kid says.

"Alexi chimes in, "Well, everyone in Russian Navy knows this. I'll bet Perchinkov is gonna try and kill *USS Alaska* next."

Jen suddenly become really, really worried. She was the first woman commander of a U.S. submarine and this is her boat. Jen now moves front and center saying, "We can communicate with her in a way I don't think Perchinkov might know about."

"Even if we tell her, how can she defend herself?" I ask.

Jen says, "I taught those guys and they taught me. We were the only boomer sub in the ICEX games. We were put up against attack subs and beat them." ICEX is the U.S. Navy's war game drills under the North Pole. Jen continues, "We simulated the sinking of several attack subs! They can do something Perchinkov can't."

"What's that?" I ask.

"A thermonuclear tsunami!" Jen says with a weird confident smile that I've never seen before.

All the guys in the room look at each other as if, "What?"

***

The "robot" humans of *TK20* are silently communicating with each other. Two of them see the *USS Alaska* parked on their large clear screen in the middle of their war room right below the conning tower.

Silent orders are said, *Ready all four torpedo tubes*, says the captain acting in a calm, robotic fashion.

Meanwhile, Admiral Perchinkov stands in a large room with a floor to ceiling, flat, wall screen watching his robot men execute his silent commands.

Perchinkov continues, *Open outer doors.*

On the large screen, the captain on *TK20* says those exact words aloud, "Open outer doors."

A weapons officer silently confirms, *Open outer doors.*

Perchinkov silently commands his team, *Fire torpedo tubes one, two, three and four.*

Before anything else can happen the large screen sees the submarine literally flip upside down and all of his men go flying into the ceiling, which is now the floor. Immediately, the huge screen shows water rushing into the submarine before the screen goes completely black.

Perchinkov stands up screaming, "What? What just happened?"

All of his other robot men stand, stoned face without any answers. Two seem to be in that frozen loop I was in and stand repeating the same, small shaking moves.

President Trump is watching a large screen in the Situation Room as *TK-20* disappears from the map.

"What the… what happened?" asks President Trump.

An American admiral smiles and answers, "We just sunk the largest submarine in the world."

A cheer goes up from the crowded room filled with military uniforms and suits.

Jennifer on the *USS Gravely* gets a standing ovation as she gives a small smile.

The president has the nuclear football in front of him on the large boardroom desk in the center of the Situation Room.

Two military men at the back of the room talk to each other, "Now get that thing away from him before he launches somethin' else."

Jennifer appears on the large screen and Trump says, "Congratulations Commander Tavana looks like your idea was a good one."

As Trump talks, the two military guys close the nuclear football suitcase and squirrel it away from him.

Jennifer replies, "Thank you, sir."

The Director of National Intelligence, Dan Coats, speaks up, "We're not out of this yet. There's reason to believe that at least three more subs are at Olavsvern, Norway. These may have nukes on them. A massive nuclear tidal wave like the one you produced will not affect these subs. They're in water but behind steel doors and under a mountain of rock designed to withstand a direct nuke strike."

Admiral Stanton, head of Naval Command speaks up, "Denning and two SEAL teams are in position."

Everyone looks at the president.

President Trump says, "Good! Denning! Well, give the order: Attack! Attack! Attack!"

The guys with the nuclear football at the back of the room look at each other. One whispers to the other, "Weren't those the words used by Japan on Pearl Harbor?"

The other kid shrugs his shoulders and they leave, carrying the nuclear football. Two Secret Service agents follow the nuclear football out the door.

Dan Coats continues, "I don't have to tell you that exploding a nuke under the North Pole will not go over well with too many people. However, since this was our only option and the alternatives were far worse, I believe we did the right thing. None of this information leaves this room."

Everyone nods their head in agreement.

President Trump stands and, as he's leaving, says, "Carry on."

All in the room give a look to each other as Admiral Stanton says to everyone in the room, "The order has already been sent to Denning's SEAL team...."

A Navy admiral in full dress whites mumbles to his young assistant, "Never thought I'd see the day when an admiral, a devout Christian, would be sending nude pix to a U.S. Navy ship."

The young assistant, appears to be gay, says, "All I have to say is they better not be my nude pictures?"

***

I'm in a mini sub in a Norwegian sea channel. The northernmost part of Scandinavia is filled with islands, water and fjords. It's beautiful here but I wouldn't be sightseeing today.

We were transferred from the *USS Gravely* in the middle of the night to the submarine *USS Dallas*. *Dallas* is a Los Angeles class attack sub. She got us within about a mile of the Norwegian coastline when we transferred into the ASDS.

The ASDS 2.0 (<u>Advanced SEAL Delivery System</u>) is a dry submersible that carries a team of six SEALs and a crew of two. So Alexi, Casmerov, Zeke, Tommy, and Spider are with me. They are all from my last assault in Utah a year ago. Fortunately, this mini sub only holds six as Jen and Stone wanted to come too.

And, as you know, Stone can't even swim!

We intend to drive this right up to Perchinkov's underwater sea doors at Olavsvern and "knock." This is a luxury! I've only used submersibles that you had to "underwater surf" to a target. The force of the water pushing on you took much of your strength.

This would have been impossible here as the channel we had to drive up is nearly 20 miles from the sea. It would have been far too dangerous to try and drive a destroyer let alone a sub into these narrow channels.

Who knows what kinds of listening devices have been hidden in these channels.

We're not detecting anything but, knowing the advances Perchinkov and The Snakes have made, that doesn't mean no listening devices are here.

The sub driver says as we look through the murky video screen, "100 yards to target, sir."

"Demo, you ready?" I ask.

Our demolition man is Zeke but he's letting the co-sub driver use this cool computer arm. The sub driver says to his co-pilot, "Deploy the arm."

The co-pilot begins working a portable joystick that looks like it came off of some video game. An arm reaches in front of the submersible as we comfortably watch from several monitors in front of the drivers.

The arm jerks and swings out rapidly.

Zeke yells, "Careful!"

Both drivers look at Zeke as if: Don't tell me how to do my job.

Zeke quickly says, "Sorry, sorry."

Sub driver says, "20 feet. All stop."

The co-pilot says, "Careful. I have a high powered oxygen - acetylene torch and I'm not afraid to use it." Acetylene torches are used to weld or cut through steel. When combined with pure oxygen the tip of the torch can be over 6,300 degrees Fahrenheit. This particular O/A torch is the .50 caliber machine gun of acetylene torches. Temperatures on this baby can reach near 7,000 degrees, even underwater!

A solid steel door appears to float into view with the mini sub's lights fixed on it. The specialized arm immediately starts "torching" the center of the door, cutting a hole only large enough for a human.

In no time a hole is cut. The inside hatch to the sub drivers is closed and, in an instant, my SEAL team is submerged in water. The entire top of the sub opens like the Space Shuttle doors and we exit, swimming toward the underwater steel door. Our weapons are pointed forward toward any threat.

Tommy and Spider are the first two to breach, weapons pointed at 45 degree angles opposite each other. Zeke now swims right after them pointing his weapon dead ahead.

I'm the last guy floating around watching our backsides when I see something moving in the water.

Since we have such a small force, the element of surprise is critical.

Unfortunately, that element was lost.

Perchinkov has his own version of a SEAL team coming at us. We have on **Dräger** rebreathers and molar mics. **Dräger**s cover your entire face and produce no bubbles to make detection more difficult. Molar mics are tiny two way radios affixed to the inside of molars in your mouth.

You don't need to say anything very loudly as the mic will pick up your vocal chords slightest movement. You can hear any incoming voice as it's transmitted through your jawbone to your ear.

Pretty cool!

I yell, "Incoming." Bullets are already firing at us from several rear positions. We return fire but shooting underwater is kinda like watching a gunfight in slow motion. The bullets never seem to travel fast enough and these guys are far enough away that they can move out of the way before our bullets reach them.

Alexi and Casmerov are pinned down in a rocky area off the side of the door. I'm worried that they're soon going to be killed. Zeke, Tommy and Spider must have their hands full as I try shouting to them in my molar mic but cannot get a response. Perchinkov must be blocking our comm systems.

I think we're all going to die as Perchinkov's men are now closing in for the kill when the mini sub's robot arm tosses something that looks like a backpack toward about 20 of Perchinkov's divers.

The explosion of the satchel charge via the robot arm was genius!

In a single blast, every single bad guy, but two, were killed.

The wave of water that comes at me turns me head over heels.

When I regain my bearings, the last two Perchinkov guys begin shooting. With two shots I take them down.

"Thanks guys!" I say with enthusiasm. I'm not sure the min-sub drivers could hear me but they must've seen me as the robot arm appears to salute as the mini sub backs away from us and into the darkness.

The reason these guys are leaving is that the mini sub has no weapons systems on board.

(Aside from the C4 plastic explosive satchel they improvised and tossed onto the "battlefield!")

As we enter through the steel doors and surface we are right alongside the twin sister of *TK-20*.

She sits in the water in an ultramodern dock. The mouth of the sub is open and trucks "were" driving directly into the hull of these Typhoon class subs.

"Were" until my team was made and started shooting. I'll bet Zeke, Tommy and Spider have made their way into the opened mouth of the sub. The plan is to destroy all of these chips. And this sub looks to have been loading chips on board. We continue firing rounds at Perchinkov's men who are truly suicidal. They foolishly keep running at us like a bunch of brain dead bad guys from some cheap video game.

I guess Perchinkov has so many guys that he can literally throw away some in hopes of killing us.

Suddenly, Zeke, Spider and Tommy come running out of the Typhoon yelling something. My mic is still not working and presumably being jammed. I can only assume they dropped a C4 satchel charge inside the sub.

I motion for my guys to seek shelter when an explosion throws flames out the port side of the sub.

They planned that!

We're on the Starboard side.

Good job!

The Typhoon groans and creaks with a horrifically loud and painful sound. The metal platform from dock to ship begins to twist like a pretzel as parts of it fall into the water.

The sub rolls onto its port side and the conning tower comes to rest on the side of the dock.

Great! Two down, two subs to go!

After more rounds, my guys are finally able to gain the upper ground. We're then able to work our way up to the main tunnel leading out of the sub dock.

It seems when you put chips in soldiers' brains they actually shoot worse. That's weird because everything else your brain does with this chip is faster, much, much faster. Maybe it has something to do with the fact these guys are operating against their will. The human body is an amazing piece of machinery yet there is a soul buried within and a conscience that keeps most people from doing truly evil things.

However, even though Perchinkov is able to override a person's conscience it seems that hesitation is costing his men their lives.

A round ricochets off the rock wall near my head.

I fire a round at the guy shooting at me and he retreats further up the rock tunnel.

Suddenly, there is silence.

Again, in a gunfight the sound of silence is not something you want to hear, especially when you can't see or communicate with your guys.

I yell, "Zeke! Tommy! Spider! Alexi! Casmerov!"

Nothing from any of them.

They were all headed up this tunnel shaft so I begin running.

And running.

And running.

I have flashbacks again of having a fever in grade school. I'm running down my grade school hall sweating. As I try to get to the outside door, the hall keeps getting longer and longer and longer.

Now I'm sweating. Even though I tossed the rebreather I still don't feel like I'm running. I feel like I'm waddling.

It's because even with this skin tight wetsuit you are still wet and carrying extra weight.

I stop at the end of the tunnel. It splits into three directions. It looks like the one on each side goes down to other sub docks. I've told the guys after you take out the chips go for Elena and Perchinkov. They would've taken the middle tunnel. I start running again and calling to each of them with the molar mic.

Nothing!

As I finally reach the end of the long rocky tunnel it opens into a large room with several doors on each side.

I feel like I'm on the TV show, "The Price is Right" with Drew Carey.

Which door do I pick?

Which door?

I don't have to pick any door as a soldier walks out with a bound and gagged Zeke.

Over a speaker rings Perchinkov's voice, "Put your weapons down JD. It's over."

I really don't have a choice here.

As far as I know, Perchinkov has captured my entire team.

And he has!

One by one Tommy, Spider, Alexi and Casmerov appear tied, bound and gagged.

"Well, that was quick. Congratulations! You took down an entire SEAL team. You must be very proud of yourself admiral," I say with some disdain.

Over the echoing speaker system is Perchinkov's voice, "I am."

"Put your weapons down," commands another voice more ominous than Perchinkov's.

I realize all my men are dead if I don't so I slowly start to put down my weapons as millions of thoughts race through my mind.

Perchinkov now appears from behind with several soldiers saying, "That's better. Now we can talk."

Talk. Ya, I'll talk. Talk over your dead body.

Perchinkov's guys take my guns and his goons throw me to my knees.

Only then does the coward walk up to me as I'm being held by two big thugs.

Perchinkov looks at me and says, "I'm reading your every thought. Don't fight it. Come join me and rule the world."

I answer, "Thanks anyway. The planet's evil enough."

Perchinkov actually smiles, a bit.

Perchinkov continues, "So you won't do this the easy way. Guess I have to make you do this my way?"

Perchinkov silently commands his men to raise their weapons at the heads of my men.

"I could shoot them all right now, you know," Perchinkov says.

I stare at him and know he could and probably will.

He really doesn't like the fact that Alexi and Casmerov defected from Mother Russia and that they are helping me!

Perchinkov smiles, looks at me and says, "Now we do this my way." I stand up and begin walking toward my men.

Perchinkov is walking behind me.

"You see, I have the power to make or break you, John. Now, I'm giving you the choice, either you're with me or I will order you to kill your men and then yourself. The choice is yours. Kinda."

I stand frozen.

"All right I'm going to let you freely make a decision," says Perchinkov.

I continue to be frozen.

"It's amazing this technology. The power you have at your fingertips. All right, let's put this to the ultimate test," says Perchinkov.

Alexi and Casmerov are bound and gagged and the closest to me.

Perchinkov walks toward me with a Beretta 9mm and says, "I want you to kill these traitors to the Motherland but I don't know if I should trust you with a weapon."

Perchinkov taunts me by putting the weapon directly in front of my body that's frozen in place. When he is close enough I pull my seven inch serrated knife from my leg band and slice his femoral artery. As he drops to his knees screaming I then slash his carotid artery in his neck.

Immediately all of Perchinkov's soldiers start to point their weapons in my direction then freeze as I did.

I say out loud on my molar mic, "Target one down. Repeat target one down."

I don't know if anyone could hear me.

I grab a machine gun from one of Perchinkov's frozen men.

I then run and use my knife to cut Alexi free.

I hand him my knife and he cuts the rest of our team free.

All of Perchinkov's men continue to stand frozen as we begin to disarm them.

Gunfire erupts but it's not from Perchinkov's frozen men.

It's coming from the opposite direction of the tunnel where we entered.

All of us are now armed and in firing positions on the threat.

There is silence and no more gunfire.

All of a sudden the next voice I hear sounds very familiar, "Don't shoot JD."

I stand saying, "Don't shoot, JD? Sounds like a plan."

It's Skull and the other team. They attacked from top side and have worked their way down to us.

Skull walks up to us with his team saying, "Lucky we had that chip pulled out of you or you'd probably be dead."

I say with some sadness, "I'm really gonna miss all that info."

Casmerov says, "Google it!"

My guys have disarmed all of Perchinkov's men and have them seated.

There is a loud noise from one of the other rooms.

I motion my men to breach the door.

They do and I follow right behind.

Inside this room is a large, surgical room. It's completely white with about 20 surgical chairs with robot arms next to 20 people seated in the chairs. The people all look to be under anesthesia and are unconscious.

Upon more careful inspection these people are easy to recognize.

I notice the Prime Ministers of several European countries.

A couple of very famous Hollywood stars and a prominent U.S. Senator are all waiting for their implant.

Maybe this explains some of the U.S. Senate's crazy, unstable, behavior recently.

And then again, maybe not.

For their sakes, I will not mention any names.

As I go down the line, the guy on the end gets up and runs for the door.

Zeke is ready to fire when I say, "Hold."

Zeke could have shot him but I need someone alive who can give us all the details of this Nazi style "death camp."

"Did anyone get a look at who that was?" I ask as I run after.

My team doesn't answer.

"Stay here and make sure these people don't move," I command.

As I kick the door open, Zeke answers, "Yes, sir."

I run down a hall to a huge metal door slowly swinging shut.

I run into a freezer like room with bodies hanging from meat hooks.

It's very dimly lit and very hard to see farther than one small light at the back of the room.

Who are these people?

Were they failed experiments?

This place gives me the creeps!

As I pass the bodies I see different kinds of incisions on the side of their heads.

I'll bet that bastard was doing Mengele like experiments on these poor people.

Joseph Mengele was the Nazi butcher who worked for Hitler in World War II. He did live experiments on Jews and others that were only "fit" for experimentation. You see the Nazi's thought that Jews, gypsies, gays etc. were the root of many societal problems because they weren't of the Aryan race. Hitler thought more of his dogs than he did many people. Hitler build air conditioning systems for his German Shepherd's dog house. Hitler was a vegetarian who gave free health care to all Germans. Well, not all, but all who were Arian or "valuable" to the 3rd Reich in their Nazi pipedream of a 1,000 years of world peace.

What a humanitarian!

"All I want is, peace… peace… peace! A little piece of Poland, a little piece of France…" What am I doing?

You're singing Mel Brooks lyrics in your head!

Why?

I don't know.

I suppose Mel and I do this as a way to relieve the pain of Nazi horrors by laughing at them.

Wait!

I don't have that thing in my head yet I did all of this in a split second.

Maybe that thing has trained my mind to use more of my brain.

The Nazi Mengele and his henchmen performed experiments on the subhumans ("Untermensch" as the Nazi's called them) which sometimes caused great pain and even death.

It's funny, how history repeats itself.

When I taught a SEAL class I had a sign in the front of the class that said:

THOSE WHO DO <u>NOT</u> LEARN
FROM HISTORY
ARE DOOMED TO REPEAT IT…
<u>NEXT YEAR!</u>

Just then there's movement. Out of the corner of my eye a guy with a meat cleaver takes a swing at me.

I don't have my weapons so this will be hand to hand.

Guess I should've brought a gun or at least my knife – way to be thinkin' ahead JD!

I say that to myself as I duck.

Fortunately, this guy is no professional fighter as he overcompensates with his swing.

He continues to follow through with his human meat cleaver like Babe Ruth swinging for the outfield fences. The guy's head follows his swing past me.

This gives me enough time to start to get up and clock him with one blow upside his head.

Didn't wanna kill him. Needed his melon intact — if only for the intel.

He goes down in an instant and lays there.

I roll him over and it's Mustafa from DARPA headquarters in Alexandria, Virginia.

All of a sudden I can hear my team on my molar mic talking to each other.

I drag Mustafa back to my team.

I ask, "Henry, you there?"

Henry immediately responds, "Go for Henry."

"It's good to hear your voice. You'll never guess who just took a meat cleaver swing at my head."

Henry, "Mustafa?"

I look at Mustafa, who's waking up, who can't hear what I hear. The molar mic sound travels through the jawbone to my ear and is the next best thing to one of those damn chips.

I look at Mustafa, "It was Mustafa all right. I believe you have a few questions for him. Maybe we'll drop him at Guantanamo Bay instead of taking him back to the U.S."

Mustafa looks around in a daze before mumbling, "You can't do that. I'm an American."

I say, "Ya, you signed that little thingy for DARPA which basically gives up all your rights as an American. Remember? You were killing Americans. I think living at a soccer field in Cuba would actually be going way too easy on you. Maybe Pakistan would be more appropriate."

Mustafa pretends to be tough.

I see through those puffy, pastry filled cheeks that he's worried.

I toss him to Spider, "Here, take out the garbage."

Spider gladly says, "With pleasure, sir."

Spider grabs Mustafa by the nap of his Armani suit and literally drags him out of the room.

My next thought is, "What about the other Typhoons?"

Zeke says, "We took care of 'em."

I'm relieved for the first time in a long, long time but that didn't last long.

Suddenly, CENTCOM blasts through our chatter, "A V-22 is waiting outside for extract. We have located Target Two. She's on the move. She's on a jet heading south. We're tracking her and…

And just then our signal goes dead again.

I walk back into the room where my team is.

I think.

This time with my "normal" brain.

I say to Alexi and Casmerov with some level of disgust, "Elena played all of us. She's been manipulating Perchinkov the whole time. While he thought he captured her, she actually captured him."

Jen says, "Where do you think she's running?"

I can guess. It's the only place on earth where you could easily hide billions, live like a king and not stand out like a sore thumb."

Jen comes through on my molar mic guessing, "Monaco?"

I say, "Bingo."

Jen sarcastically says back, "Bingo? Don't bingo me!"

I want to say something to Jen but the next thought hits me: *What if Elena already has an army of others she's implanted waiting for us?*

The police!

The military!

Everyone in town!

I really need another vacation!

32

A Bell Boeing V-22 Osprey took Skull and my team to Andøya Air Station, Norway. The Osprey had many problems over the last 25 years. Several crashes took the lives of 42 men in total.

Forty two men!

Dead!

I'm hoping it won't be 12 more.

We load through the large vertical door at rear of the aircraft.

It really is an amazing aircraft.

I see why the military really wanted this thing to work.

Maybe they should do like the "good ol' days" — You designed it, you fly it — first!

I was very, very nervous getting in this high flying, deathtrap.

What makes the Osprey unique is that it takes off and lands like a helicopter then the wings and props flip down in midair and it flies like a conventional airplane.

As this is happening in midair I start to cringe.

So did Zeke.

We look at each other as if to say, "Oh my God!"

The rest of the guys either didn't care or didn't know of the Osprey's "spotty" history.

Thank God!

We make it safely to Andøya Air Station nearby.

On the tarmac is a Boeing C17.

As we exit the Osprey, a ground crew escorts us to a warmed and running Boeing C17 Globemaster III. This giant plane flies at "only" 500 miles per hour. This will take forever to catch up with Elena.

I'm redirected by more ground crew grabbing me and shouting, "Come with me, sir."

I'm suspicious of everyone now, as who knows who has these "chips for brains."

I hear Henry on my molar mic, "JD, We've cleared your Norwegian ground crew. We're putting you in an F16. You'll be in Monaco in 1 hour."

"Good job, Henry. In fact, great job," I answer.

The ground crew takes me by jeep to a warmed and running F16. The ground crew helps me aboard the rear seat.

As I climb in, the pilot gives me a thumbs up.

I return the gesture.

In back, I immediately put on the crisscross seat belt as a ground crew member climbs behind me with a helmet.

"Oh, right, thanks. I would've forgotten," I say slightly embarrassed.

"No problem, sir," says the Norwegian flight maintenance chief as he helps me put on my helmet.

In no time he adjusts the seat belt with which I was struggling.

I yell, "Thank you," as the pilot pulls the boarding ladder out of its pins. Annoyed, he tosses the boarding ladder to the ground.

Well, that was weird.

I now realize the pilot doesn't seem too happy as I just yelled, "Thank you," in his ear.

The helmet was plugged in to the F16 comm system.

In a normal tone I say, "Sorry."

He says nothing.

Well, looks like you've gotten off to a good start with your pilot, JD.

The pilot then says, "We'll be in Nice, France in one hour."

I start to say thank you when he hits the gas — and I mean hits— the— gas!

We are airborne faster than you can say airsickness bag!

We're cruising at 1,500 miles per hour heading south.

I begin thinking: *My team is traveling at one third the speed that I am. What's the plan here? We have none!*

As I think that, the jet jerks and suddenly is heading straight down into the Norwegian Sea.

I can't breathe.

My chest is compressed as the seat belt pushes against it.

I look up and all I can see in every direction is — water.

All sorts of bells and whistles are going off.

Say, this reminds me a lot of Colorado!

I'm trying to talk to the pilot, "What are you doing?"

This is my first clue.

The pilot answers in an ominous voice, "I'm killing you."

Actually that was more like a brick upside my head.

ELENA!

The pilot has been chipped!

Didn't Henry check him?

Elena then says through the voice of the pilot, "You know John, it's too bad, I was sure we could've worked something out."

It's weird hearing a man's voice and knowing this is coming from a very evil woman.

I'm going to be fish food in a second.

218

I look at the altimeter and it says, 10,000 feet.
I can't do math but I know I have only seconds.
There are only two options:

>   1). Strangle the pilot and try and
>   figure out how to fly an F16 or
>   2). Punch out.

I chose the latter.
Fortunately, I saw "proudly built in Fort Worth, Texas, U.S.A." and right next to that was a large red "DO NOT PULL" handle on my seat which I think about pulling.
I hesitate knowing that at 1,500 miles per hour your head, arms, legs, skin or virtually anything exposed can be ripped right off your body.
I think, well at least I have on a helmet and flight suit.
Here goes nothing ———
The seat's own mini rocket engines fire and in 00:06 (6/100ths of one second) my seat's canopy breakers punch through the cockpit canopy and I'm ejected.
The pilot somehow punches out too and we are now both tangled in each other's parachutes plummeting toward the sea.
My parachute at least half opened.
The pilot's chute is completely unopened and tangled in the other half of my parachute.
Our bodies swing together in a violent fashion.
It's lucky I didn't have my arm between my body and his or I likely would no longer have that arm.
The forceful impact knocks the wind right out of me.
I can't breathe or speak.
The pilot is in far worse shape.
I quickly realize he's unconscious.
I have to quickly decide what to do as I only have seconds.

No knife!

No gun!

No idea!

My breath comes back as pure oxygen pumped into my lungs from my mask probably saved me from going unconscious too.

I realize that the side of one of the metal Koch fittings has a very sharp jagged edge, and probably scrapped something on exit. Koch fittings are the small metal latches that connect the harness to the parachute lines.

I grab the A and B parachute lines of the pilot, the ones tangled in mine. With all of my strength, I pull my arm around them and pull them toward the jagged Koch fitting.

This is impossible as the wind resistance is phenomenal. Fortunately, the pilot swings around the damaged lines in such a way as to give me enough slack to pull the AB lines across the jagged metal fitting.

I struggle at first but then the air pulls the lines tight and—Voilà! The zagged metal then rips the lines apart.

The pilot goes flying at a 45 degree angle away from me and his chute only now starts to open.

We hit the water at super high speed!

I have no idea how or why I'm still alive!

But I am alive!

I think!

I'm underwater and going to die!

Isn't an inflatable raft supposed to automatically open from under these seats?

I then realize my inflatable life vest was supposed to "automatically" open too!

It didn't!

I'm underwater and sinking.

I need to get this chute off as quickly as possible.

Finally!

Something's easy.

One belt buckle releases the chute and it floats away.

Only now do I realize that my oxygen mask is releasing oxygen but it's hanging on the side of my face. I put it back on and take what literally might be my last breath. I take a deep one as the last chute line has tangled in the mask and rips the mask clean off my face. Now I realize I'm tangled in some of the other nylon toggles that were supposed to inflate the lobes on my life vest.

I can't breathe!

My mask is floating away still tangled in the parachute lines.

Great!

I need air and need air fast so I start swimming to the surface.

Where's the surface?

It's nowhere in sight.

I don't think I'm gonna make it.

Everything begins to move in slow motion.

I realize my heart is pumping a mile a minute. We were taught to try and slow our heart rate down.

Damn!

My racing heart will quickly use up all of my lung's remaining oxygen.

I try to think calming thoughts.

That never worked in BUD/s classes and it's not working now.

I picture myself flying out of the water and taking a huge breath of air.

This seemed to work.

A little.

After about an eternity and a half I hit the surface. I take a huge breathe.

It was like a knife hit my chest.

The atmosphere on earth is only about 21 percent oxygen, far less than the oxygen in my tank, that's floating nowhere in sight. It really hurts the lungs to be deprived of oxygen for even a short period of time but that wasn't the biggest problem.

The first thing I see is the pilot's chute bobbing on the surface but no pilot.

He probably died on impact.

Now I see him.

He's underwater and his chute is dragging him down.

Do I try to save him?

He tried to kill me.

Well "he" didn't try to kill me.

All right, JD, you'd want to be saved, wouldn't you?

Yes!

I take another deep breath and start to swim to him. I can see his head as it bobs out of the water. The mask at least is still covering his mouth.

I get within arm's length of the pilot, who is slowly sinking.

The pilot's raft automatically explodes to the surface.

I'm almost knocked unconscious.

Well that's nice!

The pilot's seat was sinking directly beneath us.

As we bob around the surface, I notice his raft has a huge hole in it.

What's worse is that the pilot's mask has slipped off his face.

I put it back on him.

I realize that my raft opened but appears to be drifting away from us.

I stop to check the pilot's pupils. They are anything but normal. They are in a semi-comatose state. Something you'd see just before death.

I try punching on his chest and feel his neck for a pulse. He does have a pulse.

What difference does it make?

We're gonna die out here.

I see a plane flying over at about 35,000 feet.

I'm not sure but from here it looks like the C17 plane my team's on.

I swim toward my raft with the pilot.

If this guy wakes up we'll probably have a fight to the death.

Whose death?

Just don't go there, JD.

***

I'm still treading water as I'm holding the pilot and watching my raft now about 100 yards away and drifting further. I don't know how long we can stay alive like this but it can't be long.

In fact, I start thinking that I'll probably drown and this guy will probably go on to kill more innocent people.

Wouldn't that be ironic. I save a murderer's life and he murders again.

I should of let him drown.

As I'm thinking crazy thoughts I see an MH65 heading right for me.

Does he see me?

I'm not sure.

I soon realize the Navy chopper knows we're here. Most of these planes' seats have homing beacons on them that turn on in a crash so any NATO ship or plane in the area can pinpoint us.

Thank God! They are coming for us.

I think.

I try and raise my one free arm out of the water but realize I am more fatigued than I thought. My arm makes it to about even with my neck when a shooting pain says, "Don't do that!"

In no time a Navy diver is in the water and swimming to me.

My first words are, "Am I ever glad to see you!"

The diver says, "Not to worry, sir. You're in good hands now."

This guy looks like a giant to me. He probably was no bigger than me but in my mind he is larger than life. He looks no more than 20 years old.

I ask, "What's your name, son?"

He replies, "John just like you, sir."

Mind if I call you Big John?" I ask.

"Not at all, sir. I'd be honored." the big kid replies.

All while we're talking, he's managed to grab a basket that was lowered and has put the pilot into the basket. The kid's checked his condition and is telling his medical team the condition is red, meaning the pilot's in critical condition.

I add, "Be careful this guy has a chip in his head and was trying to kill me."

"We know, sir. We found the signal and have found a way to jam it."

"Really?" I'm once again suspicious of all high tech wizardry, especially all this chip in the brain stuff.

"We know how she's communicating and have stopped much of it. We'll brief you upstairs," the kid replies pointing to the chopper.

The kid has hoisted the unconscious pilot all the way onto the bird and now a horse collar strap is lowered for under my arms.

"After you sir," the kid says with enthusiasm.

I hate these things. You dangle precariously back and forth until you're a few feet from the blades of the helicopter. But, right now, that's far better than any other alternative.

Before I knew it another sailor/airman had hoisted me and pulled me into the bird.

Big John seems to fly up and into the chopper too.

A medic is working on the pilot who's still in the basket.

It doesn't look good.

I notice that my flight suit is cut on my left arm and that it's bleeding. The kid sees this, cuts the shirt and starts bandaging me.

When I get nervous I say stupid things. So the first words out of my mouth are, "That jagged seat down there's a lawsuit just waitin' to happen."

Big John chuckles. He looks around, picks up a blanket and hands it to me saying, "You should put this around you, sir."

I smile and politely turn it down, covering the, still unconscious, pilot with it.

I never seem to be cold.

That is unless I'm in 36 degree water in Alaska and in December but, please, let's not go there.

33

I didn't realize it until later but this chopper is off the *USS Ronald Reagan.* Normally, the aircraft carrier only operates in the Pacific region, as its home port is in Japan.

But since Russia has been antagonizing the West by flying and driving its planes and ships near U.S. and U.K. territories Donald Trump thought it only fair the U.S. did the same. He ordered the *USS Ronald Reagan (CVN 76)* to cruise through the Bering Strait. Land masses of both the U.S. and Russia are only 2.36 miles apart (See Little Diomede versus Big Diomede). Some years there is so much ice here you could walk to Russia from the U.S.!

So Tina Fey, playing Sarah Palin on Saturday Night Live, wasn't too far off. There actually are some Americans who can see Russia from their house!

Fortunately, for me, the *USS Reagan* steamed all the way through the northern waters along the edge of the Arctic Circle. Fortunately, the *USS Reagan,* did it in warmer weather. During some winters there is so much ice in the Bering Strait it would've been impossible to travel here from the Pacific Ocean by ship.

The carrier group steamed through the Bering Sea, into the Arctic Ocean and right near much of the Russian Navy's Northern fleet.

The Russians put up all sorts of complaining and began buzzing the *USS Reagan* and her full carrier strike group. This included a cruiser, six destroyers, four frigates and several supply ships.

Fortunately for me, the U.S. Navy happened to be in the right place at the right time.

A squadron of F35Bs are permanently based at Marine Corp Air Station in Iwakuni, Japan. The USS Reagan had 3 of their F35s on board to test cold weather conditions.

The F35 is the most expensive aircraft in the world. Before the Pentagon is done, it's estimated this aircraft will cost taxpayers $1.5 trillion.

After flying it, I think it's worth every penny!

This is the only supersonic short takeoff/vertical landing (STOVL) aircraft in the world.

This means the jet can take off like a helicopter and then can speed to 1,200 miles per hour in seconds. That's 1.6 times the speed of sound and again, after flying it, (I'm not supposed to say this) this jet can fly a lot faster than that!

When I lived in North Hollywood, California I could hear earlier versions of this idea whining above my house at all hours of the night.

I knew they were doing some sort of secret testing on some weird plane as Lockheed's super-secret "Skunk Works" used to be located at the Burbank Airport.

This was back in the good ol' days when they were testing the Stealth fighter.

It took them many more years to incorporate those vertical landing ideas into a supersonic jet.

But they finally had accomplished it with the F35B.

I trained on simulators for the F35B at a Marine facility in California but I had no idea that I'd actually get the chance to actually fly the bird.

But today would be the day!

After what I just went through, I didn't trust anyone.

And I had to catch up with my team who are now well ahead of me.

I was worried that I was taking a multi-billion dollar aircraft with cost overruns of billions more into the air with only a few hours of flight training, but I didn't let anyone know that.

Admiral Halsey, in charge of this fleet, the pilots and flight crew appear to be more nervous than me!

However, before I took off, Admiral Halsey was clear to explain that the cost of this jet per hour was $67,000.00.

In return, I respectfully point out: how much do you think it would cost if several cities were destroyed and hundreds of people in powerful positions were to have suicide chips running our government?

The admiral simply says, "Touché."

I'm taken up to the flight deck and talked to by multiple air officers, aircraft directors, pilots, mechanics and even some guy from the kitchen!

Maybe I'm too stupid to know what I'm climbing into.

I do know this F35 is the newest jet fighter in America's arsenal. The F22 is a bit faster but would need to refuel before I reached Monaco. Then, when I reach Monaco, there would be literally no place to land. I can land this thing on a dime — or I should say an experienced pilot can land this thing on a dime. I did it in a flight simulator.

One time.

How hard could it be?

I'd soon find out.

As I sit in the F35 going over some last minute preflight checks, I tell the air officer, "Not to worry, launch me."

The air officer looks as if, hey, it's your life but instead respectfully says, "Good luck, commander."

He walks a safe distance in his yellow jersey as the Catapult Officer takes over. He gives me the hold sign. I give him the thumbs up sign. He checks his catapult guys who goes thumbs up.

He turns to me — my adrenaline is pumping so hard that I feel like I could fly right out of this plane.

Ya right! Calm down!

Is seems to take forever for the Catapult Officer to turn his head to me.

Then it's another eternity as he stares at me.

He's making eye contact and I realize he wants me to go full throttle.

I do.

He wants something else.

What?

Oh right, I check all my flight controls on the Heads Up Displays (HUDs) and all look good — Go!

He still has the hold sign up. What else?

Right, sorry, the salute.

I salute him and he then gives me the thumbs up.

He looks back to several other checkers who are looking visually to be sure everything on my jet looks "flyable."

I sure hope Elena can't tap into these computers or I'm going head over heels into the sea again.

This is a fly by wire jet. Meaning the aircraft won't fly if the computer systems go out. The plane will tumble and tumble until it crashes as it's not aerodynamically able to fly or glide without computers.

I was told there is a backup, manual system but everyone, and I mean everyone, even the cook, gave up trying to verbally tell me what to do.

Who's idea was this again?

I see thumbs up from the checkers.

The catapult officers makes one final visual check.

They give the launch signal.

Only then does the catapult operator push the launch button.

In a split second my F35 flies across the flight deck and into the sea.

Thankfully not into but, rather, over the Norwegian Sea.

I accelerate to full throttle up and climb to 40,000 feet in seconds. At 1,200 miles per hour and Monaco 1,200 miles away, even my old bad math brain calculated that, I'll be there in — one hour!

Now, if I can remember everything I learned on that simulator!

In my earpiece is flight control giving me a boost of confidence, "Lookin' good commander!"

I'm worried about any discussion about this operation over the comm systems. So I simply say, "Thank you. Dark Lord out."

They guys wanted to call me Dark Lord.

I didn't complain.

I was too busy trying to remember everything the cook was saying.

We agreed to stay dark for all communications.

This is the hardest part of the flight.

The silence.

I started singing the old Paul Simon song, "Hello darkness my old friend, I've come to talk with you again…"[7]

A million thoughts rush my brain and I didn't even have that thing in there any more.

"… people hearing without listening…" really hit me.

"Silence like a cancer grows…"

"… and the people bowed and prayed to the neon god they made…"

All the thoughts of Elena's destructive ways and what she's capable of really hit me.

Our cities smoldering.

The Statue of Liberty gone in an instant.

So much power concentrated in such evil.

I try not to let my mind wander into all of that.

This plane is fantastic HUD (Heads Up Displays) are everywhere telling me everything.

I don't really need to look down at my instruments as they're all right in front of me.

Elena's got one better.

She thinks and people do what she says.

Well, JD, your mind has already wandered again.

I'm thinking of how this attack will go down when I keep coming back to the horrifying thought: *What if she's already implanted the local police. What if all those guys with M16s are chipped?*

It would be less than 50 minutes 'til I got my answer.

***

The coolest thing about this F35 is that, this is the only model of the three variants, the "B" version that can land vertically, like a helicopter.

I'm hovering over the city looking for a place to land.

I've told my guys to rendezvous at the F1 starting line without realizing there are thousands of people there.

Just my luck!

I forgot!

This is the day of the F1 Grand Prix in Monaco.

Smooth, JD, real smooth!

I wonder if they ever pulled out "my" Rolls from the prince's fish tank?

There's the pool.

No Rolls Royce.

Apparently, they did.

The police and government can't be too happy with me.

Maybe I should've thought this through as well.

As I'm thinking that, a shoulder fired surface to air missile is launched in my direction. Warning lights go off and, without me doing anything, metal chaff is shot out the back of the plane.

I maneuver away from the missile which explodes behind me.

I sure hope none of those people directly below me end up with shrapnel in them.

Thousands of people sitting, waiting for the start of the F1 race politely clap thinking this is an air show directly above them.

That's it!

The space I need to set this down.

I vertically drop down to the start position on the F1 track.

All of the racers are at the starting point with their engines running.

"Move!" I shout.

Like they can hear you!

As I land directly in front of the F1 cars on their track, the crowd again politely claps.

I see David Riccardo's racer and he sees me!

I think he recognizes me.

Yep, he does.

He begins shaking his head and pulls the key out of his ignition.

(Now don't get ahead of me!)

I stop.

I climb out of the jet as another surface to air missile explodes directly in front of my jet. I realize now that I've put thousands of people in the line of fire.

I jump back in the plane and take off.

The jet only needs about 100 feet to take off as it can't quite vertically lift off.

This is gonna be close.

A giant Planet Sushi sign, on top of a 10 story building, is directly in front of me.

As I look to clear the building, I breathe a sigh of relieve a little too soon.

My landing gear hits the sushi sign and all sorts of red lights go off.

The sign now says: PLAN… SHI!

All the posh people nearby paying hundreds of thousands of dollars or more to see the race, for a third time, clap politely.

They think this is all part of an act?

They're probably thinking this is an ad for "PLANSHI" and on their phones now telling brokers buy all the "PLANSHI" stock you can!"

"Landing gear damage. Landing gear damage," says the calm female voice.

Great! How do I land now?

'She' doesn't answer.

Another missile goes flying over my head and out to sea.

I've gotta get this this thing away from these people.

I spot a huge, seemingly empty, square on top of a hill.

That's good.

I fly in that direction.

What's not so good is, as I get closer, I see that it's covered with tourists.

What's worse is: I realize this is one area from where the missiles have been coming.

I decide I have to put this thing down quickly.

Another missile!

My F35 puts out more chaff as I have to break off my landing attempt.

I see exactly where the missile came from.

The F35 has aboard a GAU-22/A, a four-barrel version of the 25 mm GAU-12 Equalizer cannon on an external pod. I fire all 220 rounds into the area where the missiles have been coming. Trees, bushes and a very old fortress wall are instantly turned into sushi.

I think ya got him, JD.

I see these annoying red lights showing the underside camera of my plane.

Ok, I see I have no landing gear on the port side (*That's left. Easy way to remember this is: Port is four letters and left is four letters*)!

Now I see what the smart plane has been trying to tell me. My fuel pods and my cannon are empty. I swipe through a flashing red HUD in front of my face and the pods and cannon drop to the ground as the last tourists run for cover.

"Sorry! Sorry!" I say as if they can hear me over the sound of the very powerful Rolls Royce jet engine, inside a sealed cockpit.

I decide since the missiles came from this area and there is nothing but a huge, now empty, square below me, this would be a great place to set down.

The F35 doesn't agree.

She's fighting me and won't let me put it down.

The heads up display is showing the missing landing gear.

"Okaaaaaay... so how do you propose we land?" That I ask out loud.

No answer from the "smart" jet!

I'm only 10 feet from the ground.

I open the cockpit and jump.

I have to roll as gunfire erupts.

Fortunately, it's from the other side of my plane and my F35 is giving me cover.

I run to some building at the edge of the square.

Now the plane lands itself then explodes.

Great!

The admiral will not be happy.

I'm standing in front of giant doors looking at my smoldering mess. More gunfire hits the doors and I duck inside.

What is this place?

Wow!

Just wow!

Only now do I realize that I've landed at the Palace of the Prince of Monaco.

I thought the Sagrada Familia in Barcelona, Spain was overkill... It is but this is a close second.

A big difference being the prince's palace doesn't have a plastic Jesus ascending to heaven among 147 foot tall columns made of red porphyry, a very hard volcanic rock.

Even worse: Plastic Jesus is surrounded by Japanese lanterns, carried under a very "Gaudi" umbrella.

Guess it all depends if you're building "a palace" for God or for yourself!

Of course "the people" can now take tours through parts of both palaces — for the right price, of course.

The people's palace!

That has a frightening ring to it!

A large NATO round pings near my head.

I better pay attention.

I'm running through beautiful marble floors and priceless glass chandeliers when I'm stopped dead in my tracks.

There are millions of glass cuts on the chandeliers in here. It's breathtaking!

Mrs. Vasili is standing at the end of the great hall.

I start to walk toward her with a smile on my face saying, "Mrs. Vasili, am I glad to see you."

She replies, "I can't say the same for you..."

She raises a .45 caliber 1911 pistol and fortunately she can't shoot. The bullet misses me by a mile and hits some, probably, priceless vase nearby.

"Why didn't you tell me you murdered my husband?" Mrs. Vasili continues to fire and speak.

I'm still trying to find cover but there's nothing in this great hall that's close. "I… I didn't want to upset you any more than I already had. Your daughter is a… " I don't get any other words out as Mrs. Vasili has fired another round that grazes my flight boots.

Angrily Mrs. Vasili continues to talk and fire, "Is a what? What? Murderer? Well, so are you!"

"I'm not. I didn't know it was your husband. Your daughter hated her dad. She's hell bent on murdering millions. What the hell did you do to her?"

This stops her or so I think.

No. No, she's just reloading.

This is my chance. I charge her. Fortunately she panics as she's already reloaded. I put my finger behind the trigger so the gun cannot fire and disarm her.

She drops to the floor sobbing.

After a short eternity looking around and seeing no one else in this huge hall, I sit on the floor beside her.

"I didn't kill him… well I did but it was events that your daughter put in place that killed him."

Mrs. Vasili looks at me with a flare of anger in her eyes as if she could still kill me, now, with her bare hands.

We stare at each other as I realize, if she doesn't see the evil in her own daughter, there's nothing else I can say.

Nothing.

She seems to run a thousand thoughts past her eyes toward mine.

She stops on one and says, "Val really liked you. Maybe even loved you. Maybe more than our own son. My whole family is gone please don't take her too."

I look into her soul, through her eyes and see a mother's love that overlooks even mass murder.

How could such a rotten apple come from this tree?

After studying evil for thousands of years humans still haven't figured that out.

Cain murdered his own brother, Abel.

Murder is part of our sick condition.

How I wish it wasn't so.

The thought suddenly hits me: *What if Mrs. V. has one of those chips in her?*

I look at the side of Mrs. Vasili's head.

She doesn't appear to have one.

So how can we understand each other?

Some things in this world are unexplainable.

You say you don't believe in a spirit? A soul?

This moment is but one of many in my life that convinces me there is something more out there that we can't see, hear, touch, taste, or feel but it's real.

Like love!

You really can't use just your five senses for love you must use that sixth sense.

That's real love!

Mrs. Vasili and I hug.

This seems to last a long time.

In reality, it's only seconds.

Police officers burst through the large door.

I point Mrs. Vasili's 1911 at them.

They have M16s and say, "Drop it."

I do.

Right behind them stomps Ovwà.

He walks right up to the vase that has broken into a hundred pieces laying all over the white marble floor.

"That was a priceless Ming Vase," says Ovwà.

I want to say, not - any - more but it looks like Ovwà wouldn't be able to take it.

Ovwà sounds and acts like Peter Sellers on steroids as it is.

Ovwà then says, "So what is going on? I have a Formula 1 race with thousands of fans going on down there and I don't want it stopped for any reason.

I say, "Any?"

"That's right, any reason," replies a clearly upset Ovwà.

Nothing has made him mad so far.

Terrorists in his town.

No.

Me racing at 200 miles per hour through the streets of Monaco.

No.

But this?

Stopping the Formula 1 race, this has made him mad?

Mrs. Vasili blurts out, "My daughter wants to take over the world."

Mrs. Vasili looks to have gotten Ovwà's attention.

Ovwà studies her carefully before saying to me, "Are these the same people your 'girlfriend' was after?"

I nod my head, returning Ovwà's sarcasm.

Ovwà then quickly says, "You will stay here in the palace until the race is over. Understand?"

I try and explain, "Yes, but…"

"Don't but me… I'll have you put in jail for life if you disrupt the Formula 1 any further, understand?" Ovwà confidently exclaims, "The special forces and I shall investigate."

I look him in the eye and now notice a slight scar on the back of his right temple, exactly where Elena implanted me!

He picks up the 1911 I dropped and think he's probably going to kill me. I say, "Mr. Ovwà…"

"Die… rector! Director of Monaco Police," says the prefect in a snotty fashion.

"Die being the operative word?" I mumble sarcastically.

"Pardon?" asks Ovwà.

I do not answer.

He turns up his nose at me and says, "You vill come mit me… now!"

There are several M16s pointed at my chest.

I make it a religious habit not to argue with guys with automatic weapons pointed at me— so I follow right along.

I'm thinking of how I'm going to escape when gunfire erupts again. The Monaco police with the M16s are dropped like flies.

These are pros. They waited until we were in this narrow hall where we can't run to kill all of us.

Suddenly the gunfire stops.

The only people still alive are me (I put myself first here as that's the person who's still alive that I care about the most), Ovwà and Mrs. Vasili.

That was not an accident.

I call out, "Elena?"

Elena moves from the shadows and appears in front of us. She looks really bad. The scar I gave her looks worse than ever. She has another large scar, far larger than mine or Ovwà's on her right temple.

Has she been experimenting on herself?

She slowly walks toward us unarmed.

I know Ovwà will shoot me if she commands.

It's weird though, he points the 1911 at Elena and says, "Stop!"

Elena laughs, "You think some old gun is a match for me, old man?"

Ovwà is more offended at the old man remark than anything else, "Old man? I'll have you know I run three miles a day."

Elena starts clapping slowly and sarcastically.

"Bra… f'ing…vo, old man," says Elena.

Ya, she hasn't changed.

"C'mon mom, let's go to lunch," says Elena to her mom. "How 'bout the Blue Bay?"

Mrs. Vasili turns her nose at this, "On Princess Grace? How 'bout Joël Robuchon?"

Elena checks for stale food in her teeth before saying unenthusiastically, "Ya, okay, whatever."

I can't believe I'm about to be shot as Elena casually discusses what to eat for lunch!

Ovwà looks at me and I'm thinking he's thinking the same thing when he blurts out, "Louis the 15th is better than either!"

This is truly insane!

I look to both of the women then to Ovwà, "Before one of you shoots me, Is Louis The 15th an actual restaurant in Monaco?"

All three nod their heads in robot agreement saying, "Oh the best… great… ya"

I stand in shock.

"Well, this is the craziest Mexican standoff I've ever been a part of. But in Monaco do as the Monegasqueans." I dive to the floor and grab an M16 from one of the dead soldiers. Ovwà doesn't try to do anything.

What surprises me is that neither does Elena.

I stand holding an M16 at all three of them, thinking I'll have to kill all of them.

"All right put your guns down," I say with urgency.

Elena immediately tosses her gun onto the floor.

Ovwà says, "I'm the die-rector of police."

I say with low key intensity, "Put… your… gun… down."

Ovwà without hesitation says, "Okay" and lays down his gun.

I now say, "Okay, now, let's walk. Slowly. Very slowly."

Ovwà says, "If these are my last words I want them to be: Louis The 15th is the best restaurant in Monaco!"

I mumble, "Crazy French."

All three turn and do as I say. "I need to know where you're putting chips in people,"

Elena pleasantly say, "Oh sure. Right this way, JD. Would you like to have another chip?"

I answer, "Thanks anyway, Elena but I prefer to make my own decisions."

"Oh you can still make all your own decisions," says Elena.

"Not when you had that chip in me, I couldn't," I quickly answer.

"Oh? What are you talking about?" Elena really has no idea.

I quickly answer, "In Paris twice. First at the Eiffel Tower? Last year? Proposing to Jen?"

"But she's not right for you. I stopped you, didn't I? Why haven't you proposed since?" Elena answers.

I stare at her.

"I did you a favor," Elena offers.

"Please don't do me any more favors, Elena." I answer with contempt.

We reach the end of the hall and two large mahogany doors.

Mrs. Vasili turns to me and says, "John, please…"

She can see I am very determined to stop her even if it means killing her.

"You know what your husband's last words to me were as he lay bleeding in my hands?" I ask. No one in this room can answer that question but me and no one in the room wants to know the answer. But I gave the answer anyway, "I had a gun pointed at your heart, Elena. Much like right now. Your father stopped me. I never realized who it was. I just reacted. I put my knife through his neck. Captain Vasili, a thirty year Russian military veteran of war said coughing blood into my hands, 'Tell my wife I love her.' And then he raised his head, looked me in the eye and said, "'Finish it.' You know what he meant. He meant he loved both of you but he wanted me to stop you Elena, and that's what I intend to do."

I raise my gun toward Elena, when Mrs. Vasili yells, "No!" and runs in front of me so I can't shoot Elena.

Elena is standing in front of large wooden doors at the end of the hall. She slips behind them and out of the room.

Mrs. Vasili screams, "No, no, no!" She falls holding my leg. I have to drag her toward Elena.

I soon shake her lose and run past Ovwà, who seems worthless.

I open the door, and peek into the next room. I enter the Throne Room and stand there for a moment thinking, "People actually live like this?"

Elena closes a door on the other side of the room and I pursue.

As I come to the next door I look like Tom Cruise in "*Risky Business*" as I slide across the marble floor in my flight boots.

How is that possible?

God only knows.

Someone must polish these floors — daily!

Suddenly, gunfire erupts from the next set of doors Elena has run behind.

I'm forced to dive behind a gold and marble table.

I try to turn the table over like in some saloon in the Old West.

It's a lot heavier than I thought!

I can't even move it a little.

German Panzer tanks were probably stopped by this very piece of furniture.

The gunfire suddenly stops which likely means Elena's on the move.

I get up to run and now hear gunfire outside.

I run to the window and see Skull and my team stopping Elena's men from heading into the yacht harbor.

"Yes!" I put the *M16* in the air like a kid who just took Hamburger Hill in Vietnam.

I see Elena's men retreat back inside the castle.

I run to head 'em off at the pass.

"I hate that cliché…" But I do love the movie![8]

I run to the other side of the castle and look out the window.

A huge contingency of Elena's men make it to a second beach on this side of the castle.

No!

A $50 million yacht picks them up as I look helplessly from the top of the Prince's Palace. Just as it looks as if Elena and her men are going to escape, the nuclear Los Angeles class, *USS Newport,* surfaces directly in front of the yacht.

A couple of F35s hover over top of the sub with their cannons and missiles pointed directly at the yacht.

The yacht stops dead in the water while a couple of RIBs fly around the mouth of the harbor weapons pointed on target.

It's Zeke, Tommy and Spider!

Yes!

The terrorists on the yacht all hold their hands in the air.

God, I love the U.S. Navy!

A crowd of very wealthy beachgoers and yacht owners politely clap.

Why does everyone in this town think everything's a show?

Zeke quickly says on my molar mike, that's now working, "We're searching the yacht. She's not here."

I yell, "Impossible! Keep searching."

Zeke replies, "Yes, sir."

I run down the hall knowing Elena must still be hiding in the castle.

I begin frantically searching to no avail.

THIS PLACE IS HUGE!

Skull eventually says on my molar mic, "The yacht and both beaches are secure, John. Target 2 is not here. Repeat, Target 2 is not here."

I'm panicking.

"Then get in here. I want more bodies in here now. She's in here somewhere," I say.

Eventually, I meet up with both SEAL teams and 220 Marines from the *USS Wasp* (*LHD1*).

Nothing!

Absolutely no trace of her.

We search the premises several times, including the tunnels.

Skull and I finally meet up, "We've searched every inch of the palace. Looks like she got away."

I say to Skull, "How could she just disappear?"

I try to console my team, "Hey, not to worry, We'll get her," I try to cheer everyone up.

That seemed to help a bit.

I see Zeke, Tommy, Spider, Skull, Jen, Alexi, Casmerov and Stone all standing on the palace wall watching the Formula 1 race.

Here comes Ovwà and about fifty Monaco police.

I remember Elena has a chip in his head and probably all of these guys' heads too.

Ovwà stops dead in his tracks as his men now aim their M16s at us.

Suddenly, all 220 Marines stick their heads up over the top of the castle and surround Ovwà training their M27s on Ovwà and his men.

Ovwà smiles and motions for his men to lower their weapons.

That's a strange reaction for someone controlled by Elena.

I say, "All right everyone calm down. I know Elena put a chip in your head."

Ovwà is stunned, "What?"

"You can be controlled by Elena with that chip you have in your head."

"What chip?" says Ovwà incredulously.

That scar you have behind your right temple," I say holding an M27 at Ovwà.

Ovwà touches his scar and says, "I had a brain tumor. This is the scar from my surgery."

His men all nod their head in agreement.

This is a little too convenient.

"All right. I'm putting my gun down," I set down my M27 as I give the eye to the rest of my team and the Marines to NOT do the same. "I'm gonna walk over to you. Can I do that?" I ask.

Ovwà without hesitation says, "But of course."

Henry in my molar mic says, "I just checked. Hospital records indicate that Ovwà last year went in for brain cancer surgery in Nice, France.

I say out loud, "What?"

Ovwà says, "What?"

Henry in my jawbone mic says, "What?"

Skull behind me says, "What?"

The sound from these damn molar mics are sometimes confusing and weird.

We're all confused!

Henry continues, "I'm looking at his medical file now. The surgery is legit. I can see the before and after x-rays of Ovwà's skull."

I walk up to Ovwà and look carefully at his head. I say, "May I?" asking to inspect closer.

The scar is in the wrong place.

Mine is much further forward and higher.

Henry, "Don't start shooting, JD, he's clean. I'd bet my life on it."

I say out loud, "But would you bet mine?"

Henry doesn't hesitate, "I would."

I answer, "You would!"

Ovwà asks, "What? Who are you talking to?"

I answer, "Sorry, It's just some guy in my head."

Henry says, "Thanks. Thanks a lot."

Ovwà looks at me like I'm crazy.

I smile. Turn around and make the motion to everyone to take their weapons to low ready.

They do.

Ovwà says, "Sorry we didn't get Elena."

I smile and shake Ovwà's hand, "You're a good man Ovwà, a good man, indeed."

Both teams come together and start mingling.

Henry keeps bothering me, "What's going on? What's that noise in the background?"

Everyone has turned their attention to the Formula 1 cars that are still racing on the road nearby.

I say to Henry, "You're gonna have ta come to Monaco to believe all this. I think Jen and I might be here awhile."

Alexi and Casmerov say, "This place is paradise."

Stone says, "I gotta bring the wife here."

So I stand with them on the castle wall as we watch the rest of the Formula 1 race.

I love those cars.

But I'd really rather have that Rolls.

I wonder if it still runs?

In the back of my mind, I know Elena is plotting her next move.

Elena, her mother and Dr. Gebhardt are in the mini-sub she used to escape down the Seine River in Paris (*JDII*). She is shadowing a 500 million dollar yacht built especially for her. Skull and his guys searched this from top to bottom but they didn't see this bottom. The yacht opens its underwater hatch and Elena drives the mini-sub right into a dock inside the boat.

***

Later that night Prince Albert II, reigning prince of Monaco, invited us all to a state dinner. Before the dinner he took Jen and me on a private tour of his palace. "I'm so sorry I allowed this woman to do so many horrible things. She pretended that she was a billionaire."

I say, "Oh she wasn't pretending."

The prince is surprised, "Really?"

The prince has taken us to a large Persian rug covering the wall and continues, "Well, this is likely how she got away."

Jen and I look at each other as if, "What?"

The prince moves the rug out of the way and moves a candle nearby and a door opens. Cool air rushes out.

"Feel that?" the prince asks. "That's salt air from the water at the bottom of the castle." There are three tunnels under this castle built by my ancestors to escape invading armies. Elena said she was worried that people were hunting her. Unfortunately, I showed Elena this."

"Well, she was telling the truth. We were hunting her." I say as a matter of fact. "We only searched the other two tunnels."

As I stand in the doorway of the secret tunnel Jen is fooling with the candle and the door quickly closes on me.

My face is trapped in between the door and the castle wall. Remember when I get nervous I make jokes. So in great pain and in the great tradition of Gene Wilder and Mel Brooks, with my face pinched against the door, I say, "Put the candle back!"[9]

Jen quickly puts the candle back in its holder and the secret door fully opens.

The prince rushes to me and asks, "Are you all right?"

I do a Jay Leno line moving my jaw around, "Ya, I'm fine but I don't think the chin'll ever be the same."

The prince sees I'm smiling and Jen rolls her eyes and disgustedly says, "Oh he's fine."

The prince double checks before saying, "You're welcome to stay here or at any fine establishment in Monaco for as long as you wish. It's all on me. Just use my name."

Jen is very excited by this, "Thank you! Thank you very much."

"Thank you, your grace… I mean… I'm so sorry." I really stepped into it. His mother was Grace Kelly.

"No need to apologize. Happens all the time," says the prince.

"I wish I knew her. Everyone that did truly loved your mother," I say with sadness.

"Including me. Thank you. I miss her every day. Every day of my life," says the prince.

I want to ask him about all my crazy theories of how she died but I could tell he didn't want to discuss it further. I respect his privacy and feelings and move on.

Then I jokingly pretend to be a spoiled aristocrat from the 18th Century saying, "Well, on hot days we could always come down here for the natural air conditioning, darling."

The prince smiles and that was pretty much all that seemed to matter right then.

EPILOGUES

I placed this diary at the beginning of my first book. It still seems as relevant today as it did then:

MY PRIVATE DIARY

The following events
will sound like they're
coming straight out of some novel.
I can assure you, they are not.
These events actually took place
and brought us
to the edge of World War III.
How do I know?
I was there. My name?
John Denning (JD).
I'm not some nut writing a book to
make money.
I'm writing this to warn you...

Your government is not telling you the truth.
The enemy is already here and
We are all in grave danger.

Should I meet an untimely death under

suspicious circumstances
always remember:

Follow the money. Follow the power.
Who has the most to lose?

We lived through all of this
to tell you about the nuclear detonations,
the lies, and the cover-up.

Several of us kept detailed diaries.
This is not my story.
This is our story.

LONG LIVE THE TRUTH!

Yes, I am shouting. Are you listening?

John Denning (JD),
Former BMCS,
SEAL Team Six

Undisclosed Location

P.S. -
As the title of my first diary indicates, *The Enemy is Already Here* and it
turns out it's us!
We're our own worst enemy!

Laziness, biases, prejudices… and a million other things make us our own worst enemies.

It's not "them" it's us!

If even half the world understood that, this world would be a far, far, better place.

GUANTANAMO BAY, CUBA

Russian Agents Al Ruddy and Colonel Katrina are still rotting in Guantanamo Bay, Cuba. They both stand under the camera that's in the corner of their room plotting on Katrina's arm their getaway plan.

In some sort of sign language, they silently communicate to each other, the doors, gates, locks, guards, etc.

This goes on and on for several minutes.

Finally, they hear the outer jail door open and they scurry to their bunks.

They both pick up Chekhov books and pretend to be reading.

The same soldier, a kid, 21 years old, is still serving these guys (*JDII*), "Filet minion tonight, Mr. Ruddy?"

Ruddy licks his lips but says, "You know I don't have anything to tell you."

The kid pulls up a chair outside the jail door and says, "Well that's too bad. Guess I'll have to eat your steak and baked potato dinner, again."

He knows this is Al Ruddy's favorite meal.

Ruddy hasn't had this since he's been incarcerated here but the kid has, every night for over a year!

The kid starts eating as Ruddy and Katrina look disgustedly to each other.

The kid picks his teeth saying, "You know I think I'm putting on weight eating all of this great food every night. It's a shame you can't provide us with a little help. The quality of the food would really improve for you guys."

No answer from inside their cell.

The kid continues, "By the way, If you're gonna plan an escape make sure you know about all the cameras and mics in your cell."

Ruddy and Katrina look at each other with some worry.

The kid goes on, "Ya, there are 6 cameras and 3 mics in your cell. You apparently only know about the one obvious one in the corner."

"Not to worry though we're moving you as soon as I finish your dinner."

The kid calmly goes on eating Ruddy's steak and baked potato.

We hear a laugh from down the hall.

It's Brigadier General Bahadur, of the Iranian Defense Forces, "Haha. Finally. Now I can get some sleep."

"Pipe down Bad Odor, we're movin' you next," says the kid as picks his teeth one last time. There is nothing but the "Sound of Silence" and a whimper from the cell next door.

It's Mustafa, the DARPA supervisor from Alexandria, Virginia.

He's crumpled up in a little ball on his cot.

DIARY OF OLGA KASPAROV

I'm in a general holding area of the most notorious prison in Russia, "Black Dolphin." I know Americans pronounce articles such as "the" and I should put it in front of "Black Dolphin" but this is my diary and I'm Russian, so I won't.

This place houses worst of worst: Murderers, rapists, child molesters, insane, and Viktor Sokolov.

All have been sent here to rot and die.

I'm sitting opposite Putin's former right hand man, Viktor Sokolov.

Ugly green paint is peeling off the wall except for the green screen wall my people put behind him. Viktor is sitting directly in front of green screen. I can only assume my producer will be given instructions on what, probably something beautiful, to project behind this man.

Always remember: Russians are rarely ever what image of them really is. But then that same for a lot of people, I guess.

There was finally enough evidence to put Sokolov away and put him away "for good." He's being held here while appeals court decides if he should get life or be executed.

Crowd outside is chanting, "выполнять, выполнять," which means "Execute. Execute."

Mr. Sokolov is sitting in chains.

There are several big dudes in room with me.

There's a camera behind me.

I don't know big dudes names and I don't vant to!

The smallest of big dudes looks the toughest. He walks over to table between Viktor and me. He sits and stares at Viktor saying, "So you ready to tell world what we agreed to?"

Viktor says nothing.

Big dude looks at camera, "Turn off and leave now."

Does this mean me?

"Little" big dude looks at me.

Okay, it means me too.

My cameraman and I pick up our things and leave.

As we close door behind ourselves I ask my cameraman, "Think they are going to use more persuasive methods?"

We hear a man hit and then a subdued scream of gut wrenching pain.

Guess I got my answer.

We quickly leave.

WASHINGTON, D.C.

A discount electronics superstore in Washington sits with a couple hundred people lined up through the parking lot and down the street.

A huge banner over the side of the store says:

FREE BIG SCREEN TV
TOMORROW ONLY
FIRST 100 PEOPLE

Inside the store about 25 employees wheel out about 100 large screen TVs to the front of the store.

The employees don't seem to be too thrilled watching the sea of humanity pushed against the glass doors.

All employees have on these silly looking, way too short, blue vests with their name tags.

The store manager gets to wear a, silly looking, red vest. The manager walks to one of his employees and says, "Okay you stand right here and answer any questions."

The clearly worried employee says, "Okay."

It's Fred who was fired from the Oval Office by Donald Trump.

Fred is standing at the back of about 100 large screens, stacked like dominos.

The store manager checks his watch and yells, "Okay, let her rip!"

Two employees start to open the glass double doors and are swung open quickly by the pulsating mob of human flesh.

They crush through the door and head right for the stack of TVs.

Fred has his back to the 100 TVs. He is clearly oblivious as to what is about to occur.

He is trying to get his manager's attention but the manager is ignoring him.

Fred persists, "Sir, what if… sir, what if a customer has a specs question that I can't answer. So then do I ask you?"

Two women fight over one TV.

A man tries to intervene when another guy says, "Get your hands off my wife," and punches him in the nose.

A large woman jumps on the stack and slides her large body across the top of all the big screens.

The mob and the large woman has pushed so hard into the stack of TVs that they begin a domino chain heading right for Fred.

Fred has his back to the stack when several large screens hit him.

He is buried under the huge pieces of heavy cardboard.

But not for long.

A swarm of locusts descend on the remaining TVs and move them off Fred in no time.

Fred is then trampled by the mob as they head out the door.

Fred lays on the floor with his little blue vest over his head and his name tag stuck to his ear.

His nice black pants have hundreds of footprints all over them.

One last large man with the last big screen, steps on Fred's belly, as he juggles a TV toward the door.

Fred lets out one last, large, groan as the man catapults himself toward the front door.

The manager stands in the way of about 50 large TVs all trying to make their way out the door as if this is some sort of looting riot.

The manager says, "Wait. Wait! You must have the TV rung up first. You must…

He is tossed out of the way like a gnat in a tornado.

As the manager looks on, a sea of TVs weave across the parking lot. He and several other blue vests stare in disbelief.

Fred limps toward the front door.

The manager says to him, "Fred I need you to…"

Fred has had enough.

He calmly takes off the blue vest, which was around his head anyway, and wads it up.

He drops it into the managers hands but says nothing.

He limps toward the parking lot following 50 huge TVs that look like oversized creatures from another planet.

IN ANOTHER PART OF D.C.

An Uber driver sits at a corner looking at his phone. Some cash is thrown over the seat at Jerry who's now using a black Prius to chauffeur people around Washington, D.C.

"Here, take us to the White House. Now!"

I'm not your house Ni...... gger...." Jerry realizes the two big dudes that got in the back are both black.

One of the guys reaches up and turns off Jerry's ignition. He takes the key.

The two men then step out of the car and open Jerry's door.

One motions for Jerry to get out.

Jerry nervously says, "I'm sorry, I'm sorry... I didn't see... I mean I didn't..."

Jerry stops talking and nods, no, in a scared fashion.

One guy drops the dangling key onto the grass next to where they're standing. He takes the heel of his boot and grinds the key FOB into the grass.

These guys know that without the key FOB in the car, the Prius won't start.

Both big guys then look at Jerry.

Finally, Jerry realizes he has to get his car key.

Jerry hesitantly steps out of his Prius.

One guy says, "Now could you repeat what you said right after, "I'm not your house Ni...?"

Jerry swallows a hard fought gulp saying, "I... I...I... didn't say... I..." Jerry realizes that by lying he's only digging his grave further.

"I'm sorry," says Jerry. "I didn't mean ni... What I mean to say is...?" Jerry takes off his glasses and giving up says, "Hit me. I know you want to. Hit me."

So the one big guy winds up and Jerry as the last minute yells, "Not the face!"

The guys stop look at each other then punch Jerry in the stomach.

Jerry buckles over in pain and wheezing says, "Thank you."

The two guys walk off.

Jerry, slowly stands up, walks to his key FOB, and looks to make sure the guys have left.

He picks up his key FOB which dangles in several pieces.

He repeatedly tries to get it to communicate with the car.

Nothing happens.

He tosses the FOB.

The Prius only then does the BEEP, BEEP sound as Jerry stares disgustedly at the car.

KETCHIKAN, ALASKA

Police Chief Robert Stone is in full dress uniform.

Why?

Why not?

He's down by the cruise ships sitting in his old white Ford. His deputy is in a police cruiser.

Their cars are parked so that they can talk to each other with their driver's doors close to each other.

A very crazy acting "Former Chief Butler" is wandering around by cruise passengers in a bright red wig and Darth Vader costume.

Deputy asks Stone, "Should we take him in?"

Stone asks, "Has he been drinking?"

Deputy, "Well, no. He's a Mormon."

Stone sees tourists laughing, "Then hell no! The tourists love him. It's good entertainment, don't you think?"

Deputy watching this crazy man get a big laugh from a crowd of tourists saying, "Ya, I guess."

Stone starts his car saying, "He's certainly better at comedy than that weatherman from Anchorage but keep an eye on him. If someone looks harassed or complains, take him in, otherwise, I'm tired. I'm goin' home."

Deputy says, "Yes, sir."

Stone drives his, still, barely running 2000 Ford Escape, home.

He pulls into the driveway and walks into his house. Stone, exhausted, sits in his favorite old, duct taped, cloth recliner.

His wife, Yura, is furious with him but refuses to come into the living room to speak with him saying, "Bob, is that you?"

Stone yells back, "Ya."

Yura continues, "Well, let me say that this is the last time that you leave dirty dishes in the sink without rinsing them. The stinky salmon that you ate last night smelled up my entire kitchen. I came down here this morning and you were already gone but it still smelled like you were eating rotten, stinky salmon… Bob?"

Yura walks out of the kitchen and into the living room.

Stone's reclining chair is still rocking but there's no Stone in it.

WHITE HOUSE

Trump is sitting in the Oval Office and someone is sitting on a sofa. Trump is reading the New York Times, "Look at this! Goddamn that New York Times." He holds up the paper and above the fold it says,

TRUMP ATTACKS MONACO

The voice says, "Ya, don't worry about it. Tell me another story."

Trump gets all excited, "So this is actually kinda funny, I'm watchin' my TV and I see a sub surface right in the middle of the Monaco Grand Prix. I ask, "Is it ours?" and they say, "Yes." I say, 'What the...?' Who ordered this fuckin' thing here and they say, 'you did, sir.'" I say, "Okay, when?" They say, "Remember operation ZERO HOUR? I say, 'No, not really, I was in the hospital for a while so they could remove somethin' from my fuckin' head.' It's been a hell of a week but I think you just maybe the only guy on the planet that gets me."

The guy on the couch turns around and it's Police Chief Robert Stone from Alaska.

Stone stands and toasts The Donald with a beer bottle, "Fuckin' A, man... Fuckin' A!"

About a month or so — ish — later:

I searched for days and days.

Seventeen branches of U.S. "intelligence" have entire teams of people working around the clock trying to find Elena. Each lead turned into a dead end. I decided at some point my team needed a break.

So Jen and I are sunning ourselves on the beach. The Prince of Monaco has let us live "Anywhere in town for as long as you want!"

Jen and I decided on a billionaire's yacht... It's really more like a small destroyer. The yacht has a helicopter on the back and I've been taking flight lessons from this crazy guy who used to fly helicopters, first in Vietnam, then tours around Kauai.

The man's insane!

I thought I was crazy.

Stone's in town and wants me to teach him to fly.

Right!

The only way you can fly this helicopter onto the back of this yacht is if you touch it down on the 3 foot guardrail first then slowly inch it toward the helipad.

This— is— an —insurance—nightmare!

An accident waiting to happen!

Jen and I heard this metal on metal screeching one night and ran to the back thinking the ship had hit something.

We were in port!

This crazy pilot, Harold Potter, "Harry" was drunk and trying to land.

Lucky we're all still alive!

Jen and I made him promise to keep the thing parked at the Monaco helipad while we're on the yacht.

I learned a Russian word when Alexi and Casmerov confronted those ghosts last year, "uzhasayushchiy" meaning, terrifying.

Terrifying!

Henry then comes walking in with a Hawaiian shirt and Bermuda shorts. He has a ten plus woman in a bikini on his arm.

I'm very worried knowing what the last "ten" woman did to him.

I walk up to her and look at her temples on both sides.

Henry laughs, "Not to worry. I checked her out."

Jen mumbles as she sees my sudden interest in this woman, "I'd say my fiancée's doin' that too."

I say as I continue to touch her hair, "I'm looking for a scar in the hairline."

Jen says, "I'd say you're looking for more than that."

I give a disgusted reaction to Jen as I walk away from Henry's date.

In walks Alexi and Casmerov with two gorgeous women too.

"What is this? The Miss Universe contest?" I ask.

Casmerov does a pretty good Dan Aykroyd impression, "I think so... cause we are two wild and crazy guys."

Alexi pulls off his $500.00 Prada sunglasses, "Hey, this where party at?"

Jen can't take it, "I've warned you guys about not talking in complete sentences and dangling prepositions."

I say, "Grammar Nazi!"

Everyone laughs.

Jen is upset.

I should apologize but instead I stare at her.

Jen lightens up and laughs.

Jen then goes after Alexi on another subject saying, "By the way what happened to 'C-man' and 'A-Dog'?"

Alexi responds deadpan, "Girls didn't like it."

The beautiful woman on Casmerov's arm notices his deadpan stare and says, "Russians are so weird… I can never tell what you're thinking or feeling…"

Casmerov says with deadpan stare, "Oh baby, baby, I vant you, need you. I love you." After a long pause Casmerov then says, "Does that vork for you?"

The woman says to him after staring at him for a very long time, "Ya, okay, I guess."

Casmerov, "You crazy woman. I never understand you either."

I'm worried about these "woman" as Russia is famous for using sex as a weapon of statecraft. Some call these types of Russian women "Putin's Pussies" but I would never say that.

What this is called by the CIA is "The Honey Trap." Attractive young woman targeting vulnerable, stupid men. Usually the men are much older and aren't single.

But this is Monaco, where all the "beautiful" people are.

So, who knows?

Maybe these women want to hang with heroes?

Wouldn't that be nice?

Some at the CIA also call these type of women KGB, The Karaoke Girls' Bash. Beautiful, young women entice powerful men in key government positions to get drunk in a bar. Then the "KGB" girls coax the men home, get them in bed, and hopefully, during pillow talk, pull secret information from them.

Men are so stupid!

As Robin Williams used to say, "God gave man a brain and a penis but only enough blood to run one at a time."

Miss ya Robin, really, really miss ya!

Chinese intelligence uses the "thousand grains of sand" approach. Many doing small things eventually adds up to a "beachhead" of useful information.

I'm suspicious.

Jennifer sees this and says, "Tonight we party and tomorrow and maybe into next week. Next month we worry about all of those things flying around in that head of yours."

I smile and lighten up.

Now I'm dangling prepositions.

Some young, stupid, rich kid, somebody brought aboard tries to make a pass at Jennifer saying, "So what da you do, baby?"

Without missing a beat Jennifer pretends to be an airhead on a Miss America show. She grabs the guys hand and pretends a mic is in it. She poses and looks at a pretend camera, "Thank you for the question, Bert, my hobbies are piano, water polo and driving nuclear subs!"

I laugh. It's even funnier because the rich kid doesn't get it.

I say to her, "I love you."

The rich kid gets that! He wanders off.

Skull walks onto the dance floor (the helipad) walks right up to me and says, "Dark Lord?"

I laugh, "Hey, it's better than Bones!"

Skull yells, "Hey, could I have everyone's attention? Anyone wanna know how he got the name Bones?"

Jen speaks first, "I sure do."

Everyone else chimes in.

"You say that word again and I'm puttin' you in the water," I say with confidence.

The big dummy wastes no time to say, "Bones, Bones, Bones, Bones, Bones!"

I calmly hand my drink to Jen then attack Skull.

People start cheering including, but not limited to, Zeke, Tommy, and Spider.

You're gonna have 'ta ask one of them who won that wrestling match.

We partied all the way through the day, into the night and finally went to sleep sometime after the sun came up.

When we got up, Jen, the crew, and me were the only one's still aboard.

Anyway, we asked the captain to pull up anchor and go over to the Monte Carlo Bay Casino side of Monte Carlo.

He did.

It's a perfect day. It's 72 degrees and not a cloud in the sky.

So we're sitting here sunning ourselves on the helipad at the back of the yacht sipping margaritas when out of nowhere a submarine surfaces.

Our crazy crew is hysterical speaking in all sorts of foreign languages and pointing to the sub.

I can't understand one single word anyone is saying.

One of our crew, for no apparent reason, jumps off the ship and into the water and swims toward the beach (Guess he thought the submarine was Monaco Immigration!)!

Jennifer is the first to laugh.

I smile saying, "That your boat?"

Jennifer nods as the *USS Alaska* has completely surfaced next to us.

This really was "her" boat. She was the former commander of it.

Out steps Admiral Halsey, in full dress, from the aircraft carrier *USS Reagan.*

Jennifer walks briskly, like I've never seen her walk before, toward guys putting down a gangplank between our "ships."

Jennifer says with all seriousness, "Permission to come aboard, admiral?"

The admiral quickly smiles saying, "Permission granted, commander."

As Jen steps onto the sub I'm in tow behind her like a little kid.

The admiral says, "I thought you'd like to see your crew again and thank them personally."

Jen says to admiral, "Nice touch, thanks."

We head inside the sub to see Jen's old crew.

The commander, Bert "P man" Parks (that's really his name), salutes us.

We return the salute.

Tom Watson, Jen's old boyfriend, salutes us next.

He actually acts pretty cool since they were pretty close.

Actually, they were a little too close as Jen retired from the Navy due to an "incident" involving the two of them.

I would probably have never met Jen but for her retiring from the Navy over "the incident."

I've been meaning to thank Tom for this but never had the chance.

I hope he gets shore leave.

I see Tad Murphy is still aboard.

Boy! Have I heard stories.

But that's for another day.

On the beach nearby crazy Al Reynolds sees the sub and stands up saying, "No. No. No!" He's thinking the Navy has come for them — again like they did a year ago (*JD II*).

Tatiana doesn't even open her eyes as her beautiful body is baking in the sun, "Not to vorry darlin[k]. Not to vorry. Now zit (sit)."

The admiral gave his guys "leave" so they could party with us on our yacht.

It was sweet.

Stone walks up to Jen and I and says, "From the moment I first met you and Jennifer in Alaska… I knew you loved each other!"

Jennifer and I smile to a guy some would say is not so bright. Not me! I'd defend this guy with my life.

I know he'd do the same for me.

***

By sunset, the *USS Alaska* had left and so had everyone else.

I gave everyone on the crew "shore leave" except our crazy pilot, Harry. I locked him in a room and told Jen to make sure we keep him in there and "NO BOOZE!"

As we sit sipping margaritas on lounge chairs in, probably, the most beautiful harbor in the world, the sun dips below the horizon.

The moment seems perfect so I ask, "Will you marry me?"

Her answer is not quite what I had expected.

Jen says, "Here? Now? E gad no! You do this right, soldier boy. Paris, Eiffel Tower, sunset!... or I say no."

Jen takes another sip of her Blue Hawaiian Margarita (in Monaco?) and sarcastically mumbles under her breathe, "Not even a ring... Will you marry me?"

I'm about to apologize, again when she does something unexpected.

Jen smiles as she puts her arms around me.

In return, I wrap my arms around her.

I then say in proper Queen's English, "Right! Okay, then, The Eiffel Tower it 'tis, darling!"

As we look at the Monaco sunset everything really is perfect.

So I boldly say, "It really is a beautiful sunset."

Jen looks at me worried.

"Not to worry, you made me say that!"

Jen relaxes in my arms and I hers.

"Perfect, just perfect."

ENDNOTES

1 http://www.abrahamlincolnonline.org/lincoln/speeches/lyceum.htm

2 Listen to the song: "Sweet Emotion" (1975) by Aerosmith. Fair Use

3 https://slate.com/news-and-politics/2018/07/trump-denounces-u-s-intelligence-on-russia-hacking-praises-putin-denial-as-strong-and-powerful.html

4 "Meet the new boss, same as the old boss…" "We Don't Get Fooled Again" by The Who. Fair Use

5 https://www.independent.co.uk/news/world/americas/seattle-plane-crash-audio-footage-full-transcript-hijacking-sea-tac-international-airport-a8487491.html

6 https://www.cnn.com/2018/08/11/us/seattle-stolen-plane-audio-recording/index.html

7 "The Sound of Silence" (1965) by Paul Simon. Fair Use

8 *Blazing Saddles* (1974) Mel Brooks, Warner Bros.

9 *Young Frankenstein (1974)* Mel Brooks

www.ingramcontent.com/pod-product-compliance
Lightning Source LLC
Chambersburg PA
CBHW021952170626
46808CB00001B/123